NATE'S

REDEMPTION

BOOK THREE IN THE LAKESHORE LOVE SERIES

This is a work of fiction. All the characters or scenarios in this publication are fictitious and any resemblance to actual events, real people, living or dead, is coincidental. The author recognizes the trademark names of all brands used in this work and in each instance, the brand is used fictitiously. All views are my own.

CONTENT WARNING

Nate's Redemption includes the following:

- Detailed consensual sex scenes
- Flashbacks to past traumatic events involving the loss of a friend
- Mention of past physical abuse, not main characters
- Loss of parents, not main characters

All triggers above are briefly mentioned and are not central themes of the book

For resources and support numbers please visit:

pflag.org

Copyright 2025

Cover Design: Ashley Snyder

Cooking is like love. It should be entered into with abandon or not at all – Harriet Van Horne

PLAYLIST

Somebody to Someone by Natalie Jane

Neptune by Sleeping At Last

Bad Decisions by Bad Omens & Dahlia

Beautifully Undone by Laura Doggett

Some Things I'll Never Know by Teddy Swims

Gone Too Soon by Simple Plan

Close To You by Gracie Abrams

Before You by Benson Boone

The Very Thought of You by Michael Bublé

That's Life by Frank Sinatra

Venice by The Lighthouse and The Whaler

Silverlines by Damiano David & Labrinth

You Are In Love (Taylor's Version) by Taylor Swift

Scan QR Code for Spotify Playlist

CHAPTER ONE

Wednesday, June 12th

NATE

The love for cooking and the love for life are both passions.

I say to myself as I lay in bed. Sun pours through the windows of my loft. My alarm blares again.

"Okay, I'm up." I yawn and throw my covers off. I wrestle my messy curls and walk to the kitchen to turn on the espresso machine.

I lazily shuffle to the bathroom for my morning piss and turn on the shower. I think about the quote that popped into my head. *Love for cooking*. Have it. *Love for life*. I have no complaints. The word *love* sticks in my head. For work, yes. For a woman. No.

My dick twitches in response as if telling me *Nate, I'm lonely. Please find us someone.*

"I know big guy, you need the real thing, I do too. But there is so much work to be done," I grumble as I tug off my briefs and step into the steaming hot shower. Yes, I know I'm talking to my cock, my sanity is the cost of being so driven.

I'm a workaholic. It's safe to say I'm obsessed with running *Due Fratelli* with my older brother Nico. Cooking is an art. Having the opportunity to immerse people in a culinary experience is a privilege. Working towards earning a Michelin star is a daily challenge. Every day, every minute, everything must be perfect.

Can't you work towards your dreams and find me a nice warm home? My cock whines at me as I wash myself.

"Shut up!"

I'm losing my goddamn mind.

I rinse and dry myself off. I wrap a towel around my waist and walk to the kitchen. I reach for an espresso cup and pour myself a double shot. Years ago, I became immune to 'regular' coffee. Now it's strictly espresso in the morning and sometimes at night. I walk to my table, take a seat and a sip, and open my leather pocket notebook to resume finalizing the specials for the week. Tonight's special will depend on what I can harvest from the rooftop garden.

We feature three specials daily and change the menu weekly so it's always fresh and new. We keep our most popular and signature dishes on the menu for those who like routine and hate change.

My notebook is full of ideas, sketches, goals, random shit I need to get on paper instead of my head. The pages are stained with sauce and coffee but it's my Bible.

I scribble my to-do list and as the caffeine enters my bloodstream, I come alive.

"You got this Nate. You're not going to fail." I tell myself as I shut my notebook and finish the last sip. I wash out my cup and put it on the drying rack. I shuffle to my dresser and put on my boxers, black chef pants, socks, white t-shirt, and chef coat. I walk to the bathroom, put on deodorant, brush my teeth, and gel my hair. I secure my watch to my wrist and check the time. 6 am. 10 hours until service begins.

Could I sleep in? Yes, but every second counts. I find peace and solace in having the kitchen to myself for a few hours before Nico and the rest of our staff arrive. The first task of the day is to check the rooftop garden for fresh ingredients.

I leave my apartment and take the stairs to the rooftop. The sun shines through the morning fog. Cars honking and sirens blaring cut through my serenity. There is no peace in Chicago, so I have a spot outside of the city I go to when I need quiet to think.

I grab my basket and begin harvesting. When Nico and I opened our restaurant, I knew it was important to grow as much as I could. Fresh ingredients are always the best, and growing my own helps keep costs down.

I collect tomatoes, garlic, parsley, basil, sweet peppers, eggplant, onions, and raspberries. The aromatics of the garden tickle my senses and ideas for tonight's special start firing off in my mind. I take out my pocket notebook and scribble my ideas before Nico breaks up my solitude.

"Good morning," he yawns looking disheveled. We've had the past two days off and surprisingly I haven't seen him much.

"Rough night?" I ask, even though I didn't hear moaning from his place on the floor below mine.

"Maybe," he shrugs, "What did the garden provide today?" He asks as he peeks in the basket.

"We have enough for stuffed sweet peppers, raspberry limoncello torte, and caprese salad. I'm also going to work up an eggplant dish for vegetarians."

"Not eating meat should be a crime," Nico shakes his head. I agree. "What do you need from the farmers market? You have a list?"

I chuckle, "Of course I have a list."

He rolls his eyes at me but if it weren't for my organizational skills, things wouldn't run like a fine-oiled machine in our kitchen.

"I'll go get what we need, come back, help you unload the truck, and prepare the family meal."

"Sounds good man, the list is on the prep table downstairs."

Family meals are a tradition in most restaurants, and for Nico and me, Wednesdays before service are dedicated to this practice. During these meals, we set the tone for the week, announce the weekly specials, review the daily specials, and provide the staff with an opportunity to voice any concerns. Fortunately, there are rarely any issues.

***

Nico and I prepare a test run of tonight's specials for the staff and the food is served family-style. We are lucky to have the most loyal staff around. In March 2020, the pandemic shut the city down for two weeks. It's the last time I've had that much time off work, and while a two-week vacation seems great, it turned into the most stressful year of my life.

Our fine dining restaurant, which we built from the ground up, suddenly became obsolete. We could no longer offer dine-in seating and had to pivot to takeout orders only. When restrictions were lifted to allow for outdoor seating, our only available option was the rooftop, which wasn't set up for serving guests. We improvised by hosting private parties and taking reservations for the limited seating we had, but we still relied heavily on takeout.

Through it all, Raul, Julian, Leah, Amira, and Megan stayed at Due Fratelli. Nico and I took care of them and I'm thankful every day. From April 2020 to April 2021, over 385 food businesses in Chicago closed and I'm grateful every day that ours wasn't one of them.

"Chef, everything smells delicious," Megan our lead server compliments me with a sparkle in her eye, snapping me back to reality.

"Thank you," I smile.

"Ohh, I love the sweet peppers!" Amira says with a full mouth.

"I only like spice in my books," Megan nudges her and they laugh together.

Megan is quiet, reserved, and professional. Her comment about the spicy book surprises me. It's no offense to her, but I don't picture her as the frisky type. However, I've noticed that she seems to be flirting with me lately—perhaps she's just being friendly? I haven't dated in years, and I won't even admit how long it's been since I've gotten laid. Too long. I have to connect to my partner to get off and a connection is damn near impossible when I work and live in this building. Business is my life.

Nico announces the specials and reviews each chef's responsibilities. Tonight, I am monitoring the kitchen and keeping an eye on the guests.

"Let's have a great service!" Nico toasts.

Megan

"Oh my God!" I groan as I come around the corner to input my table's order, "I feel so bad for that woman."

"Which one?" my co-worker Amira asks.

"The pretty brunette with the handsome guy wearing glasses."

"What's wrong?" Our boss Nate asks as he peaks his head between us.

"She is so bored, Mr. Glasses will not let her talk or get a word in, she is downing that wine like it's the last bottle on Earth." I chuckle.

Amira laughs, "Do you think she will make it until the end of the meal?"

"Doubtful." I shake my head.

"Which table?" Nate asks, he is overlooking the front of house and his job is to ensure that everyone has a great experience.

"10."

Nate sighs, "I'll take care of it, bread and salads out?"

"Yes, Chef."

"Raul! Can you rush table ten please?"

"Yes, Chef!" Raul acknowledges. Nate washes his hands and makes his way to the dining room.

I round up drinks, fresh warm bread, and salads for my new table. As I deliver the orders, I notice Nate turning on the charm. Those dimples that appear when he's trying to suppress a smile peek through; his dress shirt is rolled up at the forearms, and his dark, naturally curly hair is styled perfectly. He looks gorgeous and charming—and he's winking at my customer.

Her eyes follow Nate as he subtly nods his head, signaling her to follow him to the back. What the hell is he doing?

I refocus on my guests and repeat their orders back to them, ensuring I've heard everything correctly. I smile kindly and then return to the kiosk to enter their main course.

Nate whips past me with the brunette in tow and they head out the backdoor.

I find his older brother who is also my boss and smack him, "What the hell is Nate doing? That is my customer!"

Nico laughs at me, as he rubs his arm, "Ouch! I don't know."

Nate opens the back door and yells, "Chef! 86 Table 10, Seat 2 table service, make it to go!"

"Yes, Chef!" the line hollers in acknowledgment.

"It looks like he's bailing her out of that boring date," Nico rolls his eyes. "Go make her date feel better. You haven't been on a date in… how long? Hijack hers."

"I hate you," I grumble under my breath.

"Orders up for one!" Raul laughs as he looks at me and slides Mr. Glasses' plate of carbonara. I take a deep breath and put my best smile on. I can feel my heart beating against my black uniform dress shirt.

"Dinner is served." I smile as I set the plate in front of him. Steam billows from it, and he has to take off his glasses to see. His eyes are a gorgeous blue.

He half smiles at me, "She left, didn't she?"

I nod, "I'm sorry, yes."

"Shit! I was so nervous, she was so beautiful I couldn't think, when I'm nervous, I ramble…"

I cut him off, "Hey…"

"Mark."

"Mark, I'm sorry she left, it just wasn't meant to be." I lift a shoulder, "Look on the bright side, you get to enjoy fabulous homemade pasta, so tonight isn't all bad, right?"

He smiles and his teeth are perfect and glimmer in the candlelight, "You're right." He sits up and straightens his tie.

"Would you like me to bring another bottle of Syrah?"

"I'd like that, thank you…"

"Megan."

"Right, Megan, sorry."

"It's okay, I'll get that wine." I nod and scan my other tables to see how they are doing before heading back again hoping to see Nate so I can give him a piece of my mind.

"Where's Nate?" I ask Amira.

"He told Julian he would be back."

"Fuck." I mutter under my breath. I retrieve Mark's bottle of Syrah and make my way back to the table. I uncork it and pour him a glass.

"Thank you, Megan, this carbonara is incredible, give my compliments to the chef?"

"I will, he will appreciate that." I smile, trying to salvage my tip. "Is there anything else I can get for you?"

"A date," he jokes as he points to the empty chair across from him. That makes me laugh out loud. He is cute and witty.

"I'll check back." I tap his table.

I continue excellent service for my other tables and everyone is full and happy when they leave. It's nearing closing time and Mark is my last table. He finished his pasta, bread, dessert, and a bottle of wine. He is studying his phone screen when I tap the table to get his attention, "I'd ask if there is anything else I can get you, but I have nothing more to offer," I joke.

He looks around and says, "Sorry, I didn't realize the place had practically cleared out. I'm not holding you up from leaving, am I?"

"Nah, I still have to clean up." I wave him off.

"Do you like it here? Working here?" He asks.

"Yes, I do. The owners are great, it's always busy, the pay is good…I like it."

"Have you always wanted to work in fine dining?"

I let out a sigh. "No, I went to school for elementary education, but then the pandemic hit. I saw how little teachers made and how they were treated. I make more now than I would as a teacher, so here I am, living the dream of being a high-end waitress." I playfully bow.

Mark laughs. "What's your passion?"

His question takes me by surprise. "Um, I don't think I have one. That's sad, isn't it?" I scrunch up my nose.

"Not as bad as your date leaving before your entrée comes."

"She missed out. It's her loss." I half smile, "I'll go get your check."

Instrumental music fills the dining room and it's almost reset for tomorrow. Nate still isn't back. I go to the server kiosk and print Mark's check.

"Are you finally getting rid of that camper?" Amira asks.

"It's fine, he's not so bad."

"You've been cranky since Nate left, are you okay?"

"Yeah, I'm fine." I lie. The truth is, I've had a crush on Nate since my first week working here almost six years ago. He's my boss so I've never made a move or pursued him, but I was working up the courage. The past few weeks I've been less subtle with my flirting, and I've been trying to make it more obvious that I'm interested but he isn't picking up on my signs.

I return to Mark's table and hand him the black padded book containing his check. He doesn't even glance at it before handing me his card. I swipe the card, and when I return, he is standing, ready to sign and leave. He scribbles on the receipt and reaches into his suit jacket.

"This may be out of line but, here's my card."

I glance at it and the words, 'financial', 'investment', and 'retirement planning' stand out.

"If you're ever looking for a change, I know people. Give me a call." He smiles.

"Thanks, but…" I try to hand him the card back and he refuses.

"Even if you don't want a change, if you don't skip out on dinner dates, call me." He winks and heads towards the exit.

I grab the black booklet, and when I get to the kitchen, I open it. He left me a $500 tip. *That's four times more than what dinner came to, what the fuck?* At the bottom of the slip, he wrote:

'Thanks for keeping me company tonight, I hope you find your passion- M'

Passion. I love what I do here. We get to celebrate birthdays, anniversaries, engagements. We get to share in special moments in people's lives. I thrive in controlled chaos. I like the hustle. I give 100% of myself and my effort and it's why I'm the best. It's the Capricorn in me. Loyal, dependable, hard-working.

I have a passion for making people smile. I wish I had a different kind of passion in my life. The kind that ends in an orgasm.

"Nate! There you are, we didn't think you'd come back." I hear Julian tease Nate and I shake my head out of my daydream.

He's back. Nate's black t-shirt clings to him perfectly and his tattoos peak from under his sleeves. His cheeks are rosy beneath his tan skin.

"Boss man is blushing!" Raul teases.

Amira joins them in laughter and so do my co-workers, even Nico gets in on it. Nico puts his arm around Nate's shoulder and tussles his hair, "How'd it go little brother, did you screw her?"

Nate shoves Nico, "No I didn't fuck her, Jesus Christ man, I just met her, and if I did…I wouldn't have come back here to help close up."

"What happened?" Raul nudges him and wiggles his eyebrows. My stomach churns.

"I took Olivia to…"

"Ooohh she has a nameee," Nico interrupts.

"Nope, that's it…I'm not telling you guys shit." Nate throws his hands up and starts walking towards the office.

"No, no, no, you ditched work for her, we need to know." Nico stops him.

Nate blushes, "As I was saying… I rode us to Navy Pier, where a jazz band was playing. We ate together on the lawn as we listened and talked. When the fireworks started we kissed."

Everyone whistles and claps for him but me.

"Did you get her number?" Julian asks.

"I did." Nate smiles. *God, you're so lucky Olivia.*

I exit the kitchen and go to the dining room to finish resetting my section. When I'm almost done, Nate joins me. It's just the two of us.

"How'd Olivia's date take the news?" Nate asks as he runs a hand through his hair.

"How'd you feel if a woman didn't stay for the entrée?" I snip, I can't even look at him.

"You said she was bored out of her mind, I was trying to help you," he tries to rationalize.

I turn and poke him in the chest. "Never take my customers' date again. Do it with Ava or Hayes, not me, understood? What if Mark was an undercover reviewer or worked for Michelin? You need to think things through, Nate!" Okay, maybe I'm being a little jealous and dramatic, but I have a valid point.

Nate puts his hands up to surrender, "Fine. You're right. Are you really mad at me?"

I scoff and push past him. I untie my apron and walk to the office door, "Can you cash me out so I can go?"

Nate digs his keys out of his pocket and unlocks the office door, he powers up the computer to run reports for the night.

There is an awkward silence between us. When Nate runs the reports he clicks his tongue, "Holy shit, you cleared more tips than anyone today, and one for $500? I need to steal *more* women from your tables. I did you a favor."

I stand in anger, "You know I work my ass off for you and Nico, right? Mark could have been planning to tip that much *before* you stole Olivia away, that guy is loaded."

"Mark? You're on a first-name basis with him?" Nate cocks an eyebrow at me.

"That's what happens when you have to make the best of your boss ruining your customer's night!" I snap.

Nate stands, "I'm teasing you, relax. You are the best server we have; you work hard and I'm thankful you kept him calm." He smiles softly at me before unlocking the safe and counting out my tips for the night. He hands me my stack of bills, "You're still coming to work tomorrow, right? After making this much today you're not going to call in sick, are you?"

I count my money and don't answer.

"Megan, I need you," Nate says softly, and my eyes meet his chestnut-colored ones. "I need you to hold things down while Nico and I are in Aspen. Please say you'll be here tomorrow." His bottom lip juts out, and he clasps his hands together in a pleading gesture.

I lighten up, "I haven't missed a day of work in five years, I'm not starting now."

He breathes a sigh of relief, "Whew, good, do you want a ride home? I don't want you walking home with that much cash on you."

Of course, I want a ride home! I have wanted to ride on the back of his motorcycle for years!

"Don't you have to finish up here? Nico will kick your ass if you leave again."

Amira pops in the doorway, "Side work is done, dining room is swept, I'm ready to cash out!" She cheers.

Nate glances at me with an apologetic expression as Amira interrupts us. "Amira, could you drive Megan home tonight?"

"Of course! She is on my way!"

I unlock the door to the apartment I share with my older sister Hayley. She must have been working on a painting because our apartment reeks of oil paint and brush cleaner. I hear the muffled sound of angsty music coming from her room. I knock lightly on her door, just in case she has company. "I'm home, sis. Goodnight!" I holler and hear her faintly say goodnight back to me.

I take off my work uniform and release my posh bun. I undress completely and count the cash I'm stashing under my bed, as well as the money I'm depositing into my checking and savings accounts. My under-the-bed stash is my 'play money'. I've paid off my student loans, I don't have any credit card debt, and I'm not making car payments. I'm also not saving for a house or children. I tend to save most of what I earn since I rarely go out or travel; I guess you could say I'm a bit boring. Could that be why Nate hasn't noticed my flirting? Am I just too boring for him to pay attention to me?

As I recount my bills, Mark's business card falls out. I'm curious about who he knows. Is there something better out there for me?

CHAPTER TWO

Thursday, June 13th

NATE

Nico and I are flying to Aspen to be featured during the Aspen Food & Wine Classic. It's been a dream of ours to get invited.

"Are you sure you ordered enough?" Nico asks as we review the sample tasting plan for the next few days.

"I spoke to my contact, and everything we need is ready. The refrigeration and burners are set up, and the tent is prepared. We just need to prep, show up, and do our best."

"Hell yeah!" Nico and I fist bump.

We land in Colorado and Nico picks up our rental SUV. On the drive to Aspen, I list everything we need to prep for the next two days.

"Tomorrow we will do our sample-sized chicken cacciatore paired with a dry red wine sample."

"And Saturday?" Nico asks.

"We will change it up and make chicken Genovese with a pesto cream sauce and pair it with a sample of dry white wine."

"You ordered enough wine, right? And sample cups?"

I look over my list, "Yes, everything is ordered and Wyatt double-checked everything arrived."

"I can't believe we are doing this," my brother beams with happiness. Our Nonni and Mom are the reason why Nico and I love and appreciate food and our Italian heritage. Some of my best memories as a child were cooking with my Nonni. I remember loving the smell of fresh-cut basil on my hands, picking fresh tomatoes from her garden, and being covered head to toe in flour from making fresh pasta. I loved it. The sound of bubbling boiling water, the sight of steam rising from freshly baked bread, the sound of a knife chopping on the cutting board, and the aroma of garlic. Heaven.

While my Nonni and Mom instilled in me a love for food, it was Nico who inspired my passion for the art of cooking and the joy of serving homemade meals. He is the reason I became a chef and co-owner of Due Fratelli.

The pine trees rush by as Nico drives to Aspen, and my mind flashes back to the night when Nico saved my life and changed it forever.

I was devastated when Nonni passed away. I was sixteen, lacked a solid friend group, and chose to cope with my emotions by partying. I was drinking a few weekends each month, smoking pot whenever it was available, trying cocaine, and even snorting some pills just to fit in and experience what my friends were doing.

I went to a rundown house with my best friend Trey. Thinking back now, I don't think it had electricity or running water, but it was somewhere to listen to music and drink. Trey and I sang angsty songs as he drove us to the house. We felt like we were the coolest. Trey got his older brother to score us cheap vodka and some weed. We weren't picky when it came to what we got our hands on. We were teenagers who wanted to be cool like our older brothers who were 21.

Trey and I took turns drinking right from the bottle, we smoked a couple of joints, listened to music, danced with some girls, made out with a few, and one slipped a pill in my mouth as we kissed. I didn't care what it was. I wanted to be numb. I wanted to escape reality.

Kissing that girl was the last clear thing I remember before waking up in a fog with Nico slapping my face and putting his fingers down my throat to make me throw up on the lawn in front of the house.

"Thank fuck I found you! You scared the shit out of me you asshole!" Nico yelled and I remember feeling like my brain was rattling inside my skull. He slapped me on the face to keep me awake, and when my eyes finally focused, he hugged me, tight. I've never had a hug like that since.

My stomach churns thinking of why my brother was so thankful he found me. He broke our embrace and used my shirt to wipe my face. He practically had to carry me to his car. I was confused about why he was there, how he found me, why he was putting me in his car and not Trey's. I couldn't form words, if I did, they didn't come out coherently because Nico didn't answer me. He put me in his passenger seat, leaned the seat back a little, and strapped me in.

I woke up the next afternoon at Nico's apartment and when I stumbled into the living room, he was sitting on the couch looking like hell.

"We need to talk."

I knew I fucked up.

"Go shower then we will talk, I put clean clothes in the bathroom."

I rejoined him smelling much better, "Nico, I'm sorry you had to see me like that...I just...wanted to have fun and not think about Nonni not being with us anymore, it was stupid. I—"

"Trey was in an accident last night," Nico cut me off, "He got behind the wheel all fucked up, he wanted to take some girl home and..."

I didn't hear anything after that. My ears rang so loud, and my legs gave out. Nico caught me before I hit the floor.

"Hey asshole I'm talking to you! Hello!" Nico snaps me back to reality.

I clear my throat and refocus on the present, "Sorry, what?"

"Can you call and let Ma and Pops know we made it?"

I call my parents and let them know Nico and I are heading to the hotel and that we will be busy the next few days and when I hang up with them, my mind drifts back.

I spent four days at the hospital with Trey's parents, siblings, and the family of the girl who was the passenger. Unfortunately, she didn't survive. Machines were the only thing that kept Trey alive. My parents and Nico came to keep me company when they weren't at work.

I'm grateful that Trey's parents didn't hold me responsible for his choices. He was heading down a dangerous path in life, and I could have easily gotten caught up in it with him. I like to believe I wasn't foolish enough to get into a car with someone drunk and high, but I would have followed him anywhere.

The parents of the girl who passed away didn't blame Trey. We found out that Trey was driving her to the hospital because she had been sexually assaulted and needed help. He was trying to be the hero.

During my darkest days, I often wondered if her death was God's way of protecting her from having to raise her rapist's child or make the difficult choice of having an abortion. He took both her and the unborn baby to heaven so they would never have to witness the darkness of humanity again. I knew that if I voiced this thought aloud, my Catholic parents would disown me, so I kept it to myself all these years.

My parents didn't punish me or ground me for drinking and using drugs. Losing my Nonni and seeing my best friend from elementary school on a ventilator was punishment enough.

Carrying his casket was the ultimate punishment.

My parents and Nico were worried I'd use partying to cope. The three of them kept guard over me. My parents switched me to cyber school. Walking the halls that Trey and I grew up in was too hard. Nico got me a job as a dishwasher at the restaurant he worked at. On slow nights when the management wasn't there, he'd pull me on the line and teach me how to cook. Cooking, crafting dishes, and trying new recipes became a healthy addiction.

Nico saved me and changed my life.

I graduated from high school with honors and then attended culinary school. I worked my way up at the restaurant alongside Nico. I even filled in as a waiter when others called off work, and I bartended as well. This experience allowed me to learn everything about running a restaurant.

A sign for the Aspen Food and Wine Classic catches my eye and it's unbelievable how far Nico and I have come together.

"You said Hannah is going to be here?" I ask. Hannah Summers is a famous surfer and influencer in her industry and Nico's fuck buddy. Anytime she's in Chicago, they hook up.

"Yeah, she had some time off and always wanted to come so we are meeting up."

"Just let me know so I can leave the hotel room first," I grumble.

"Have you heard from the hottie from the other night?"

"Olivia? No."

"Dude, what? Have you texted her?"

"I've been busy and aren't there rules about texting too soon or something?"

"A woman that hot, and I only caught a glimpse, you throw out the rule book."

"Shit."

"Let's focus on getting service done and then you're texting her."

"Deal."

CHAPTER THREE

Friday, June 14th

NATE

Nico and I checked into our hotel last night and immediately got to work preparing for today. We found our rhythm serving samples, and people flooded our tent. I'm so grateful that I over-prepared.

"Restocking," I call to Nico as I get him more bottles of red wine and sample cups. When I turn around, Olivia and Hannah stand there, waiting for their samples. Olivia looks gorgeous in a flowy olive-green outfit; her hair is styled beautifully, and she appears nervous. *What is she doing here?*

I shake off my surprise, and a smile spreads across my face.

"Olivia!" I walk to her and reach across the table to hug her, God her hair smells so good. I politely kiss her on the cheek. Hannah greets Nico and my focus shifts back to Olivia.

"Hi Nate," Olivia smiles nervously, "Congrats on being featured this weekend."

"Thank you, sorry I haven't texted you. We have been crazy busy traveling and getting things ready for today…" I prep a sample of our signature modified version of chicken cacciatore to keep my hands busy.

"It's cool," she shrugs. I know it's not cool, I should have texted her or told her I was coming to Aspen. She takes the sample from me and sips, "This is amazing." She licks her lips, and I want to kiss them again. She tilts her head back and finishes and fuck, I want to be in her mouth.

"It's our twist on chicken cacciatore, I'm glad you like it." I try to focus and not check out her plump breasts and perfect legs.

Hannah pops over next to Olivia, "Nate, this is perfection! Are you busy this evening?" She blurts out.

Her question catches me off guard, "Uh, I'm free."

"Would you like to come to a party tonight with Olivia? Nico is coming with me." *He is?* He didn't tell me about the party. I look over at him and he smirks. *What is he up to?*

I rub my neck, "I'd be honored."

Olivia fights a smile.

"Olivia, you in?" Hannah asks.

She nods and her emerald eyes bore into me, "Yeah, I'm in."

"Perfect! We will see you guys tonight. I'll send your brother the details. Come on Liv." Hannah directs

Olivia away and I want to run after them, but I have work to do. For the rest of the service, I'm on autopilot. All I can think about is seeing Olivia tonight.

Megan

When I arrive at work for my shift, it feels strange not having Nate or Nico there. One of them was always around. While they are in Aspen, Raul is in charge. Since Nate and Nico didn't ask, and because I'm the waitress who has been here the longest, I take responsibility for the front of the house.

Raul goes over the specials with the waitstaff, and cooks, and Julian is the lead chef tonight. They are like big brothers to me; all the staff are. We all want to make the Rossi brothers proud while they are away. They never take a break or vacation, they deserve this.

After Raul's rundown for the night, I pull him aside before we open. "Have you heard from Nico or Nate today?" I ask as I tie my black apron.

"Day One was a success; Nate planned everything perfectly, as always. They should be posting pictures soon, and they got invited to a party, so that's a good sign."

My heart flutters, I knew they would do incredible.

"That's amazing," I smile at him, "Let's make them proud tonight."

NATE

I'm feeling nervous as I prepare for the party that Hannah's friend is hosting. I texted Raul to update him on how my day went and to let him know to text me if any issues arise during dinner service.

I give myself a fresh shave and put gel in my hair to tame my curls. I spritz on cologne and check myself out in the mirror. I'm slim, but fit and have abs thanks to unloading the trucks twice a week. I also try to work out a couple of times a week with my makeshift home gym. I look over my tattoos and the cross on my shoulder that memorializes my grandparents and Trey catches my eye.

"Thanks for looking out for me today, I know you were there," I tell them.

I hear the door to the hotel room open and Nico and Hannah are giggling.

"Nate, you ready?" Nico asks as he knocks on the bathroom door.

"Almost!" I holler. Nico and Hannah got ready at her hotel room. God only knows what they did before. I hear kissing noises and her yelp so I have a good idea of what went on.

I put on my white undershirt followed by my navy blue dress shirt. Since the summer air is warm, I roll the sleeves up a quarter of the way. Next, I slip into my dress slacks and shoes. I check my breath one last time before joining Nico and Hannah.

Nico parks the black SUV in front of the condo complex that Hannah directed us to, and she texted Olivia to meet us outside. I get out of the SUV and anxiously wait for her. As soon as she turns the corner, all the air leaves my lungs. Olivia is beautiful, her loose curls frame her beautiful face, and her makeup is natural except for stunning eye makeup. Her knee-length black dress fits her curves perfectly. Olivia radiates a bright smile and she greets me with a hug. Her floral perfume surrounds me like a spell.

"You look stunning," I whisper and kiss her cheek before diving into her green eyes, "I can't believe you are in Aspen. You never mentioned anything on Wednesday."

"It doesn't come up," she smiles, a pink blush rising to her cheeks. "You didn't say anything either, you know?" Her eyebrow quirks.

Fuck she is so damn cute, focus Nate, "True. Are you ready to go?" I reach my hand out to take hers and she accepts it. I lead and open the door for her then slide in beside her. My hand rests on Olivia's thigh and my fingers twitch wanting to touch every inch of her.

Hannah and Olivia engage in light conversation to get to know each other better, while Hannah guides us to the lodge where the party is taking place. When we arrive, I help Olivia out of the car, and she loops her arm through mine.

Hannah and Nico lead the way inside. The room is dimly lit, everyone is mingling, and waiters are going around with food trays. Light acoustic music plays setting the Aspen vibe in the rustic log lodge. I scan the room and there are so many chefs I admire here but first, I need to focus on Olivia.

"How was your day of tastings?" I ask as we grab a food sample from a passing tray.

"It was great, I tried so many kinds of food and wine. I got starstruck a few times meeting some of the chefs I recognize from television."

I chuckle, "I get that way too sometimes. People in the culinary world are so chill and normal in real life, don't be nervous." I kiss her cheek, trying to seem cool and calm, but really, I'm just as nervous as she is. I fake my confidence and lead us around the room. I introduce Olivia to one of my old buddies from culinary school.

"Denzel, hey! Good to see you, man!" I greet him with a handshake. His hands are the size of baseball mitts, and he makes me look short, standing at 6'5". Not the guy you want to run into when trying to impress a woman. If Trey got to live, this is how I'd picture him at this age.

Denzel's deep voice rivals Morgan Freeman's, "Nate, good to see you. I wanted to stop by earlier but I'm featured too."

"Hey, no problem, that kicks ass that we are both here, how have you been, where are you working now?"

"The Palisade in Los Angeles, we are hoping to be nominated for a Michelin Star. Who is your guest?" Denzel asks.

"Oh sorry! This is my friend Olivia." They shake hands. "Working on a star huh? Nico and I are trying too."

Denzel and I compare notes and catch up, once I start talking about food and cooking, I get lost in it. I notice Olivia getting antsy so I say goodbye to my friend.

"I'm sorry...Once I start talking about food, I lose myself, I didn't mean to ignore you," I apologize, "I promise I'm all yours now." I whisper in her ear over the music, trying my best to resist the urge to kiss her neck, "Do you want to get some air?"

"Sure."

I take her hand and lead us outside to the patio area. A fire is lit, and the mountains are so close it looks like it could be CGI. Olivia moves past me to take it all in.

"Wow, this view is breathtaking." Olivia admires the scenery.

I take a mental picture of her and I have to touch her. I move her hair off one shoulder and kiss it. Her sun-kissed skin is so soft, and a hint of jasmine and daisies floats from her. Olivia pulls away from my lips and faces me, catching me off guard. I move closer and rest my hands on her hips. "I'm so glad you are here. I could have passed out when I saw you earlier." I confess.

Olivia smiles softly, "I'm happy too, it's nice to travel somewhere and not have to enjoy everything alone."

I have to make up for not texting her since Wednesday. I have to let her know I'm interested, "If it's okay with you, I can keep you company this weekend. Nico and I have samples to hand out again tomorrow, but I'd like to take you out Sunday. Would you want to do that?" I flinch.

"That sounds nice, yes," she nods, "But I don't understand why haven't you texted me? You said you have been busy traveling and preparing for the festival but...I thought you and I had a great time?" She asks sweetly but I hear the annoyance in her tone, "I'm the one who put myself out there and gave you my number..."

She's right. She made all the first moves, the least I could have done was fucking text or call. I take her hands in mine, "I'm sorry, I didn't want to seem too eager and scare you off. It's been a long time since I've dated. I am out of practice, forgive me?" I stick out my bottom lip like a sad puppy. It works on everyone else, will it work on her?

Olivia takes a long pause before finally relaxing., "Fine, I forgive you." She kisses my cheek and I'm thankful for her forgiveness.

"Perfect, I'll plan something. I promise." I want to show her a good time. She deserves it. Right as I am ready to pull her in and kiss her, I feel a hand clench my shoulder.

"Can I steal my brother? I just spotted someone I want to introduce him to." Nico asks Olivia. *Fuck.*

"Of course, go!" Olivia lets go of my hands and shoos me away.

Nico takes me back inside and as much as I love talking about the restaurant and all our goals, I want to be with Olivia. I politely introduce myself and make quick small talk then excuse myself.

I spot Olivia at the bar with Hannah and a man who is maybe a few years older than Nico. Olivia is blushing and smiling from ear to ear, sipping her wine and batting her lashes. I try to stay calm, but she came here with me and is leaving with me.

I make my way through the crowd and she doesn't even notice I'm behind her, I let out an audible, "Ahem." That gets her attention.

Hannah takes notice, "Oh Brad, this is our friend, Nate, his restaurant is being featured this weekend. Nate, this is Brad Walker." Hannah introduces us.

Olivia grips Brad's arm, "He follows my blog. We were talking about traveling."

Seeing her touch him makes me seethe, "Nice to meet you." I say in an even tone and reach out to shake his hand. I eye him up and down.

"Are you two here together?" Brad asks as he points between Olivia and me. *Why does he have to be Australian? I can't compete with that!*

"Yes, she is with me."

Brad's jaw drops, "Livy! I didn't know you had a boyfriend, you never posted about traveling with someone." *Livy, they are comfortable enough to have nicknames now?*

"We aren't a couple," Olivia says quickly.

"Yet." I cut her off and snake my arm around her waist. I want Brad and Olivia both to know that I intend to make her mine.

"Isn't that her choice, mate?" Brad smirks cockily and I shoot daggers out of my eyes at him.

Luckily, Hannah grabs Brad's hand and starts to pull him away from us, "Come tell me about your trip." Before he goes with her, he places a hand on Olivia's hip and leans in to kiss her cheek and it's a little too long for my liking.

"See ya' 'round darlin'." He says seductively and Olivia blushes and smiles. *What the fuck?* I know I didn't text her or tell her I was going to be here, but do I deserve to have her flirt with a guy right in front of me?

"He's a fan huh?" I cock my head to the side.

"I've never had someone recognize me before, don't take that from me, okay? You have been talking to people since we got here. Maybe, if you stayed with me, he would have assumed I was with you." She has a point. She is sassy and strong and puts me in my place. She reminds me of Megan.

"I don't want anyone eying you like he did." I blurt out.

Olivia huffs, "Nate, he was just being nice. If you don't want him or other men to look at or talk to me, act like you are here with me."

Hannah scurries to us, "Come on you two, let's get outta here!" Hannah links her arm with Olivia's and starts walking away with her. Nico walks beside me.

"What the hell was that? You looked like you were ready to punch that guy."

"She was flirting with him like I wasn't even there."

"It's her job to socialize, don't take it personally."

I try not to, but Olivia opens the door and climbs in the SUV. She doesn't wait for me to open it for her. I climb in beside her and this time, I keep my hands to myself. She doesn't want me.

Twenty minutes later, Nico pulls up in front of Olivia's condo complex. I try to be the bigger person and apologize so I get out with Olivia.

She starts to walk away before I get out of the car, "I'm sorry. I didn't mean to act like a jealous prick. Can we start over tomorrow?" I offer.

She turns to face me and snaps back, "I don't want to wait until tomorrow, I've been waiting for you since Wednesday." The words spew from her pouty lips and take me by surprise.

I can't let her get away. I reach out and cup the back of her neck, pull her to me, and kiss her passionately. Our tongues wrestle and I can still taste the champagne on her. Our kiss is desperate and needy like we have both been wanting this. I break our kiss and rest my forehead against hers, "Brad wanted you. It looked as if you wanted him too and that drives me fucking crazy," I admit. I gaze into her eyes with lust and desire, "I want you."

"Prove it."

CHAPTER FOUR

NATE

I follow Olivia, her perfect ass looks incredible in her tight dress. My hands are all over her as she punches the code into the keypad to unlock the door. As soon as we are inside, we attack each other with kisses. Olivia pulls my dress shirt out of my pants and I help her unbutton it. She takes my shirt off and tosses it to the floor. I pull her against me and kiss her. She reaches back to unzip her dress, wiggles it off and it falls to the floor.

"Fuck, Olivia you are sexy, my God." I drool at seeing her in a black strapless bra and thong. She's perfect. Olivia unhooks the bra and her big tits fall free. I bury my head in her chest and breathe her in. I kiss her chest while her hands work at my belt. Her back arches in pleasure giving me access to licking and sucking her peaked nipples. Olivia's moans and whimpers make me rock hard.

I work my way up her neck and then back to her mouth. Her lips are pouty and perfect. Olivia wrestles my belt free, unzips my pants, and crouches to pull them down. I step out of them and my hard-on is raging in my boxer briefs. From the look on her face, she is impressed with my length.

Olivia is ravenous and kisses over my tattoos and chest. I grip her tit and plump ass and take in how incredible this feels. It's been over eight months since I last had sex with someone, and I don't have time to jerk off either. I'm too exhausted by the time the day is done.

The kisses move down to my stomach and happy trail then make their way back to my lips. I grab Olivia's ass and hoist her up. She wraps her legs around me and nibbles on my earlobe while I find the way to the bedroom.

I lay Olivia down on the bed and run my hands up her smooth legs, I grip her thighs and goosebumps form on her skin. I move my hands to her thong and slowly slide it off, admiring every inch of her. Her bare pussy is glistening, begging to be fucked.

We lock eyes and I slowly ease two fingers inside her wet pussy and a gasp of pleasure escapes her. I want to make her come a few times before having sex with her because I'm not sure how long I'll last. I caress her g-spot with the 'come here' motion gently and I lean down to kiss her while I work my fingers. "Tell me you are mine for the night," I moan. I want to know she only wants me. Not Brad or anyone else.

Olivia moans and looks me in the eye, "I'm yours tonight. Fuck, that feels so good."

"It's from using the clutch when I ride," I tease and her tight pussy clutches even tighter. My cock twitches. I increase the speed and pressure, and an orgasm erupts from her. Her legs are shaking, and she grips my wrist to make me stop fingering her. I let out a sinister chuckle, pull my fingers out, and lick them clean. Fuck she tastes good.

"I want you," her eyes plead.

"I want you too. I'll prove it to you, over and over again." I lean down to kiss her and go back to my dress pants to dig a condom out of my wallet. I put it on as I walk back to the bedroom. I need more of her so I get between Olivia's thick thighs and lick her pussy. She comes again. I love how responsive she is to me. My cock is screaming for release. I drag my tongue one more time through her juices and then I spit on my condom-covered dick. I rub it in and rub my tip over her clit before sliding in nice and slow.

I pump in and out trying to get a feel for how much Olivia can take. My cock is eight inches and decently thick. I don't want to hurt her. She looks gorgeous as she looks up at me, she grabs her tits, and I love watching them move. Fuck it feels good to be inside her.

Once her pussy starts to get used to me, I pick up my pace and start pounding into her, hitting her cervix. Our moans fill the room. I slam into her and hearing how wet her pussy is, seeing myself going in and out, I don't know how much more I can take. Olivia lets go of her tits and seeing them bounce drives me wild.

"Lay down, I want to ride you." Olivia pleads.

I pull out and lay back on the bed. I'll do anything she wants. I clasp my hands behind my head to let her have her way with me. My ego gets a little inflated when she slides down my shaft and isn't able to take all of me. I love watching her bounce up and down on me, her juices running down the condom. Seeing her moan and bite her lip. I'm barely hanging on.

"Come here, closer to me," I lean up and pull her against me. I grab her ass and thrust into her and Olivia lets out a loud earth-shattering orgasm. "Fuck your pussy is so tight," I grunt through gritted teeth, "I'm going to come, come with me," I thrust faster. My body tingles. A warmth washes over me. I give her every inch, bottom out in her, and hold myself there. My balls empty into the condom and my cock twitches as it's buried deep. My legs get weak and I lower my hips and relax.

I hold Olivia against me. Our hearts are racing. I trace my fingers over her skin and breathe her in. I could hold her here forever.

Sadly, she rolls off me.

"Fuck, I needed that." She confesses, panting.

Was this just sex, to satisfy a need for her? I can't ask her that, so I just say, "I needed that too, it's been way too damn long," I tussle my hair. I get up from the bed and toss my condom in the trash. It felt like she couldn't roll off me fast enough. If I crawl back into bed, will she think I want to stay the night? I'd love that, but will she?

"I should probably get back to my hotel, Nico and I have planning to do for tomorrow."

Olivia lies on her side, propping her head up on her hand., "Yeah, sure, do what you gotta do."

How can she be so casual about this?

I gather my clothes and bring them to the bedroom to get dressed, hoping she likes what she sees enough to ask me to stay. She doesn't. "I hope you sleep well tonight," I lean on the bed to kiss her in one last attempt, "Are you going to try to stop by the tent tomorrow?"

"I'll try, keep in touch about our plans?"

"Of course," I kiss her again. I make sure I have my phone and wallet and before I leave, "I had an amazing time with you, get some rest, goodnight."

"Goodnight." She smiles.

I make my way out and call Nico, but he doesn't answer. He's probably balls-deep in Hannah. I guess I'll walk to the hotel. I could use a walk to clear my head.

I check the time and call Raul. Dinner service is done and he answers on the second ring.

"Hey Boss, what's up?" He asks.

"Just checking to see how service went tonight." I sigh as I start walking toward the town center.

"You left me in charge so you know it went amazing," he laughs, "Nah, in all seriousness, it was awesome, and you and Nico must have made an impression today because we are booked through the end of the year."

I stop in my tracks, "What?"

"Yeah, all the reservation slots are full."

"That's insane." I am speechless. "Have you told Nico?"

"I sent him a text, but he hasn't replied yet."

"I'll let him know, did everything with front of house run smoothly too?"

"Megan stepped up and took the initiative since you didn't appoint anyone, do you want to talk to her?"

My heart beams with pride, "Yes if she's not—"

"Megs! Nate's on the phone!" Raul hollers for her, "One sec, she's coming."

I hear rustling then Megan's voice, "Hey Nate, how is Aspen? Are those crickets I hear? Are you outside?"

I chuckle, "Yes, I'm uh, on a walk. Aspen is great. We are looking forward to tomorrow. Raul said everything went well tonight. He said you stepped up and ran the front?"

""Well, you didn't ask me to, but someone had to take charge," she says, a smile evident in her voice. "Raul, Julian, and Callum did an amazing job. All the courses were served at the perfect time, and the customers were thrilled. Did he tell you our reservation slots are full for the year?"

"He did, it's crazy. Thank you for looking after things while Nico and I are here, can you do it all weekend? If you have any problems, I'm here for you if you need me."

She is quiet for a moment and then replies, "I can."

"Perfect, can you make sure the waitstaff gets tipped out?"

"Already taken care of."

"You're the best."

Megan

He said I'm the best and that he will be there if I need him. Yes!

I try to contain my excitement as I hand Raul his phone back, "Front of house is clear, do you guys need help with anything?"

"All good, getting ready to lock up, we are heading to the bar, you wanna join?"

"Nah, maybe tomorrow?"

"I'll hold you to it," Julian teases, "Get home safe!"

"I will." I toss my apron and uniform into my bag and step outside. The summer air is thick. I only live three blocks from Due Fratelli and the walk will help me clear my head.

As I walk, I check Nate's Instagram and he posted pictures of the samples they served today and a selfie. Fuck he is handsome when he is in chef mode. Hopefully, Nate realizes that I would do anything for him and his business. What man wouldn't want a woman who supports his dreams?

When I get home, my sister Hayley is curled on the couch watching a documentary.

"You're home late. How was work?"

I spin around and toss my bag to the floor, "It was amazing! The tips were great, I ran the front perfectly. Nate thanked me for stepping up while he's in Aspen."

"Are you going to ask him out?"

"I'm going to when he gets home, I'm done being shy and scared."

She laughs, "It's about time. You know if he rejects you, you can always switch to girls like me," she smiles, "Gay bars are the best and serve the best drinks, I promise."

"Oh, I know, you've made me go how many times over the years?" I laugh.

"It's Pride Month, we have to go at least once!"

I roll my eyes at her, "I'm going to shower and go to bed. Enjoy your boring documentary."

I turn the faucet on lava hot, strip down, and release my hair from its bun. I need to wash the smell of parmesan and garlic off me. Hayley's lavender-scented organic body wash fills my nostrils and relaxes me. As I wash myself, my hands linger over my tits and I tease my nipples and then I move my hand to my clit. I fantasize about seeing Nate all wet in the shower. I've seen him shirtless before and my God is he a sight to behold. I dream of what his dick looks like and how big it is, how it would feel. Mmm. Is he sensual in bed, rough? Is he more dominant or submissive? I want to know.

The more my thoughts drift the harder my fingers circle my clit and I let out a silent moan of pleasure and bite my lip. I need laid. I need Nate.

CHAPTER FIVE

Saturday, June 15th

NATE

I wake up early and decide to have champagne and orange juice delivered to Olivia. I stop by the store to pick everything up and then head to the condo's office to arrange for delivery. Along with the drinks, I write her a note expressing my excitement to see her. I want her to know that I'm interested in dating her, even though I got the impression last night that she was just looking for a casual connection.

A half hour later while I'm finishing prep with Nico, my phone lights up with an incoming call from Olivia. I fight my smile.

"Do you like it?" I ask seductively.

"Yes, thank you." I hear her pop the champagne and pour herself a glass.

"You're welcome! I figured you could use a mimosa or two."

"I can always use a mimosa. Are you and Nico getting set up?"

"Yeah, almost done then the fun begins," I chuckle, "I hope you have a good time today, enjoy it. I'll call you later today when I'm finished, okay?"

"Sounds good." She chimes.

***

People came to our tent non-stop, even more than yesterday. Luckily, Nico and I worked so well together that we kept the service running smoothly. I hoped to see Olivia stop by, especially after my sweet gesture this morning, but she didn't. I wanted her to know I was thinking about her, so I decided to video call her.

After the third ring, she answers looking like she just got out of the shower, fuck.

"Hi Nate, don't mind me, I just got out of the shower. How was your day? I was going to stop but the line was so long!"

That would explain her absence today I guess, "Unbelievable, we ran out of samples quicker than yesterday. So, either more people attended today, or word got around to try us."

"That's great! I'm happy for you guys!" Her gorgeous smile fills her face.

"Raul my sous chef informed me we are booked for the rest of the year. Can you believe that?"

"You better make room for me," Olivia says seductively and my stomach flutters.

"You'll always have a table," I assure her. "Are you up to anything now? I can come over." I ask boldly.

"Sure, come on over, "she flirts, opening her robe to give me a little flash.

"Fuck, I'm on my way. Stay just like that."

I rush to Olivia's before she can change her mind and she answers the door in her little silk robe, "Oh my God," I tip my head back and moan. I back her inside and close and lock the door behind me. I devour her mouth like it's a five-star dessert and I feel her up over her white silk robe. Whimpers escape her. I slide her robe off her shoulders and suckle her perfect nipples.

Olivia's moans echo in the entryway and I back her against the wall. I feel down her body and slide my fingers through her wet folds before inserting two fingers inside her needy cunt. It causes her to stand on her tiptoes and wince in pain so I slow my motion and work her g-spot until she orgasms. Once I make her come with my fingers, I get on my knees and lick her sweet pussy.

"Someone missed me," she moans and bites her lower lip as she looks down at me. She grasps my hair and grinds into my mouth. I moan while sucking on her clit and the vibration sends shockwaves through Olivia making her weak.

Olivia drops to her knees with me and works the button on my shorts. I stand up and take my hard cock out. If she wants it, she can have it. Her tongue teases the tip of my head and then she takes as much of my length as she can down her throat.

"Fuck Olivia…goddamn that feels incredible…just like that…yes…" I pant as I focus all my attention on her mouth. I thrust into her mouth and fuck I feel like I could drain myself right now. She sucks the crown of my cock and I tense up, "If you keep doing that…I'm going to burst."

Olivia giggles, "Mmm…do you want me?"

"Fuck yes, please." I help her to her feet, kick off my shorts, and slide my t-shirt over my head. I have to feel her naked body against mine. I pull her against me for a kiss, but she pushes me away and saunters her ass into the living area. She walks to the couch and seductively peers back at me.

"How do you want me?"

I want to feel her up, feel her against me, kiss her, smell her hair and perfume and savor the moment but she wants fucked.

"Bent over with that perfect ass in the air," I growl.

She bends down and gets on all fours and arches her ass in the air, "Like this?"

"Perfect," I say as I rip the condom packet open and sheath my cock. I position myself behind her and rub my dick over her slick lips and ease into her center, "I've been thinking about being inside you all day," I moan as I press inside her, taking long strokes in and out.

When she opens for me, I start pounding into her pussy. Her ass ripples with every thrust. I dig my fingers into her hips and put her back onto me.

"Nate…" she moans as she grips the cushions with both hands and buries her head into the couch to muffle herself. Her pussy is pulsing and gripping me so tight I can't hold it.

"Yes Olivia, come on this cock." I fuck her harder and she turns around to watch me fuck her. Her green eyes get glossy. I thrust so hard my hair falls across my face, but I don't stop. I gather her hair around my fist and pull back gently. Seeing Olivia's head tilt back, the curve of her spine, her ass clapping against my hips, I can't wait. I have to blow my load.

"I'm close Liv, oh…fuck…" I whine and release her hair. My body caves in and I lean forward on Olivia, using her ass and back to prop me up. I kiss her shoulders and down her spine as I empty every drop. She is silent and her body tenses up. Once I go soft, I pull out and grab a tissue to wrap the condom before tossing it in the trash.

I join Olivia on the couch, wrap my arm around her shoulder, and pull her into me.

"Please tell me you don't have to leave right away?"

"Not until this evening, Nico and I got invited to a private dinner tonight." I move Olivia's hair and kiss her head, "Do you have any plans this evening?"

"Not yet. Hannah is having dinner with her friend who hosted the party yesterday. I'll find something to do."

We cuddle naked together for a while on the couch. I love just existing here with her. We don't need to talk or do anything sexual to enjoy our time together, "Do you want to shower together? I need to get cleaned up before I go, I'd rather shower with you than alone in my hotel room."

She stays quiet and nods. I stand, take her hand, and walk to the paned glass shower. I turn the faucet on and step inside first, then help her so she doesn't slip. I get her under the shower head so she can be warm, and I kiss her She doesn't touch me or deepen our kiss though. *Maybe asking to shower together was too much?*

I splash water on myself to get wet and start washing myself off. Olivia does the same. When I offer to help, she declines. We rinse and the shower is over. I get out first since I'm closest to the door. I grab a towel to dry off quickly and toss Olivia her towel so she can dry her hair and body in the steam left over from the shower instead of getting cold.

As I towel dry my hair, Olivia lets out a heavy sigh that catches my attention.

"Nate is this just a weekend fling with us?" she blurts out catching me off guard.

I smile out of confusion, she's the one who has been cold to me, shouldn't I be the one asking this? "What?" I ask as I pull on my boxers and shorts.

"This thing between us, is it just a weekend thing or do you want us to continue when we are home?"

This is anything but a weekend thing to me, but I also want to set expectations, "I'd love for this to continue when we are back in Chicago, but I can't promise I'll have the time for a relationship. I'd love to date you and see where this goes when we are home." I think having a couple of dates before putting a label on this is reasonable, right?

Olivia stares blankly at me, so I continue, "Tomorrow, Nico and I aren't being featured because of the cookout on the mountaintop, come with us. Afterward, I'll take you on a proper date, how's that sound?" I slip my shirt over my head, "This isn't just sex to me if that is what you are thinking." I cup her face in my hands and kiss her tenderly.

"Okay," she smiles softly, "You better get going. Have fun." She walks me to the door and pecks my cheek. I'm not sure she is convinced I want to date her, but I respect her boundaries and leave.

Megan

Saturday is always the busiest night of the week and of course, every asshole wants to come out tonight when Nate and Nico are out of town. Reservations were booked, and we set aside tables for walk-ins and those were full too and we had an hour wait for those. Due Fratelli is not a restaurant where people come to eat quickly and leave. Guests visit to enjoy the food and atmosphere, to socialize, or to have a special night out with their spouse. We never rush our customers to turn tables.

We did our best to keep people waiting outside calm, we made room at the bar for people to have drinks while they waited for an open table. Some people you can't please no matter how hard you try.

I helped the best I could, and the kitchen was firing out appetizers and entrees in record time. They were in a flow and at times had food up so fast that they helped deliver to tables. When the dishwashers got backed up, everyone pitched in and helped put things away to clear more racks. I have never witnessed teamwork like this at any other job. We all did it because we took pride in our work, and we all loved the Rossi brothers.

At the end of the night Raul opened a bottle of wine and those who stayed behind shared the bottle except Julian, who chugged water from a plastic prep container. Come to think of it, I don't think I've ever seen him drink.

"Nico called to check on us. He said Nate is out with Olivia."

My brain short-circuits, "Wait, Olivia? The girl he bailed out of the date Wednesday. What is she doing in Aspen?"

Raul and Julian shrugged, "I dunno, Nico said she's some big-time travel blogger and she and Hannah are friends."

I pulled my phone out and went to Hannah's profile to find Olivia and there she was. Naturally beautiful, natural big boobs and curves, a world traveler. *Fuck.* There were pictures of her and Hannah and selfies of her at the Food and Wine Classic but no pictures with Nate. I scrolled her feed and she never had pictures with guys so at least she's not a whore. Maybe Olivia wants to promote local restaurants in Chicago and since Nate rescued her from Mark, she wants to do something nice for him in return?

I need to make my move when Nate is back.

CHAPTER SIX

Sunday, June 16th

NATE

As soon as I wake up, I text Olivia to see if she wants to meet me at the gondola. I think a romantic gondola ride up the mountain will woo her. I get ready and Nico's nosey ass asks a million questions about last night. I let him know Olivia and I hooked up and that I was trying to win her over. I tell him about the gondola and somehow it leads to him and Hannah tagging along.

Nico offers to pick up Hannah and my dumbass lets him go inside to get her; this causes us to be late. I can see the disappointment on Olivia's face when Hannah runs to her, and Nico and I are there.

When Hannah is done hugging her, I scoop her up in a hug, "I was trying to keep them on schedule, sorry we are late." I grumble, "I wanted it to be the two of us, but they invited themselves."

"Hey, it's fine. I was enjoying the view."

I take her hand, and the four of us board the gondola. She is gripping my hand so tightly that my fingers go numb. "Are you alright?" I ask, shaking to loosen her grip.

"Sorry, I don't like heights."

I put my arm around her and pulled her close, "There is nothing to be afraid of. We aren't that high up, we are safe. Look at that view." I say soft and reassuring. I point out the window at the mountains. The sky is clear, the sun is out, and it looks like a damn magazine cover. Olivia cuddles into me and I rub her arm with one hand and her thigh with the other. I feel her melt into me.

When we get to the mountaintop barbeque, Hannah takes off to talk to someone and I want to be a gentleman and get us drinks. While I wait in line, I try to play out how I want today to go. I want everything to be perfect. I try to plan everything in my life. I steal a glance back and see Olivia and Nico talking, they seem to be getting along.

One important requirement I have in a partner is that they must get along with my brother and parents, and be able to handle my hectic work schedule. I haven't met anyone yet who could come second to my career.

Olivia spots me coming back with drinks and her face lights up like a child on Christmas morning, she's happy to see me, "Nico mentioned the dinner turned out great last night?"

"It was awesome, it was at this huge log cabin up in the mountains. A famous chef invited us and cooked for us and a few other chefs. It was surreal. One of the best meals I've ever had."

"That's amazing! What an experience!"

I put my arm around Olivia's waist and sip my beer, "What did you get into last night?"

She hesitates to answer, "I went to dinner at this pub downtown, had a couple of cocktails, and an amazing steak sandwich and fries. I went to my room and fell asleep." She sounds like she is trying to convince her parents why she's home late. I shake it off.

"You look well rested," I smile and kiss her cheek. I'm not entirely convinced she is telling the truth, and it makes me want to put my guard up.

Hannah rejoins us and the four of us make our way around the festival eating and drinking.

Nico and I pick on each other and dare one another to try spicy foods or weird foods we have never tried. We take shots together and I stop Nico from telling Olivia embarrassing stories about me. Hannah and Olivia find us entertaining.

"We have to take pictures!" Hannah cheers as we reach an overlook. The view is beautiful. I offer to take pictures of the girls for their socials. I take pictures of Nico and Hannah, and Olivia solo.

"Your turn! You and Nico get over there together!" Olivia cheers and Nico and I take professional style pictures first and then silly ones.

Nico forces Olivia and I to take pictures together too. We wrap our arms around each other's waist, kinda couple-ish but not really, and in one picture I steal a kiss on her cheek. All the drinks are hitting us and all four of us feel good.

We ride the gondola back downtown and Hannah and Nico make out most of the way back since it is private. Their friendship confuses me. I hold Olivia's hand again and we admire the view together.

When we reach the bottom, Nico and Hannah take off together. The sun is setting, but I don't want my time with Olivia to end. I smile down at Olivia, "Let's take a stroll and walk off some of that food," I swing our hands as we make our way into town.

We pass vendors selling art and handmade goods and we hear acoustic music. A folk-style band is playing. I find an empty seat on a bench and motion for Olivia to sit beside me. We watch them in silence, enjoying the ambiance and atmosphere together when an older couple, who reminds me of my grandparents, gets up and starts slow dancing.

"Aww that is so cute!" Olivia coos.

Her appreciation makes me smile, I lean over to her, "My parents still dance together, in the kitchen, usually after a bottle of wine at dinner but, I love watching them," I whisper.

"That is the kind of love I want, I want to be dancing at 85, surrounded by people and not having a care in the world."

I don't want us to wait until we are 85. I stand up and extend my hand to her, "Dance with me?" Olivia takes my hand and I pull her into me. I start to lead us swaying to the beat.

"Where did you learn to dance?"

"My Nonni taught me," I smile. Olivia rests her head on my shoulder and other couples join. I love having Olivia safe in my arms, swaying with me to the music. The summer air whips her hair in the breeze. The song ends, and I politely kiss Olivia's cheek. The crowd claps for the couples and the band. I take Olivia's hand in mine again and continue our walk-through town.

"When do you fly out?" Olivia blurts out, reminding me that we have to go back to reality, and we won't always be in this Aspen bubble where I work short hours and have time to go on walks and dance.

"Tomorrow at 6 am. You?"

"I was thinking about staying here a few more days. I'm so relaxed here. I can go hiking and make more content for my blog and socials. People are liking all my posts about Aspen."

She wants to stay longer? What about our life back in Chicago? I fake my enthusiasm, "That sounds badass, you should do it!" As the words come out of my mouth, Olivia starts to turn pale and begins fanning herself, "Are you alright?"

"Yeah, just a little warm."

As I walked to the hotel the other night, I passed fountains that shot up from the sidewalk. I take Olivia's hand and guide her through the crowd down the street. Jets of water erupt from the ground, and kids play in them to escape the summer heat. "Go on," I point at them, directing Olivia to cool off.

She looks around at the people around us, "Nate, I am not going in there!"

"But you are hot, cool off, you're red," I press the back of my hand to her face and it's hot as a flame.

"Are you crazy? It's for kids!"

"Fine." I shrug, pick her up into my arms, and carry her into the fountains. The water is freezing and hitting me more than her, but she is laughing and yelping as she puts her arms around my neck, so I don't accidentally drop her.

I spin her around and we are both laughing.

"Nate come on!" she whines.

"Are you cooled down?" I tease, "I don't think she is wet enough kids, do you?" I ask the children who are laughing at us.

"No! She needs more!" They tease and I spin and a jet shoots up the back of Olivia's shirt and soaks her hair.

"Put me down!" She begs and I finally do. A game of tag breaks out and we run through the jets with the kids. We play until we are both out of breath. I lead us to the dry part of the sidewalk and we wring ourselves off. I shake my hair and move a piece from Olivia's beautiful eyes.

"Playing in the fountains and puddles reminds me of when my brother and I were little. I always got into something, you're lucky it was water and not a mud pit in your parent's driveway. I thought our Ma was going to kill us when we came into the house covered in mud!" I confess to Olivia as I get us bottled water to hydrate.

"Aww! In the summer, I played in our pond, catching frogs and using a stick as a pretend fishing pole. I had to use my imagination. In the winter, my Dad would teach me how to ice skate, for as much as he loved hockey, I am surprised he never put a hockey stick in my hand. I loved ice skating with him."

"He should have, that would have been badass. Are you ready to go back to your room?" I ask as I shake out my hair sending water droplets everywhere.

She replies with a huge smile, "Yes."

We get to her condo and once again we attack each other with kisses as soon as we are inside. Olivia peels off my wet shirt and I get naked down to my briefs. Olivia raises her arms so I can take off her wet top and bra. Her nipples are hard, and her skin is damp and cool to the touch.

"Do you know how hard it was not to touch you all day?" I ask her as I study her face. Freckles appear on her skin from being in the sun all day and her nose is slightly sunburnt. I caress her arms and grab her ass and pull her to me.

"I like the gentlemanly side of you," she whispers as she wraps her arms around my waist and lays her head on my bare chest. My heart thumps. I play with her hair which turns wavy when it's wet. I trace my fingers down her spine. I wish I could bottle this feeling.

"You know what I loved most about today and this weekend?" I ask as I tilt her head up to me.

"What?"

"Having you to share it all with, it wouldn't have been the same without you."

Olivia's emerald eyes twinkle like she has stars in her eyes, "I feel the same."

I want to kiss her, savor her, and take my time making love to her.

"Nate?"

"Yeah?"

"Fuck me."

Oh. Okay. Lovemaking isn't in the equation with her. I turn my emotions off to protect myself and turn on horny Nate. This is the version of me she wants. I put on a condom, bend Olivia over the bed, and pound her within an inch of her life. We orgasm together and then I make another attempt at being softer with her.

I toss my condom in the trash, crawl into bed beside her, and hold her until she drifts off to sleep. I can't stay the night with her. I need to pack and be awake early for our flight home. As Olivia sleeps, I post the pictures of Nico and me and the one of Olivia and me to social media After an hour, I gently roll Olivia off me, and she stirs in her sleep.

She lets out a tired groan and her eyes slightly open, "Nate?"

"Hey sweetie, I need to go. I need to pack and catch my flight, okay? I'll text you when I'm back in Chicago Go back to sleep."

"Okay," she yawns, "Have a safe flight."

I pull the covers over her, pet her hair, and kiss her forehead.

"Goodnight Olivia."

Megan

It was another long night, but I made it through. I'm so glad we are closed on Mondays and Tuesdays because I need a break. Nate and Nico will be back tomorrow. They have never been away together for three days.

In the kitchen, the guys are giggling and passing a phone around.

"They are a bunch of children," Amira rolls her eyes.

"What are they going on about?"

"Nate posted a picture with Olivia," she grumbles.

I feel like I got a punch to the stomach, "He did?"

"Mmmhmm, he posted one of Nico and him together and a bunch of food too, but they are fixated on him with Olivia."

I take out my phone and find Nate's Instagram. I want to see the picture for myself. Nate and Olivia have an arm wrapped behind each other's back. They look cozy but not too lovey. *Maybe I still have a chance?*

"Is everyone going out tonight?" I ask Amira.

"Yeah, are you coming?" She squeals.

"Count me in. My sisters' friend is the bartender and I need a fucking drink."

Amira and I change outfits and get ready at her house then meet everyone at the bar.

The guys do shots, except Julian, and Amira and I partake before switching to girly drinks. Lilah the bartender hooks me up and makes my drinks extra strong. Raul, Amira, Julian, and I play pool in teams while the rest of our coworkers are on the dance floor.

"Are you okay?" Amira asks as I finish my third drink, "You rarely come out with us and you're done with your drink already?"

"I'm great!" I smile, "I need another one!"

Amira grabs my arm before I can walk to the bar, "You're lying, what is going on?"

"I'm fine." I smile and yank my arm from her, "Who wants another shot?" Amira and Julian shake their heads.

Raul, Callum, and Leah yell, "Hell yeah!" Callum is Irish, he moved to America for opportunity and Nate hired him. He's a flirt and loves to drink and get in fights.

I get Lilah's attention, she has shoulder-length raven-colored hair, a badass vibe, and tattoos.

"Back for more?" She asks as she pops tops of beers and cashes people out.

"3 shots of tequila and mix me up another, please? And do you know what he drinks?" I point to Julian.

She looks around me and smirks with a slight blush on her cheeks, "Julian? Yeah, I'll make his for you too."

I wave Raul and Leah over and we clink our shot glasses together and tip them back. I suck the lime in my mixed drink and carry it back to the table near the billiards table along with Julian's clear bubbling drink with a lime. Gin and Tonic maybe?

I hand him his drink, "Got you a refill, she made it special for you." I nod back to Lilah and she gives him a thumbs up.

"Thanks," he says as he sips his drink and we start our game.

Julian and I win the first two games. Raul and Amira give up and head to the dance floor with Callum, Ava, and Hayes.

"What's going on? Now that it's just us, you can talk to me." Julian presses.

"Nope! I don't want to talk about it."

"Meg, we have been friends since you started…"

"Friends?! You ignored me completely!"

He laughs, "I had a lot going on."

I scowl at him.

"Come on, you're worrying Amira, she's right, you rarely come out with everyone and when you do it's for one drink and you go home. Tonight…"

"Am I not allowed to have fun? We just pulled off *four* services without the Rossi brothers! We need to celebrate!" I cheer.

Julian studies me with his ocean-blue eyes, if I wasn't so hung up on Nate, I'd probably find him dateable. His face lights up like he figured it out, "Oh shit, you like Nate."

My face scrunches, "What? No!"

"You do, you totally do!"

I punch him in his tattooed arm, "Do not." I sip my drink a little too fast and give myself a head rush.

"I can ask everyone else what they think…or you can fess up." He runs his hands over his short dark hair.

Fuck. This is a battle I won't win.

"Can you keep this between us?"

His brows knit together, "Wait, Amira doesn't know?"

"No. Nobody but my sister knows."

Julian moves closer, "Alright, I won't tell a soul, you need to talk about this, you can't keep it all in or drink it away."

"If I tell you, I want to know what's in your special drink."

"Fine, now spill it." He says as he takes a sip.

I take a deep breath, "I've liked him since I started." I mumble.

"Why haven't you told him or said anything? You're a catch, you're hot, and he'd be stupid not to date you. I think you're one of the few people that could handle being with Nate."

"What do you mean?"

"He never has time to date. He's married to the job. But you're there every day. You've never missed a day of work…you have the same days off, you care about DF like you own the place."

I sigh, "I know, but if he liked me, don't you think he would have said something by now?"

Julian shrugs, "Not really, he's the boss, he's five years older than you…he probably doesn't want to mix business and pleasure. Just tell him how you feel!" I trust Julian. Besides Nico, Julian is like a brother to Nate. I've heard rumblings of how Julian got hired. Nate gave him a chance when nobody else would.

"The past few weeks I've been flirting and hinting I like him…"

He holds his finger up, "Wait, in Nate's defense, you're *really* nice and when women are nice, sometimes, we don't think you're flirting with us."

I hang my head in my hands, "What do I do?"

Julian puts my arms down, grabs me by the shoulders, and forces me to look at him, "You have to be honest with him and tell him how you feel." His eyes search mine and I don't know if it's the alcohol hitting me or what, but I feel attracted to him. "Make him notice you." He releases me.

"Make him notice?"

"Jesus, didn't your sister teach you anything about men?"

I laugh out loud, "She's a lesbian, has been her whole life, so no."

He smacks himself on the forehead, "Ok, look…you're always at work in uniform, it's not flattering on anyone, right? You barely wear makeup, your hair is in a bun to keep it out of the food, and you smell like garlic and marinara. You need Nate to see you. *The real you.*"

He has a point. In the five years I've worked at Due Fratelli, Nate has only seen me in work clothes. I don't post on social media and even if I did, I doubt he has time to look at it. I think the only time Nate has seen 'The Real Me' was at our annual July 4th parties.

"Here, take the pool cue and bend over, pretend you're shooting." Julian hands me the cue and I do what he asks. He takes a picture. "Ok, now pose with it, cute, not too posey though." I again, do as he wants, "Perfect, now dance with Amira and I'll take a picture of you two having fun."

"Is this going to work?"

"Yes, trust me. I'm a dude, I know these things."

I weave my way to Amira and slither between her and Leah, our pastry chef. The three of us dance and sing and grind with each other and then Julian wiggles his way in and dances with me.

"I got the pictures, now, we need the final one, the one that will drive him crazy." Julian says in my ear, "Amira! Take a video of Megan and I dancing." He says and hands her his phone, she doesn't ask any questions, "You ready? Dance with me like you want me. Pretend I'm Nate, okay?"

I nod. The perfect song comes on and I put one arm around Julian's neck and then with the other, I hold his bicep. I press close to him and start grinding on him while I look up into his eyes.

He smiles down at me devilishly and holds my waist. Grinding on him, and the friction in my tight jean shorts is doing something to me. His hand glides to my ass and he squeezes, pulling me into him and it makes me laugh, he turns me around and I'm against him. We couldn't be any closer. I lean my head back on his chest and roll my ass in circles. He's hard, I can feel it.

"Is it working?" I crane my neck to ask.

He leans down and whispers, "Oh fuck yes."

His comment makes me blush and Amira and Leah cheer us on. Raul watches in shock. When the song changes, Amira hands Julian his phone back and we all dance and take group pictures together. For the first time in a long time, I'm having fun.

Julian and I dance for a few more songs and our sexual tension builds. For the first time in days, I'm not thinking about Nate being with Olivia.

"Who wants to take the party back to my place?" Raul cheers and Amira and Leah start to follow him along with the rest of our crew.

"Come on Meg, it will be fun!" Ava dances behind Hayes, holding onto his shoulders like she's in a conga line. Hayes fist bumps Julian.

"You wanna go?" Julian asks.

"What happens at Raul's place?"

"We usually play cards, listen to music, and everyone passes out somewhere. He makes a killer pancake breakfast in the morning."

"Sounds fun," I smile. Julian takes my hand and leads me out of the bar to his Jeep Wrangler. I buckle my seatbelt, and he starts up the engine, "Wait, you've been drinking…"

"Sprite with lime. I don't drink. He says as he looks in his mirror and pulls out of the parking spot.

"You don't?"

"Nope."

"Is there a reason why? Not that being sober is bad or anything, I'm just…"

"Surprised because I'm tattooed and look like I drink and do drugs?" He smiles devilishly at me before turning his eyes back to the road. He does have that cocky bad-boy vibe. "I'm on probation, almost finished. It's been five years."

"Shit, I'm sorry…"

"Hey, it's cool."

"Does everyone know?"

"No, just Nate and Nico, and our bartender. Everyone is cool about me not drinking when we go out. I'm usually the DD."

"It doesn't bother you to be around it?"

"I never depended on alcohol so it doesn't bother me.."

"I – never mind…"

Julian snickers, "You want to know why, don't you?"

"Kinda," I shrug.

"I beat my Mom's abuser to within an inch of his life and *she* pressed charges against me. The judge felt sorry for me for having such a shitty mother, so I didn't get jail time."

"How could she do that? You're her son!"

Julian rests his hand on my thigh, "Chill, I'm fine. It sucked trying to get a job, but Nate took a chance on me, he probably saved my life."

Another reason for me to love Nate. He cares about people. He takes care of them.

"I won't drink at Raul's if it bothers you."

"Fuck no, you need to let loose and have fun. Take my phone and send yourself the pictures you like and post them."

I grab Julian's phone from the cup holder, "You're letting me in your phone?" I flirt. He holds his thumb on the screen to unlock it.

"If you want to see shirtless gym selfies and the rest of my tattoos, just ask Meg." He blushes.

Picture 1: Me posing cute with a smile

Picture 2: Me bending over playing pool, my ass looks great

Picture 3: Julian and I dirty dancing with me facing him, us looking at each other smiling

I quickly scroll down his camera roll out of curiosity and see nothing but abs and beautiful plates of food. I send myself the pictures and put Julian's phone back. I use #nightout #afterparty when I post the pictures to my Instagram account.

At Raul's, I drink more since tomorrow is our day off. It's nice hanging out with everyone and not having conversations between waiting tables. Raul turns his living room into a dance floor and all of us dance together. Julian and I continue dancing, and Amira gives me a wink.

All the alcohol hits me at once, this is what I get for rarely drinking. I stumble to the bathroom and peeing is the best feeling ever! I text my sister and tell her I won't be home but that I'm safe because I know she will worry. I wash my hands and rinse my mouth out with mouthwash before stumbling back to the dining room where a roaring poker game is starting.

Julian walks down the hall, "You good?"

"Yeah, just needed to use the little girls' room," I hiccup.

"Alright just checking," he walks past me and we brush against each other. Our eyes lock. I hold onto the wall to steady myself. Julian continues past me into the bathroom. I gasp for air.

I watch my co-workers play poker and when I go to the kitchen for a bottled water, Julian follows and catches me as I trip over my feet.

"Whoa! Are you okay?"

"Yeah, I'm fine," I giggle.

He puts an arm under me, "You need to lay down, come on." He leads me to the stairs and looks up them, it looks like I'm about to climb Mt. Everest. I start swaying.

I groan, "I can't do it. Just lay me on the couch."

Amira joins us at the bottom of the stairs, "Meg, you cool?"

"She needs to lay down. I'll take her upstairs."

Amira coo's, "Aww little Megs, time for beddy bye."

I want to punch her in the face. I hate being treated like a child. Julian picks me up and carries me upstairs to a bedroom. He lays me on the bed and turns the lamp on.

I strip off my shirt and wiggle out of my shorts and he looks away. *Why?*

Julian pulls the covers over me and disappears from the room. He comes back with two bottles of water and a small white trash can. "Drink water and if you need to puke, aim for the can, if you miss, Raul will make you clean it up and charge you a cleaning fee."

Julian sits on the edge of the bed next to me.

"Did you look away because you didn't like what you saw? Is that why you covered me up?" My insecurities emerge.

His head whips towards me, "Are you fucking kidding me? I told you earlier you're hot."

"Do you think Nate will ever like me?" I ask as I yawn.

Julian sighs, "If he doesn't, he's a fucking idiot. Get some sleep."

I think about kissing Julian. I think about asking him to fuck me just because I know he'd tell me if I suck, and he'd let me know how to improve so I could be my best. But I don't. There is only one man I want.

***

A scream wakes me in the middle of the night. It's not anyone partying. I run into the next room and close the door behind me and Julian is groaning and tossing in the bed. Another scream rips through him. He looks like he's in pain. His muscles are tense and his skin looks slick with sweat.

"Shh, it's okay…" I say as I cautiously approach the bed. I climb on it and rub Julian's arm and he begins to calm down. I brush my fingers over his cheek.

He leans into it before jolting awake and yelling, "STOP!"

"Hey, hey…it's me, Megan…you're having a nightmare, you're okay…" I get him to focus his eyes on me in the darkroom that's only lit by the moon coming through the window blinds.

"Megan?" His voice cracks.

"Shhh. I'm here. You're safe." I climb under the covers and he pulls me into him, "You're safe, okay?"

His breathing is labored and he squeezes me tightly, "I'm sorry for waking you."

"Don't be. Do you need to talk about your nightmare?" I offer.

"No. Just…stay here with me. Please."

"I'll stay, I'm not going anywhere."

CHAPTER SEVEN

Monday, June 17th

The flight home is long. I sleep most of it and when we land in Chicago, the first thing I do is text Olivia that we made it safely.

Nico and I make our way home. The workaholics in us check the dining room, kitchen, and reports before we go upstairs to unpack and relax. Our entire staff, especially Raul and Megan, did incredibly well in our absence. Maybe I can take days off and make time for Olivia if she wants to date me.

As soon as I enter my space, I kick off my shoes, strip down, and shower off the airplane smell. When I'm dry, I plug in my phone and crawl into bed. I get a text from Olivia with a picture of her in bed. The sunlight coming through the window casts her in an ethereal light. She looks like an angel.

I don't want to reply right away so I check my emails, reply to the important ones, and answer texts from various people congratulating me on my successful weekend. I jump on Instagram and scroll my feed and I see

Megan's post. *She went out with the crew last night. She never goes out.* I almost didn't recognize her. I swipe to the next picture, and she is bent over, shooting pool. *Has her ass always looked that good? Damn.* The last picture is her dancing with…Julian?! I jolt up in bed. "What the fuck is she doing dancing with him? Are they a thing and I've been too busy to notice?" I ask myself out loud. "I could have sworn she's been flirting with me lately but maybe she was just being nice? Why does this bother me?" *There I go talking to myself again.*

Technically, Nico and I don't have a policy against dating in the workplace. In my experience, it never ends well, and I can't lose Julian or Megan.

I scroll through Amira and Leah's Instagrams next; it looks like they all went to Raul's after the bar, but I only see Megan in one picture. They better have taken care of her or else they will have hell to pay.

It's early enough that they are probably all waking up and Raul's cooking his famous pancakes. So much for relaxing. I text Raul.

> NATE: Crew still at your place?
>
> RAUL: Yes, Boss, do you need something?
>
> NATE: Pancakes
>
> RAUL: Mixing up the batter now, come on over

I get dressed and ride my motorcycle to Raul's. I speed there and as soon as I park, I can smell the heavenly aroma of fresh pancakes. I knock on the door and Callum answers, "Oh shite, are we in trouble or something?"

"Just need some food," I push past him and scan the room, taking notice of who is here and accounted for before I get to the kitchen.

"Hey Boss, here's a plate, I added French Toast Moonshine to the maple syrup and it's amazing!"

"Sounds awesome, and don't call me Boss, we aren't at work," I huff. I take a seat and dig in.

"Soooo, how was Aspen, and your time with Olivia?" Leah sings.

"It was good," I nod as I shove another fork full into my mouth. Raul sets a glass of orange juice next to me and I take a gulp. My mind flashes back to fucking Olivia like she wanted. I wanted to take my time and make love to her, but she wanted railed. I loved having her fall asleep in my arms. I held her, cherished having her close to me, and then kissed her goodbye before I left. I'm holding out hope that she will want to pursue something with me when she is back from Aspen that isn't just sexual.

I inhale my pancakes and empty the glass of OJ. I refocus on why I came here, "How did things go while Nico and were gone? I saw you all partied last night."

Amira clasps her hand on my shoulder as she sits next to me, "Everything was awesome and we left the place pristine for you, I know you and Nico checked when you got back, right?"

I smile, she knows us well.

"We partied hard last night!" Leah laughs, "Megan came out to celebrate too, and she danced!" Her eyes widen.

I clear my throat, "Where is Megan?"

With a full mouth, Raul answers, "Upstairs asleep."

"Anyone else still sleeping?"

"Nope, Julian left before Raul started cooking so just Megs."

I want to ask if Julian and Megan slept together but I bite my tongue. I take my plate and cup to the sink, wash them, and place them in the dish rack. I grab a coffee mug and fill it. I add two ice cubes and a splash of creamer, just the way Megan likes, and I plate up a short stack of pancakes for her. "I'll go wake up Sleeping Beauty," I grumble.

I carefully make my way upstairs and find the room she is in. Megan is laid out like a starfish taking up the whole bed, half a pillow over her face, and wearing nothing but a bra and panties.

I clear my throat loudly. It gets her to toss onto her side and a groan a zombie would be jealous of comes out of her. I stifle a laugh. Her ass is perched up in the air and I feel guilty for checking it out. I walk to the end table and set down the coffee and plate of pancakes. I sit on the edge of the bed and move her dark brown hair out of her face.

"Dinner Rush!" I yell and Megan snaps open her eyes and then bolts upright. I can't help but laugh. My trick worked.

Her eyes meet mine, and then she swings a pillow at me, "Nate? Nate you fucking asshole!" Megan insults me then brings the blanket over her, "What the fuck are you doing here?"

I smile, "I brought you coffee and pancakes, assholes don't do that, do they?" I tease and she rolls her eyes at me then grips her temples, "Drink a little too much last night?"

Megan slowly nods her head.

I hand her the coffee mug, "Drink this, made just how you like it. Two ice cubes and a splash of creamer."

Her brows furrowed over her hazel blue eyes, "How do you know how I like my coffee?" She asks then takes a long sip.

"Pfft, you have worked for me for almost six years now? I know a lot of things," I shrug. What I didn't know was how nice of an ass she has, that her eyes have flecks of silver in them, or that she is beautiful, even when she's hung over. "Eat. The carbs will help with the headache."

She doesn't argue; instead, she starts eating, and color returns to her face. Why have I never noticed her lips before? Her upper lip is thinner than her lower lip, and her nose is perfectly proportioned for her face.

"Why are you staring at me? Am I in trouble or something?"

I shake my head, "No, you're not in trouble."

"Why are you here Nate?" She asks with a sigh.

"I told you I wanted Raul's pancakes, it was a long flight from Colorado, I saw everyone had fun partying last night, I wanted to check on my crew."

Her eyes narrow at me, "You look at our social media pages?"

"When I have time I keep up with what's going on in the world, you and Julian looked cozy last night, do you two have a thing going on that I didn't know about?" *Stupid. Stupid. Stupid.*

Megan practically chokes on her bite and needs to wash it down with her coffee, "No, I don't have a thing with him …or anyone."

Why does hearing that excite me? I like Olivia. Dammit. I need to get out of here, "I should get going…"

"Wait," she grabs my wrist before I stand up, "Can you give me a ride home?"

Fifteen minutes later, Megan is on the back of my bike. I give her my helmet, and her smile beams, showing her dimples. I get on first and help her climb on. She wraps her arms around me, I fire up the engine and speed off towards her apartment building. I shouldn't but I like feeling her hanging on to me. I hear her whoop and giggle, she loves riding.

As I arrive at her apartment, I slow down the bike and turn off the engine. I help Megan off, and she unbuckles the helmet and hands it back to me.

"Thanks for the ten-minute ride, it was great!" She smiles as she combs her fingers through her hair.

I don't want to say goodbye to her. "If you put on jeans and sneakers, I'll take you for a real ride."

Her eyes light up, "Really? You have time?"

"Yeah, go," I nod, "Hurry up before I change my mind," I tease. She runs inside and she's back in five minutes wearing a t-shirt, jeans, and black combat boots. I hand her my helmet and she puts it on.

"Where are we going?" She asks.

"One of my favorite spots."

Megan

I hold onto Nate as he speeds through downtown Chicago, and we head west on the interstate. I have no idea where he is taking us, but I'd go anywhere with him. I hold on tighter when Nate makes a right onto I-94 and fifteen minutes later Nate slows down to pull into the Chicago Botanical Gardens.

This is one of his favorite spots. I mean, there is a garden on the rooftop at Due Fratelli, so I guess that makes sense. Even though we are about a half-hour northwest of Chicago, I feel much further away. The grass is a vibrant emerald green, the sun is shining through the trees, and we aren't even near the gardens yet, but the air is sweet and floral.

We pull up to the parking booth and Nate takes his wallet out and pays before we continue. He finds a place to park and then shuts the bike off. He helps me off the bike and puts down the kickstand. I hand him the helmet, and he leaves it with the bike.

"Aren't you afraid someone will steal it?"

"Nah, come on," Nate waves for me to follow him. The grounds are perfectly manicured and landscaped and for the first time in too long, I feel like I am breathing fresh air. I follow Nate inside, and he pays for our admission. He then asks me where I want to go.

"You lead the way. I've never been here before."

I follow Nate outside and he goes to the right. We are surrounded by seasonal flowers as we walk the paved path and the view of the small lake is breathtaking.

"Why is this your favorite place?" I ask as we walk side by side.

"I love gardening, it was my idea to turn part of the rooftop into a garden area. It's more cost-effective to grow what we can and preserve what we cannot use."

"I love that, fresh is best, right?"

Nate smiles, "You've heard me say that a million times, huh?"

I shrug, "Eh, maybe."

"This is the Heritage Garden. It's modeled after a garden in Padua, Italy. That statue is Carl Linnaeus," he points, "He looks over the garden."

"He looks kinda creepy, and melted," I chuckle.

"He developed the modern system of naming plants and animals."

"Still creepy. Oh, look! Fountains!" I run to them like a child and Nate slowly follows me. "Aren't these great? Look at that view!" The wind blows and a cool mist hits my warm skin. I look back and Nate has a somber look on his face. I run back to him, "You okay?"

"Yeah...I...fountains remind me of someone." He pulls his phone out and unlocks the screen. His face flashes with an emotion I don't recognize, and then he looks up at me, "I'll take a picture for you," he waves his hand, and I stand in the middle of the lawn and pose.

I sense something isn't quite right. "Let's keep going," I say with a smile. I walk ahead of him and notice model trains chugging through the plants and flowers. I turn around and ask, "Do you have any soft spots for trains that I need to worry about, or should we just keep walking?"

He chuckles, puts his phone away, and returns to me. "No bad feelings about trains; I have a funny story about them. Want to hear it?"

"Duh!" I flirt.

"One Christmas my Dad was dead set on having a train under the tree, I think watching The Polar Express woke something in him, anyways, he bought a train set that looked identical. Nico and I spent hours helping him set it up," Nate smiles softly as we walk along the exhibit, "I remember how magical our tree looked with the train chugging along, we put on The Polar Express and my Ma made hot chocolate."

I choke back tears, "That's cute."

Nate starts to laugh, "Oh, it was glorious, until Nico crawled under the tree to water it, and the Express crashed into him, the damn thing never chugged the same way after that." Nate rubs his chin.

I can't help but laugh when I picture Nico being scolded by Nate's parents.. I have to grab my ribs from laughing so hard, "I gotta ask your Dad about this when they come to the July 4th party." I howl.

"Oh god, please don't, he might hurl Nico from the rooftop." He smiles brightly making his dimples come out and I try my best not to gawk at him.

Nate leads the way through the native plants, we explore the fruit and vegetable garden, and he takes pictures of plants he wants to research later. He also takes a picture of a vertical wall garden he wants to add to the rooftop. Nate also records voice memos of special ideas for the restaurant. He never stops thinking about work.

"You're going crazy without your notebook, aren't you?" I tease. He always has his brown leather-bound notebook within arm's reach or in the office at work during service. God forbid anything ever happens to it.

Nate smirks, "I'm fine, that is why I have voice memos and pictures so I don't forget anything. When I'm inspired I have to make a note of it before my wacked-out brain moves the next thought in."

I shake my head at him.

"I think that's why I love it here too, it's quiet."

"Yeah, it's nice to think sometimes, I get what you're saying about wanting to turn your mind off though, I'm a chronic overthinker."

"Me too, I've never seen you at a meeting."

I look over at him confused, "Meeting?"

"Overthinkers Anonymous."

I huff out a laugh, "At least your thinking creates beautiful one-of-a-kind dishes and desserts."

"Not all of my thoughts relate to food," he says in almost a whisper like it wasn't meant to be heard.

We come to a brick trellis and Nate and I take pictures of one another.

Nate changes the subject as we continue our walk, "I got the idea for two of my tattoos here."

"Oh yeah? Which ones?"

He lifts his pant leg and near his ankle is the phrase 'From The Ground Up' in cursive.

"I love that, why that phrase?"

"Nico and I built our careers and the business from nothing, and we are growing."

"You two sure are," I smile, "I'm honored to work for you and Nico, I hope you know that."

"I know," he nods. "Thank you again for stepping up while we were in Aspen. I should have asked you to watch over the front of house, I'm sorry. I need to talk to Nico but I think you're due for a promotion."

I wave off his apology and offer, "Whether you asked me to or not I was going to do it."

"I appreciate that you care for the restaurant as much as we do," Julian said Nate would. *Fuck.*

I change the subject, "What about tattoo #2? What inspired you?"

Nate points to the water where lotuses are blooming.

Nate lifts his shirt and there is a tribal lotus near his right pec and collarbone.

"I know guys getting flowers is kinda lame, but the lotus resonates with me."

"How so?" I ask as we lean on the railing and look down at them.

"Lotus' grow in muddy and murky waters and yet they come out on top, unphased and pure, beautiful."

"Did you have a muddy past?" I lean closer to him. For as long as I've worked for Nate, you'd think I'd know more about his past.

"For a brief time in my teenage years, yes."

"I'd never guess, you're always so…"

"Asshole-ish?" Nate jokes.

"No," I chuckle, "I mean, yes, you have your asshole moments, and you're a sarcastic prick, but you care about people, you look out for people."

"I had Nico look after me and it saved my life so I guess I want to be that for someone if I can."

"Like Olivia?" I blurt out and his eyes lock on mine.

"She's strong, she doesn't need anyone looking out for her."

"So, you want someone weak?" I ask confused.

"No, that's not what I meant…I don't know if she wants anything with me."

A quick puff of air comes out of me, and I begin walking again.

"Hey, what the hell was that?"

"Forget it, Nate," I sigh.

"No, seriously, you don't believe me?"

"Nate, why do you think she doesn't want you?" I walk faster.

"I think she just wanted sex," he blurts out and an old couple scoffs at him, "Sorry."

"Oh look, another fountain, should we keep walking?" I ask sarcastically and Nate runs in front of me to face me.

"Stop."

I cross my arms over my chest.

"I shouldn't be talking to you about my personal life or sex life okay, I'm your…"

"Boss."

"I am, yes, but you're my friend too. You're my friend right now, okay?" His eyes plead for me to elaborate.

I take a deep breath, "Nate, you're a fucking idiot, respectfully, any woman would want you. Whether that's just a friendship or a fuck buddy or a relationship, if you two hooked up, I highly doubt she wants casual."

"She stayed in Aspen longer instead of coming back and trying to date me, she couldn't roll off me fast enough the other night, she flirted with a guy right in front of me, she communicates in selfies…she doesn't want me."

How can I be mad, jealous, and feel sorry for him all at the same time?

"I played in the fountains with her in Aspen, before that we slow danced to this little acoustic band…I held her hand on the gondola, I sent her champagne, we were alone last night after a beautiful day together and when all I wanted to do was take my time and make love to her, she wanted me to rail her."

My stomach churns. Olivia is a fucking idiot just like him. I want to stick my face over the fountain and waterboard myself hearing this. I'm officially in the 'friend zone'.

I see the hurt in Nate's eyes. What the hell do I say without pouring out years' worth of feelings I've had?

"Megan, say something…"

"I can't think with the fountains spurting…let's keep walking."

He nods and we walk side by side. I walk across a large boardwalk suspended over the water leading to a more secluded area. "I can think here," I tell Nate. I pace around fighting with myself and rehearsing what I want to say to Nate. I don't want to complicate his situation further, but if I never express my feelings, will I lose my chance to be with him?

CHAPTER EIGHT

NATE

Megan is pacing. She is cracking her knuckles and I can see the wheels turning in her head. *Why is she wrestling with what to say?* She's always been a tell-it-like-it-is type of girl…woman.

"Megs…"

She takes a deep breath, "Nate, I can't speak for all women here so take my advice with a grain of salt. If you and I had a beautiful day together, like the one you described, I would have wanted to make love all night until you had to leave for your flight."

I clap my hands together once, "See! So, I'm not crazy to want that right?"

"But…"

"Shit, there is a but…"

"But did you text her Thursday? Because I know you were traveling all day, and I know you likely threw yourself into work the second you arrived." Megan holds up a finger like she is going to count off something, "Two, did you tell her you were going to Aspen? How the hell did you both end up there?"

"I didn't tell her I was going, pure coincidence, I swear."

"So, she just popped up in Aspen and found you there?"

"Yes, and then we got invited to a party and I was her date and I kinda got jealous of her talking to this Australian dude."

"Uh-huh." Megan nods, "And did you apologize?"

"Yes, yes I did, and I asked for Olivia to give me a chance to start over fresh the next day and instead she told me to prove I wanted her, and she led me to her condo, and we had…"

"Ahhh, I don't need details!" She covers her ears and I shut my mouth. She puts her hands down and starts pacing again, "You didn't communicate worth a damn."

"I take responsibility for that."

"I think she has her guard up because you can't communicate so she got what she could from you."

"That's how I feel, yes. What should I do?"

Megan bites her lower lip in thought and for a moment I wish it was me doing it.

"I think Olivia is an independent woman who wants to explore, she runs a travel blog, and she's likely taking time in Aspen to work and escape. Do you like people bothering you when you are menu planning or doing inventory?"

"No."

"I'd give her space. She knows you're focused on your career. She probably wants to focus on hers…let her chase you. If she texts flirty messages or shows interest then pursue it, if she doesn't then maybe she wanted a fling."

Times like these I wish I had a sister to ask for advice because it shouldn't be my best server. But I do consider Megan a friend, we've never talked like this before, but I like it. "Thanks for the advice."

She shoves her hands in her pockets and puts on a fake smile, "Mmm-hmm."

It seems that she is holding back what she really wants to say, "Is there anything else you want to say?"

"This therapy session is free but if you keep asking for advice on women, I'm charging you."

Her sarcastic comment makes us laugh out loud and it breaks the awkward tension a little, "Come on, let's keep exploring. Tag, you're it!" I bop her on the head and take off across the boardwalk. I can hear her combat boots thumping across the boards behind me and when I don't hear them anymore, I stop and look back. She is gasping for breath.

"I give up…" She holds her hands up in surrender and collapses into the grass. I lay beside her, uncertain if we were allowed on the grass, but I didn't care.

Megan's chest heaves and the hot summer air has turned her skin slick with sweat. I watch the rise and fall of her chest and note the way her long hair clings to her. Her eyelashes are naturally thick and dark. She doesn't need mascara or makeup. She's beautiful.

I blurt out, "Are you sure nothing is going on with you and Julian?"

She squints her eyes and looks over at me, then closes her eyes and lays her hands on her stomach, "It felt nice to dance with him and have him look out for me last night. He got me up to bed and brought me water. He was respectful, which was nice. He could have made a move, but he didn't."

"Good, I don't want to fire one of my best guys."

"You wouldn't fire him," she chuckles.

"If he tried something with you that you didn't ask for, I absolutely would fire him and take him out back and kick his ass."

"He had a nightmare, it seemed really bad and I held him until he was okay, he would have been there beside me when you got there but he left at some point."

So I should still be jealous of him but at the same time, I'm glad she was there for him.

"He had a really fucked up childhood and teen years and he got punished for doing the right thing. I'm glad you were there for him." I stand up and offer my hand to Megan to get her off the grass before the Grass Police come. I dust off the grass blades on her and we keep walking. We pass the Sensory Garden which smells like chocolate today, and the basin. We stroll on Evening Island and stop to take pictures.

"My favorite part is coming up."

"Why didn't we go there first?"

"I wanted to save the best for last," I smile. I take her hand and lead her to the Japanese Gardens and she gasps.

"Nate…" she whispers, "I don't feel like we are in Chicago anymore."

"I come here when I need to think and block out everything. You're the only person who knows about it so don't tell anyone, okay?"

"I won't."

"Do you see that island over there?" I point.

"Yeah, can we go over there?"

"No, it's not open to the public, it's called The Island of Everlasting Happiness, it's symbolic of paradise, you can see it, but you can't touch it."

I look down and see Megan wipe a tear from her cheek. I hear her sniffle and another tear slowly falls.

"Did I upset you? I'm sorry."

"No, it's just…"

"No words can describe it right?"

"Right."

Megan and I sit in the Japanese Garden in silence. We needed an escape since we both responded to it. The early evening sun shines.

"Where is your other favorite spot?" Megan asks. I grab her hand and we hear the waterfall before we see it. "Nate, this is beautiful, I think I've said that a million times since we have been here." She laughs. She skips over and skims her fingers in the water and the way the sun hits her, she looks like a fairy. I have this urge to kiss her. I want to so badly, but she doesn't deserve a kiss until I know what's going on with Olivia.

Megan and I walk through the English Rose Garden. We look at the Bonsai Trees, and as we admire the view one last time, a butterfly lands on her shoulder.

"Hold still," I tell her.

"What? Why?" She freezes.

"Do butterflies creep you out?"

"No…why?"

"There is one on your shoulder, don't swat at it I think they have rare ones here."

She slowly moves her head and looks at the butterfly. The butterfly seems so calm and comfortable on her shoulder. "Can you get a picture? I think it likes me," she whispers. I get my phone and take pictures. "Do I keep walking or just stand here?"

"Just stand there, I think this is good luck."

I move to stand in front of Megan to see the wonder on her face and when she looks at me, she smiles, "Nate, you have one that landed, right there," she points. The butterfly lands right where I have my memorial tattoo, and it takes everything in me not to cry. I felt Trey with me in Aspen and I feel him now.

Megan gets her phone out of her pocket and when she does, her butterfly flies away. She takes a picture of me. "Are you okay Nate?"

Fuck, she knows me too well, "My memorial tattoo for my best friend Trey and my Grandparents is in this spot. Trey passed away when I was a teenager, I should have been in the car with him, but I was passed out drunk in someone's yard."

"Oh fuck…Nate, I'm so sorry."

As soon as the butterfly takes flight, Megan crushes me with a hug. Her hands run up and down my back to comfort me. "I've never told anyone that before," I confess. Only Nico and Julian.

She pulls away and looks up at me, her eyes glassy, "I won't tell a soul, I promise." She squeezes me again, "For what it's worth, I'm glad you're here."

Her voice has a tinge of something I can't quite place and I hug her back. I hold her in my arms and something feels right about it. I rest my chin on the top of her head, she's the perfect height. I feel like a strong protector for her. Her touch calms my nerves and mind, like a drug. *What is this?*

Our stomachs growl and I break our embrace and lead Megan to the café to order dinner. We eat outside overlooking the gardens.

Megan and I eat next to the water and watch the sunset together. The ingredients are grown on the grounds here and my Ahi Tuna Poke bowl is delicious, and Megan lets me steal a bite of her Summer Berry Salad. As we eat, we talk about her parents, who I've met a few times, we talk about my parents who she knows from our annual July 4th and Christmas parties over the years. My parents love her, and I think her parents like me. Her Dad is a cop so he's a tough cookie to crack but her Mom is sweet as pie.

As much as I don't want this evening to end, I have to get home to sleep. "You ready to head back to the city?"

Megan groans, "Ugh, I guess. Do you think they would find out if we set up and tent and camped here forever?"

I laugh, "Well, I don't know about camping here *forever* considering our winters are sub-zero, but I like where your head is."

I drive Megan home and the urge to kiss her comes back. I have déjà vu. I'm reminded of when I dropped Olivia off and she kissed me. Luckily, Megan takes off the helmet and gets some space between us.

"Thank you for taking me to your top-secret spot Nate. This is the best day I've had in a long time."

"I enjoyed it too, very much."

"I'll see you at work Wednesday."

"I'll be there." I joke.

"Goodnight," she waves.

"Goodnight."

When I get home I'm exhausted. Happy, but exhausted. I strip off everything and text Megan and Nico that I'm back home. I send Megan the pictures I took and she does the same. I send Nico the picture of the butterfly on me and he replies right away.

NICO: He's always looking out for you, and so is Nonni

I lay my head on the pillow and my eyes drift closed and I'm transported back to the day Trey's parents pulled the plug.

His parents cried. A lot. But then once the hospital told them Trey's organs, even his corneas, and skin, could be used to help people, children, in need, they expedited taking him off life support. In my mind, they were butchering my best friend like an animal. To this day, I usually assign butchering meats to someone else.

My parents were appalled by my comparison. I never said it in front of Trey's family. As an adult, I see now how beneficial organ donation is. We were never getting Trey back so why not help people in need? I get it. But trying to grasp that as a teenager. No.

I didn't eat meat for months after that and lost weight because I wasn't eating protein. I wasn't born to be a vegetarian.

My phone pings just as I'm about to drift to sleep. It's a picture of Olivia on top of a mountain. I haven't heard from her all day, and I get a selfie, one she'll post on her Instagram anyway. I type out a quick reply

NATE: Cute

Then my eyes are heavy, and I fall asleep.

CHAPTER NINE

Tuesday, June 18th

Megan

"Meg! Get up! It's almost noon!" My sister Hayley pounds on my door.

I roll out of bed and stumble to the door, "It's my day off who cares, I groan."

"You didn't come home on Sunday night, you were gone like all day yesterday, on your day off, that isn't like you, are you okay?"

"Oh, so I'm not allowed to have a social life?"

She puts her hands on her hips and cocks an eyebrow at me, "And did you wear my combat boots, there are scuffs on them."

"I did, do you need a new pair?" I yawn.

"What? No, they look more badass, I just never knew you as the combat boot-wearin' type."

I walk to the coffeemaker and start a pot, "Do you paint animals by chance?"

Hayley laughs at me, "I paint sapphic art, so no, why?"

"I have a picture of Nate I want you to paint, one of me too if you can."

Hayley shakes her head at me, "Your obsession with him crosses the line when you want an oil painting of him."

"I'm not obsessed with him, okay? I have a beautiful picture I took yesterday of him at the Botanical Gardens."

I pour myself a cup of coffee, add two ice cubes and a splash of creamer, and join my sister on the couch. I got my phone and showed Hayley the pictures from yesterday.

"Wow, you have a great eye. You're right this is beautiful."

"One landed on my shoulder and then one landed on Nate's where he has a memorial tattoo."

"Really? Wow, that's some spiritual shit."

"It's heavenly there, you have to go. I know you only paint women but, crop his head out of it and focus on the butterfly?"

"Send me the pics and I'll see what I can do, okay?"

"You're the best, thanks." I smile as I sip my coffee.

"Was yesterday a date? Botanical Gardens, flowers, romantic setting…sounds like a date to me."

"Nope, just friends. But it has to mean something that he's never shared the story behind his memorial tattoo or the fact that the Gardens are his secret getaway spot—yet he told me about them, right?"

Hayley shrugs, "Maybe it does. Did you tell him how you feel?"

"No. It's complicated."

"It's been complicated for what, six years now? It's never going to get less complicated with Nate, ever."

"I'll tell him soon, okay? If I ask you to take me to that cool plant place you love, can you drop it?"

"You want to go plant shopping with me?" Her nose crinkles.

"Yeah, come on please!" I whine.

"I thought you'd never ask."

I return home with two small bonsai trees, one for me and I'm giving Nate the other tomorrow at work. I also got a small fountain to sit next to the bonsai on my end table. Now I can have a mini version of heaven on earth—a little slice of paradise. I type out a text to Julian:

MEGAN: Your plan worked

NATE

Another selfie from Olivia. This time she's on a mountain top holding a yoga mat under her arm.

NATE: Beautiful

She is. She is stunning. Maybe I'm old fashioned but I don't communicate in selfies. I want to type out more but what do I say?

I go to the rooftop and harvest everything I can for tomorrow. I spend hours harvesting and planning specials. Nico joins me and I tell him more about yesterday.

"Our Megan?"
"What do you mean *our* Megan?"

"She has worked here for years and you're just now noticing the full-blown hottie she is? Are you blind?"

"You've noticed?"

"I'm a straight man who has a dick, of course I've fucking noticed, Julian has heart eyes for her so bad dude, I'm surprised she went with you."

"What the hell is that supposed to mean?"

"You're kinda a dick, I can't believe you asked her for advice about Olivia, are you stupid or somethin'?" Nico smacks me upside the head, "Megan likes you. She flirts with you all the time. She probably posted that picture with Julian to get your attention and it worked."

"She's not like that," I scoff.

"Bro, women are the masters of mind games. She's a mastermind."

Did I fall into a trap?

CHAPTER TEN

Wednesday, June 19th

Megan

I walk to work carrying the bonsai tree I bought for Nate. I know the guys are prepping so I get there early hoping to have time to catch Nate. When I walk in the back door the guys say hello to me and my eyes scan the kitchen. I don't see Julian. Maybe Nate sent him on an errand? Nate looks up and smiles when he sees what I'm carrying.

I gesture with my thumb towards the office and he tips his chin in the air in response. I try to look busy until he is ready. He unlocks the door and waves me in. I close the door behind me.

"I have something for you," I sing. I put the tree down on his desk.

"Is it real? This is awesome, thank you." He smiles brightly.

"I also got you the itty-bitty scissors you need to trim it, and I emailed you instructions on how to take care of it just in case. They require regular care and maintenance." *Like a relationship.* "I got myself one too and a little fountain, I put them on my nightstand and it's heavenly."

I hand Nate the pruners and our hands graze each other. I try my best not to blush.

"This is sweet of you, thank you." Nate hugs me and we hold on a little longer than is boss/employee appropriate.

Julian got to work in time for the family meal. I didn't have time to ask him why he was late. During the meal, I caught Nate looking at me a few times and it gave me butterflies. I also noticed Julian's eyes on me and the tension in his jaw when he noticed Nate being more friendly than usual with me.

The high from getting Nate's attention put me in a good mood and carried me through dinner service. At the end of the night when I'm in the office getting my cash out, I decide to inquire about Olivia, "Now that I'm clocked out as an employee, can I clock in as a friend?"

I get a smile out of Nate, "Sure, what's up?"

"How are things with Olivia?"

Panic floods his face.

"You didn't text her today, did you?"

"I was so busy prepping and unloading the truck, shit!"

"Did she text *you*?" I ask, hoping he will get the hint that phone communication goes both ways.

He pulls his phone out, "Nothing, not even a selfie." He taps his phone a few times and holds it up for me to see Olivia's Instagram. "She posted about food and a spa treatment so she had time, should I text her?"

"I mean, isn't it a little late now? See if she texts you tomorrow and if she doesn't…"

"I blew it." He sighs.

"You did not, and even if you did, learn from this and communicate better next time you like a girl," I smile.

Nate sighs, "Yeah, you're right. Live and learn isn't that what they say?"

"That's what I hear," I chuckle.

There's a knock on the doorframe, "You ready Megs?" Julian asks.

"Ready for what?" Nate plasters a fake smile on.

"It's raining, I'm driving her home," Julian answers matter-of-factly.

"Ready." I nod and follow Julian to his car. I didn't want to walk in the rain and if I could make Nate a little jealous and notice me, so be it.

"Thanks for the ride," I say to Julian as I slip in the passenger seat.

"No problem, he looked jealous, didn't he?" Julian says cockily as he starts his car, "I kinda like that Nate is jealous of me."

I lean my head back on the seat, "Oh God, is this a game for you now?"

"I'm teasing," he smiles and the streetlights cast shadows over his square jaw and perfect cheekbones. I check out his sleeve tattoo on his right arm. It's a mix of skulls, roses and snakes.

"Do your tattoos have a story?"

"Doesn't every tattoo?"

"I wouldn't know, I never got one."

"Really? You don't have a foot tattoo or something?"

"Did you see any when I stripped my clothes off at Rauls?"

Julian clears his throat, "Um, no but maybe you had one that was hidden," he lifts a shoulder.

"Are you avoiding my question?" I scoff playfully.

His grip tightens on the steering wheel, "Tattoos are permanent but so are scars and I had some I wanted covered."

"Oh, sorry."

"My first love was pain, then alcohol, then pot and pills." Julian adjusts his grip on the steering wheel, "I think that's why I haven't kissed you."

The words almost get stuck in my throat but I croak out, "What do you mean, what do your scars and tattoos have to do with you kissing me?"

"No, not that, my past. You don't know this, but Nate is the only person in my life who ever believed in me. He took a chance to hire me. Because he did, my life changed for the better. I can never repay him. He was the first person in my life who ever gave a shit about me. Nico was second."

"So… because Nate gave you an opportunity, you won't kiss me? I'm not his property you know?"

"He likes you and I'm not moving in on his girl." Julian pulls into an empty parking spot in front of my building. The fact he is now refusing to kiss me makes me want to kiss him even more.

I take off my seatbelt and adjust myself so I'm facing him. He drums his fingers on his lap and his leg bounces in nervousness. I lick my lips and lightly bite my lower lip.

"I'm not kissing you Megs," he chuckles and looks away.

Rain pelts the car and it's all I hear besides the pounding of my heart. Nate is caught up in Olivia. I'm allowed to kiss anyone I want. It's been nearly six years. I have to give up on the idea of Nate. When Julian looks back over at me, I grab his chin and force my lips to his. I move my lips on his and he starts to kiss me back.

"What are you doing?" He whispers.

"Something I should have done a long time ago."

Julian and I make out and fuck can he kiss. We kiss until we are both panting and the windows are foggy.

"Megan…" he whispers and then pulls away.

I pinch my lips together and take a breath, "Yeah?"

"I've liked you for a year…and I love kissing you…but, I'd never be able to give myself to you until I know there is no chance of you and Nate being together. I care about both of you so much. I want what is best for you."

"What are you saying?"

"I can wait longer. Figure your shit out with Nate and once you do, then we can figure us out."

God, I'm glad one of us is rational. I kiss him again, this time more sensual and less needy, "I can respect that."

He nods towards the door, "Go get some sleep."

"Goodnight."

CHAPTER ELEVEN

3 AM, Sunday, June 23rd

I'm drained after our Saturday shift, but it was another successful night. I strip off my clothes and pour a glass of wine, letting the warmth settle in. I want to text Olivia, but it's been days since I last reached out. She hasn't messaged me since Wednesday, and I can't blame her. She was the only one putting in the effort. I need to make time. I need to stop trying to follow these imaginary rules I've set for myself.

I check Olivia's Instagram and see a picture of her with Hannah. They are at a nightclub. *Fuck Olivia is dressed like a vixen tonight.* That red top and lipstick, fuck me.

Hannah is tagged. I click her profile and see pictures and video clips of Hannah, Olivia, and a redhead dancing. I watch the video she posted. I catch a glimpse of Olivia. I watch it again and pause it. There's a guy with his arm around her waist and his head is buried in her neck. *Is he kissing her?!* My heart rate increases. I go back and look at the rest of the pictures Hannah posted. There is a picture of Olivia on stage singing what appears to be a rock song with a live band. *Olivia can sing?*

I scroll back to earlier in the evening. There is a group picture of the girls with four guys #Chicago #hockeyhotties. *She's partying with hockey players?* She mentioned that she loves hockey. *How the hell can I compete with that?* One of the pictures is Olivia with the same guy who had his arm around her, and they are taking a shot together. I try not to get jealous but he's tall, has a sleeve tattoo, quiet confidence, fuck!

I swipe. In the next picture, she is holding onto his arms and smiling. He towers over her, I'm 5'11", and I'm not short but Christ. I can't help it. I'm jealous.

I throw my phone on the table and run my hands through my hair. I slump in my chair and my blood is boiling and it's nobody's fault but my own. *How do I ask about this without coming off like a jealous asshole? Can I even ask?* I'm the fucking idiot who hasn't texted or called her.

I try to breathe. I'm not totally to blame here, I can't communicate with selfies. Nico warned me that a girl as driven and beautiful as Olivia wouldn't put up with my bullshit and overthinking. Her orbit pulls people in. Two minutes with her and she makes you feel high, makes you feel better, makes you want to be better. *Fuck!*

I pick up my phone and recheck Hannah's post. She looks cozy with Ethan Hall. He is tagged as well as Trevor Armstrong. They play hockey together. I'm not proud of it but I check their Instagrams too. It's mostly all hockey shit but there are some pictures with Olivia's mystery man. From what I can tell, he doesn't play hockey. *Whew, maybe*

I have a chance. I wonder if Nico will even care that Hannah is posting about a guy. They have an odd situationship. I text him to tell him to browse her Instagram.

NICO: I'm not stalking her Insta. Hannah is happy. I can't give her all of me so she deserves to find someone who can. Olivia does too.

I don't care what he says, I need to try to redeem myself.

Sunday Morning

I barely sleep but the first thing I do when I wake up is text Olivia.

NATE: Thinking of you, call me when you can

I wait for a reply and don't get one. I wait an hour and then take the initiative and call her. It takes three rings, but she answers.

"Hi Nate," Olivia's voice is perky. Okay, this is a good sign.

I clear my throat, "I saw you moved into your new apartment. How is it? How are you feeling after last night?" I sound pathetic.

"Yeah, the new place is great, I love it…oh, last night? The girls and I went out. I kinda overdid it, I'll be spending the day recovering."

I let out a little nervous laugh, "Since you're taking today to recover, would you like to go out with me tomorrow?"

She hesitates, "Tomorrow?"

"Yeah, I want to take you on a date."

I hear her sigh and fumble for words, "I'm busy, I have a lot of work to do."

"I do too but I'm willing to take time off for you."

"I understand Nate, but--"

"Babe, the shower is ready!" I hear in the background.

"Oh, you're not there alone." I feel like the air is punched from my lungs. *He* is there with her. *He* called her babe and is waiting for her in the shower. I'm fucked.

"Yeah…sorry, maybe some other time, I gotta go."

She is being polite. There won't be 'some other time'. I don't even get to say goodbye before she hangs up.

The rest of the day at work, I'm pissed off, annoyed, jealous. I'm kicking myself for not calling Olivia sooner. To make matters worse, my best sous chef drove Megan home last night and she's been smiling all day. I don't want to say Megan is my backup, but she is #1 on my list of potential partners.

When we close for the night, I grab a bottle of red wine and head to the rooftop. I need to think. I'm a glass in when I hear the door creak. I don't care who is joining me, so I don't bother to look. I stare down at the street below.

"Don't jump." I hear Megan joke.

Part of me is relieved it's her and not Nico. I turn to face her, "I'm not going to jump, it's not high enough to kill me." I return her dark comment with my dark humor. I pour another glass of wine and offer her a sip. She takes the glass from me and takes a gulp, then hands me the glass and I take a long drink.

"You okay?"

"Yeah," I sigh. I look down at her and by the expression on her face, she knows I'm lying.

"You're lying, what's going on? I'm clocking in as your friend right now."

I take a deep breath, "I blew it with Olivia."

"I'm sorry, I'm not the best at advising on relationships."

I wave off her comment, "It's fine, I'm glad you tried to help, it was nice to get a female perspective."

"You could always try a grand gesture, take her by surprise, it works in the movies," Megan shrugs and takes a swig of my wine, "Or you can give up."

"I've never given up on anything in my life."

CHAPTER TWELVE

Friday, June 28th

Megan

"Is Nate ever going to stop being an asshole? I hate this version of him!" Amira grumbles.

Nate's been a dick. I won't even try to cover for him.

"I know he's stressed and wants everything to be perfect, but he needs to chill," Leah adds.

"Whatever has him in this funk, it needs to stop. Please talk to him." Ava chimes in. If she's begging me to talk to Nate, it has to be bad.

"Why me?" I scoff.

Amira rolls her eyes, "You're the only one who seems to get through to him. Go! I'll watch your tables."

"I'll have Nico and the guys watch the kitchen. Please!" Leah begs.

"Fine. I'll try."

I intercept Nate while he's in the cooler grabbing something that needs to be stocked, "Hey, I've been appointed to talk to you, and I need you to listen."

"I don't have time for this Meg—"

I grab the pan from him and set it on the rack, "This can wait."

He reaches for it and I slap his arm away, "No. Listen to me."

"What? What is it?"

"You're driving everyone crazy with your mood. You've been a dick to everyone and that isn't you Nate. You're like, Ramsey level bad."

Nate tries to talk and I cut him off.

"Hush! These people have stuck with you through everything and you're going to lose them if you don't stop being an asshole. You don't get results that way. Go clean yourself up and make your grand gesture with Olivia. Even if it fails, you can have closure."

"Megan—"

"Olivia posted about an art gallery event for her best friend, she'll be there. Go."

"It's too late…"

"Nate. *Go*. Hear it from her yourself or you're going to keep overthinking and treating people you love like shit."

It kills me to send him to her. I want him. I've always wanted him. If his grand gesture does work, I can finally move on. If it doesn't, maybe I'll finally have my chance.

NATE

I didn't realize how much this Olivia thing was affecting me. I'm not a Ramsey type. I give up the fight and take Megan's advice. I go upstairs and take a quick shower. I spritz on cologne and put on dress clothes. I try to tame my hair and then take the car to the gallery. The rain is pouring down.

When I park, I try to calm my nerves. I need to be confident like her tattooed Viking guy. I scroll her Instagram, she documents everything, and there haven't been pictures with that guy so that's a good sign, right?

The rain has slowed to almost a complete stop as I walk to the gallery. It's packed. My eyes scan the room, and I see Olivia standing next to one of the guys in the group pictures she was in. *Oh shit, she sees me*, she does not look happy. *Abort, abort, abort!*

"What are you doing here?" She asks with no expression in her voice. She looks beautiful tonight, her shoulder and neck are exposed on one side and I want to kiss her neck so badly.

"I knew you would be here supporting Kenzie…"

"Stalker."

"I'm not stalking you, I am making time for you, I'm making an effort," I try to defend myself.

Her eyes narrow, "How did you get the night off? What about work?"

"Nico has it covered," I assure her in almost a whisper. I get lost in her eyes, "I wanted to see you, talk to you, explain myself."

She takes a deep breath, "Nate, tonight is for Kenzie. I'm not going to make a scene. I'll show you around, you will buy one of her pieces, and leave."

I'll take any time I can get with her, "Understood." I nod. Olivia leads me around the room and tells me about Kenzie's paintings. If this travel blogging doesn't work out for her, she should work in a museum because her descriptions and viewpoints on art hypnotize me.

"She is very talented," I compliment and take a sip of champagne from my flute glass. I scan the room and the gallery is full of people mingling and everyone is having a good time, "Great turnout."

Olivia smiles, "She worked hard for all of this, I'm proud of her," her lips meet the rim of her glass, and her lipstick leaves a print. *I miss her lips.*

As I'm admiring her instead of the art, a bubbly blond greets Olivia. I finish my glass of champagne while they chat and grab another. My nerves need alcohol.

"Nate, what would you like to purchase?" the peppy young woman asks.

I scan the wall of abstract paintings in front of me, "Uh, how about the red one? It would look great in our restaurant."

"It's $900."

"Okay." I nod. Money isn't an issue. I give her my contact information and put it on the business account. I'll explain to Nico later. I catch Olivia smiling at me. I think supporting her best friend won me some forgiveness.

"We only have that corner left," I nod towards the area glowing red.

Olivia shakes her head and starts blushing, "Oh, no, you are *not* going back there."

"What? Why?"

"My best friend's naked body is on display back there," she whispers close enough to my ear that I can feel her hot breath on my neck.

"It is art, isn't it?" I ask as I step closer to her. I see her face flush and her breathing pattern gets shallow. I still affect her.

"Yes, but I don't want you seeing her like that, and her new man may get jealous," she nods behind me.

My eyes trail over Olivia. The champagne is kicking in. I lean in close and whisper in her ear, "I'd rather see you naked." Olivia's skin bubbles with goosebumps and I kiss her bare shoulder.

"Nate, stop." She pulls away blushing.

I kiss her shoulder again then her neck.

"Nate," she pushes me gently, "No."

"Olivia, I miss you, all of you…" I rub my thumb over her lightly freckled cheek, "I was a fucking idiot for not texting you, I regret it every day." Olivia doesn't move, I see the wheels turning behind her eyes, "You are beautiful tonight, you're the most breathtaking thing in this gallery. I want to show you that I can make time for you."

I see something behind her eyes switch and she pokes me in the chest, "If you thought you could just show up here, flirt with me, and try to turn me on to get me to have sex with you after making time to see me, you were wrong."

Does she think I'm here to try to fuck her? "Olivia…" I reach out and caress her elbow, she is trying to make me out to be the bad guy here, she isn't seeing this as a grand gesture to win her back, she thinks I want to fuck her. "Is this about the guy in those pictures with you? And who was calling you to the shower when I called you Sunday? Is something going on with you two? Is he my competition?"

Olivia huffs out a breath then turns around and starts heading for the door. I take a deep breath and follow her outside. I'm a few feet behind her and almost bump into her when she turns around and starts yelling at me with tears welling in her eyes.

"This has nothing to do with him! You are not in competition with him, you compete with me! Me and my peace! You have made this all too hard, too confusing, you're not worth it to me. I like my sanity!"

She is the one confused? I'm confused. I thought she just wanted sex.

"Are you jealous I may be with him? Is that why you came? You and I *fucked*. That does not mean you have a right to know my business."

It was sex. That is it. That's all this was to her. And yes. Yes, I'm fucking jealous of the guy who she's with because she doesn't see him as just a lay.

"We could have been more, but I match effort with effort. You are only here because Anders is in the picture. I should have had your time and effort before he was a factor."

My blood boils, she's right, we could have been something if she didn't think I was only interested in her pussy. The hurt in my voice spills out, "I'm jealous of anyone who gets to spend time with you!" I snap. "You weren't just sex to me, okay? I fucked up. I'm terrible at this, but this is me trying," I pace the sidewalk, I'm shaking, "I've been having this internal battle with myself all week to give up how I feel about you and just be happy that I even got the chance to have time with you. I keep telling myself to leave you alone and let you move on with someone who won't fuck up from the start, but I had to let you know hoping that maybe you'd give me another chance, I'll change, I promise…" my voice cracks. I don't even recognize my voice.

Olivia squares her shoulder and lifts her chin, "If you wanted me, you should have texted or called, not given me one-word answers when I sent you pictures of me in Aspen. You dropped the ball, not me, don't make me out as the bad guy here! You're worried about competition instead of connection." She sighs, "You don't get another chance Nate, I don't trust that you will change at all, learn from this and do better with the next woman you meet."

I'm speechless. My phone vibrates in my pocket. I stand up tall and breathe in the sticky night air. My hands itch to answer the phone. *What if there is an emergency at the restaurant?*

"Answer it," Olivia sighs, she looks exhausted. The phone goes silent.

"They can fucking wait!" I shout in frustration that I can't have a few hours without thinking about work. "Nothing is more important than you." I grab the back of Olivia's neck tenderly and pull her into me for a kiss. I burn in my mind how her pouty lips feel on mine, I feel her body relax in my arms. She fists her hands in my shirt and pulls me in …then pushes me away. She wipes my kiss from her lips and tries to catch her breath.

The phone rings again.

"Fucking answer it!" She yells and starts to back away from me.

I pull my phone out of my pocket and answer, never taking my eyes off Olivia, "What?!"

"Nate, you won't believe the call we just got, we have been asked to be on Food Network!"

I blackout. "I swear to God Nico, you better not be pranking me," I can't breathe, I hunch over bracing myself with my free hand on my knee. I look down at the sidewalk.

"I wouldn't joke about this bro! They want us to compete against each other and with others and they asked us to be guest judges on a couple of other shows!" Nico laughs and I hear our crew cheering in the background.

My eyes sting with tears, "Stop, Nico, are you being serious?" I stand upright, pinching the bridge of my nose to try to hold back tears. I fail.

Olivia grabs the phone from me and I run my hands over my face trying to process everything that Nico said, "Nico, it's Olivia, what is going on?" I hear panic in her voice.

Of all times for the call to come, it had to be now?

"Congratulations. You both deserve it. He is on the way." Olivia ends the call and hands my cell phone back to me. I can't stop crying, fuck. I wipe my eyes. I'm overwhelmed with emotion. I lost Olivia but gained a career achievement. One that I never thought was possible.

Olivia is holding back tears too, she smiles, a genuine smile, she wipes a tear from my cheek and her touch burns, "I am proud of you." She chokes out.

"I'm so…"

"Don't be sorry, just go." She takes her hand back, "This is your time, go celebrate with your brother and staff."

I nod and turn to walk away.

"Nate…" she calls my name. I half turn around, "Don't show up where I am again. Let this go."

I nod and start walking back to the car.

This was a terrible fucking idea. *Why did Megan give me this idea dammit?*

I speed faster than I should back to Due Fratelli.

Slow down, I hear Trey's voice.

"Shut up!" I yell at him.

Dude, it will be okay. Slow down. You can't compete on Food Network if you're dead.

I take my foot off the gas and slow down. Trey's voice hasn't changed. He still sounds like a sixteen-year-old.

This is all you've ever wanted and more.

"But I don't have someone to share it with besides Nico. You're gone. Olivia is gone. My parents don't count. I want someone to be my cheerleader."

You already have one.

"Like I said, you and my Nonni don't fucking count. Who do I have?" I ask but the ghost of Trey is gone, "Fucking answer me asshole!" I yell into the void. Nothing.

I compose myself in the car after I pull it into the garage. I look like shit. I can still smell Olivia's sweet floral perfume on me. I lean back into the headrest and mentally go to the Botanical Gardens.

I'm in the Japanese Garden, my happy place. The bees are buzzing, the air smells like fresh-cut grass and the wind gently kisses my skin.

"Are you going to come inside and celebrate or just stand in the garden?"

I look over and Megan is in the garden with me, she looks like an angel. A teenage Trey joins her.

"She's right, you need to celebrate," he smiles. His brown eyes shine brighter than the sun. He has eyes, he is whole. Nothing about him looks different, "Megan is right." He repeats.

"She's always right," I say aloud. I snap myself back to reality. Megan said I needed to make a grand gesture or get closure knowing I tried. I have that closure now and now I can move on.

I take a few deep breaths and overwhelming joy comes over me. I perk up and make my way inside. I can't help the smile that is on my face and Nico is the first one to spot me. I jog to him and hug him so tight. "We did it."

"We did it together." He laughs and pats my back.

"Did you call Mom and Dad yet?"

"I was waiting for you." Nico wraps his arm around my shoulder, and we walk to the kitchen.

Megan

'Happy Nate' is back. I get choked up seeing him and Nico so happy. There were times during the pandemic when their dreams could have died out but instead, they thrived. Like a lotus in muddy waters. Nate makes his way around and gives everyone a high five or hug. He saves me for last.

I wrap my arms around his waist, and he hugs me, tight.

"Congrats, I'm so proud of you."

"We wouldn't have made it this far without you. Thank you. I'm sorry for being an asshole, forgive me?"

"I forgive you."

Before I can ask him how things went with Olivia, he breaks our embrace and calls everyone to the kitchen.

"I'm not one for speeches but I want to tell all of you how much Nico and I appreciate every single one of you and all the hard work you do. I'm sorry I've been…"

"An asshole." Raul fills in the blank for him.

Everyone laughs and Nate nods his head in agreement, "Yes, an asshole. I promise I'm back to normal now, okay? Let's rock out the rest of this service and celebrate!"

Everyone claps and Nate and Nico go to the office and close the door.

Amira nudges me, "See, we told you that you have the magic when it comes to Nate."

"Megan drinks for free for a month!" Raul cheers and everyone comes to hug me then, it's back to business.

Right before we close for the night, the phone to the restaurant rings. I'm the only person left in the dining room so I rush to answer it.

"Good evening, Due Fratelli, how may I assist you?" I say in my best customer service phone voice.

"I need to speak with Nate Rossi, it's urgent." A deep voice demands on the other end.

"May I ask who's calling?" I ask as politely as possible.

"Just put him on, he's expecting a call from me."

What the hell? "One moment please, I need to put you on a brief hold."

I press the hold button and walk to the office. I knock on the door and Nico opens it. "Nate, there's a guy on the phone asking to speak with you, he said you're expecting his call? He didn't give me a name, but it sounds important."

Nate and Nico exchange glances and Nico leaves the office. I shut the door to give Nate privacy.

NATE

"Hello, Nate Rossi speaking."

"Nate, this is Anders, I know you know who I am. Don't fucking hang up, you need to hear what I have to say."

Anders? Olivia's man? Why the fuck is he calling me? "Olivia already made it very clear that she wants nothing to--"

"She didn't ask you to be there tonight, you showed up, uninvited like a fucking creep! Was it not clear enough the first time Olivia told you not to put your lips on her in the gallery? Because she said you kissed her again on the sidewalk against her will? Is that the kind of man you are Nate? Do you stalk women and force yourself on them because you think you're charming? It'd be a shame for rumors of that to get around."

"What?! No!! It wasn't like that, I swear…" I try to defend myself. *Is this really how Olivia feels about tonight? What the fuck?* "I was just trying to show her I can make time for her…I was trying to get a second chance…"

"You don't get a second chance! You were too much of a pussy to know what you had with her. I'm not letting her go for as long as I have air in my lungs. You stay the fuck away from Olivia, if I find out you have any contact with her, if you're even in the same zip code as her,

I'll fucking end you and your business. Do you understand me?"

I have no words. This is how Olivia spun tonight? I have nothing to say to Anders. I hear him loud and clear. I hang up the phone, punch my desk with both fists and run my fingers through my hair. I try to take deep breaths and open my eyes; they land on the bonsai tree. Megan.

I push back from my chair and scan the back of house to see if she is still here and of course, she is.

"Megan, a word." I nod for her to follow me outside. I need air.

She looks confused but follows me.

I pace the alleyway.

"Nate, are you okay?" Megan reaches for me and I pull my arm away.

"That was Anders."

"What?"

I raise my voice, "Anders! The guy that Olivia is dating. He called to threaten me. He thinks I'm stalking Olivia and she told him I forced myself on her."

"What the fuck?" She scoffs, "Nate, you would never…"

"I did kiss her, but I was desperate to show her I wanted her. Once she made it crystal clear she wasn't interested, I backed off. So much for a grand fucking gesture. It was a stupid fucking idea and now I'm getting threatened by him to end me and this business if I contact her or happen to be in the same place as her."

"Nate…are you blaming me?"

"I…I don't know. I got closure alright and might lose everything now!"

"He's not going to do anything. He's just defending her." Megan tries to ease my worry.

"Nico is going to flip the fuck out, you know that?" I grip at the roots of my hair in frustration.

"I'll explain everything was my idea, okay?" Megan's voice cracks, "I didn't know it would escalate to this, okay? I just wanted you to get another chance with Olivia, get closure, and move on."

"Oh, I got that." I huff.

"I'm sorry Nate." Megan wipes a tear from her eye and runs inside.

Shit.

I put my hands on my hips, tilt my head to the sky, and try to breathe. I close my eyes.

Trey and I are passing a joint back and forth in the yard at the party. The party the night of his accident.

"What do you want to be after high school?" He asked me as we laid in the grass under the stars.

"I have no fucking idea...I'm not sure I'll even graduate."

"Dude, we have to graduate at least."

"What do you want to do?" I asked him as I took a drag. A hit so big I almost coughed myself unconscious.

"I think I want to be an EMT or something. I want to help people, but I don't want to be a cop or social worker or some shit like that and I'm not smart enough to be a doctor, so that is out. Most doctors are just legal drug dealers, ya know?"

"That would be cool, I bet you get to see a lot of gory fucked up shit."

He laughed, "Yeah like a guy with a tree limb up his ass or something."

We laughed together. Probably too much but we were stoned out of our minds and drunk.

"It's cool you want to help people. I admire that you have some fucking idea of what you want. I'm lost."

"You'll figure it out."

"What the fuck is the matter with you?" Nico comes stalking towards me and punches me in the stomach.

It knocks the wind out of me. He grabs me by the hair and punches me in the ribs. I swear I feel one crack.

"Stop! What the fuck? I'm your brother!" I choke out.

Boom! A blow to the other side of my ribcage. This punch makes me fall to one knee. Nico towers over me. I've never seen him this pissed off.

"Nathaniel Anthony, I swear to fuck that if you ruin this opportunity for us, I'll kill you."

"I'm not going to see her, okay?"

He points at me, "I'm not just kicking your ass because of that chick, you made Megan fucking cry and feel guilty for trying to help you! What the fuck is wrong with you?"

I hold my ribs and collapse to a sitting position on the pavement. I'm the worst.

"If she quits and we lose our best server…I swear…"

"I get it, okay?" I raise my hands in defense, "I'll apologize to her, alright?"

"She left."

I lay down on the pavement and cover my face. *Fuck.* It hurts to breathe.

"Bro, take smaller hits," Trey laughs at me, "I'm going to find snacks."

I close my eyes.

That was the last time I saw Trey without tubes coming out of him.

CHAPTER THIRTEEN

Saturday, June 29th

NATE

I'm sore. It hurts to move. The hot shower helped a little. I wrap my ribs and make my way down to the restaurant.

"Hey Boss, Megan called in, she's not feeling good and won't be in today. It must be bad because she's never called out of work."

Fuck

Nico shoots me a death glare, "Go apologize, *now*."

I take off my chef coat and run to the garage. I put my helmet on, fire up the bike, and speed to Megan's apartment building. I look at the names on the buzzer, find her last name, and frantically press the call button.

"What the fuck? Who is it?"

"It's Nate! Is Megan home?"

No response.

"Is she sick, is she okay? She called out of work today."

"Maybe she just wanted a day off."

"She never takes a day off…" I mumble to myself. Neither do I. Fuck. "Please tell her I need to talk to her. I'm free all day."

Nothing.

Fuck.

I rub the back of my neck to ease my tension and walk down the stoop. I sit on the step and clasp my hands together tightly in frustration. I shouldn't have taken my frustration out on Megan. I fucked up. I hear the door open behind me and don't bother to move.

"Nate?"

Megan. I get off the step and dust myself off.

"What are you doing here?" She looks annoyed. Her arms are crossed over her chest. Her hair is in a messy bun, her eyes puffy, her t-shirt hangs off her shoulder and her grey sweatpants have coffee stains on them. She's beautiful.

"I fucked up, I shouldn't have taken what happened last night out on you. I apologize."

"I was just trying to help you, Nate. I had no idea Anders would threaten you."

I move closer and take her hand in mine, "I know, I know…you're right, you're always right…it's kinda annoying actually."

I get a half-smirk from her before she pinches her lips together to hold back a laugh.

"I got the closure I needed with Olivia, and I should be thanking you. Before I met Olivia, I was finally ready to be in a relationship with someone. My life needs to be more than work. Last night should have been one of the happiest of my career but Nico beat the shit out of me…"

A snicker emerges before she turns her expression back to stone, "He did what?"

"He beat my ass for upsetting you and the threat from Anders. But that's not my point, you weren't there to finish celebrating with me." Nate lowers his voice. "I missed you."

Megan looks away and then back to me, she pulls her hand from mine, "I've worked for you for years and you have *never* yelled at me…" Her chin quivers, "I'd never do anything to put the restaurant at risk."

"I know. I'm sorry."

"I'm not working tonight or tomorrow so you can plan for that." She squares her shoulders.

My heart sinks.

Megan takes a deep breath, "I'm thinking about quitting."

I shake my head in confusion, "What? No." I grip her upper arms in desperation, "Please, take the time off…don't come back until after July 4th if you want just please, don't quit. I need you."

Megan shuffles out of my grasp, walks down the steps, and starts pacing the sidewalk, "Nate, it's hard to work with you."

"I know, I've been an asshole lately, I just needed to work through…"

Megan starts walking away from me. "You don't get it do you, are you fucking blind to flirtation?" She snaps and pokes me in the chest.

Once again, I'm caught off guard.

"I like you Nate! I've had a crush on you since the day of my interview. I never made a move because I didn't want to be unprofessional."

She was flirting with me all those times.

"I thought maybe, you liked me too, you came to Raul's and gave me breakfast in bed, and we had a beautiful day together…"

"I was there because I was jealous of Julian. I saw the pictures you posted and how…close you two are, I showed up at Raul's to see if you and Julian are together."

I want her to know that her feelings for me can turn into something.

"Julian and I aren't together. I gave you advice on Olivia because I was hoping that once you got closure with her you would see that I've been here all along."

Megan has been there all along. Why didn't I see it? She is the one Trey was talking about.

I slowly move towards Megan. I gently cup her face and look down into her big kaleidoscope eyes. "I'm sorry I never picked up on your flirting. You *have* been here all along and I'm so sorry I didn't notice." I lean down and kiss her softly like she is made of porcelain. A long overdue kiss. Her lips are so soft. Megan starts to kiss me back before pulling away.

Megan clinches her eyes closed and then opens them as she gently shakes her head in disbelief, "You're only kissing me to change my mind. I'm not changing my mind, Nate."

Her words take my breath away, "Megan, that's not my intention. Take all the time off you want but, tell me you'll give me a chance. I can't promise I won't fuck up. But I'll learn from the mistakes I've made. I want to have a life outside of the restaurant and I want it to be with you."

Megan's posture relaxes.

I continue, "I've been chasing my dreams, but I came here to chase you. Can you please forgive me for last night?" My eyes plead for her forgiveness.

She contorts her face and bites her lower lip. It's a long moment before she says anything. The corner of her mouth twitches, "I guess." Her smile beams and I pull her into me and kiss her again. We kiss for a long time like if we stop we won't get the chance to again. Megan breaks our kiss and hugs me tightly around my ribs.

"Ouch! Not the ribs…" I wince in pain.

Megan pulls back, "Shit! Sorry, kinda."

"You're not going to make this easy, are you?"

"Nope." She smiles up at me, "Can I kiss you again? I've dreamed about it so many times that now I don't want to stop."

My smile is her answer and Megan grabs my chin and pulls me down to kiss her.

Megan

I'm kissing Nate. After all this time, Nate and I are kissing. All it took was me calling off work. I deepen our kiss before pulling away, "I should have taken a day off years ago," I joke and Nate and I laugh.

"Would have saved us both a lot of heartache."

"Let's not waste any more time, okay?"

"Okay," Nate kisses my forehead.

"Did you mean what you said, that you're free all day?"

"I can be. Nico has things under control."

"Do you want to go back, take care of things and tonight, you and I can have a celebration dinner somewhere?" I ask boldly.

"I'd love that, I know the perfect place."

"Go let Nico know we talked so he doesn't beat you up again," I laugh, "We can work out the time and details later." I walk Nate to his motorcycle and he pulls me in for a kiss before putting on his helmet.

"I'll text you the details," Nate says before turning the ignition, revving, and taking off.

When I get in the apartment, my sister Hayley has her hands on her hips scowling at me, "What was he doing here?"

"Trying to redeem himself." I smile softly. There's a knock at the door, "You get that, I'll be in my room."

A half-hour later, Hayley comes bursting into my room.

"I have to tell you what happened!" Hayley says as she shakes me by the shoulders, "Lilah and I went to the art gallery open house last night and Kenzie delivered my portrait!"

Olivia's best friend Kenzie. I wonder if she was there at the same time as Nate.

"Yeah…" I say, knowing Hayley has more.

"Kenzie, fuck she's gorgeous! Her abstract paintings are incredible, and she had these stunning nude body paint photographs too, I bought one, it's hanging in the hallway now." Hayley grabs my arm and yanks me off my bed to see it. It's erotic and sexy without showing anything.

"I love it Hayley, this is definitely your taste."

"I gave her my card and let her know I'm an artist too. I showed her my paintings, and she offered to show my work in her gallery!" Hayley squeals as she throws her arms around me in excitement. "Can you believe it? My work in a real gallery!"

I hug her back. "I'm so happy for you, this is huge."

"I know!" She squeezed me harder then pulled away, "She loved my sapphic pieces so I get the impression she may float my way, bi at least. We exchanged numbers and she told me to get in touch with her when I'm ready to bring pieces over."

"That's awesome Hay, but take my advice and don't crush on who you work with," I said as I walked to my room and plopped on my bed. "I finally told him how I've felt about him."

"And…"

"He had no idea."

"Did he freak out?"

"No, we kissed."

Her jaw dropped, "How was it?"

"Magical."

"You haven't had a Saturday off in forever, let's go to the club. It's the last Saturday of Pride Month and we need to celebrate!"

"Nate and I were supposed to have our first date tonight."

"Oh come on! You've waited this long, what's one more night?"

I text Nate and let him know we will have to reschedule.

MEGAN: Hayley is making me take advantage of finally having a Saturday off, we are going out tonight for the last Saturday of Pride, can we change our date to Monday?

NATE: Of course, Meg xo Be safe, call me if you need me

CHAPTER FOURTEEN

Sunday, June 30th

Megan

Older sisters are supposed to set an example. Mine made me do shots. I swear each one was a different color of the rainbow. I'm suffering from it today.

I stumble to the bathroom and catch a glimpse of myself in the mirror, my makeup is smeared and I'm covered in glitter. I relieve my bladder and get in the shower. The hot water eases my muscles from dancing all night. I smell the aroma of coffee brewing mixed with my citrus-scented shampoo. Hayley's awake.

After my shower, I change into a tank top and pajama shorts and check my phone. I have three texts.

JULIAN: Missed you tonight

AMIRA: Tips were great tonight, is it a full moon or something? Get your cute ass to work!

I laugh at her text.

The last text came in when I was showering.

NICO: Nate is trying to give you space so he's not texting you. He missed you last night. We have a film crew coming in tomorrow when we're closed to interview us and I'd like you to be there. We also asked Raul. Consider it. Please. 10 am.

I like being missed. I get slight satisfaction from it. I shuffle to the kitchen and Hayley looks human. How can she feel A-OK while I feel like death warmed over?

"I poured you a cup and there are two pills next to it for your brain-splitting headache," she teases.

"How are you so bright-eyed and bushy-tailed?"

"I'm high on life!"

"High on something," I grumble under my breath.

"Nah! I got work to do. I have to make my work perfect before taking it to Kenzie."

I chug my coffee, take the pills, and wash my mug, "I'll be in bed if you need me."

I stumble back to my bedroom and text Nico.

MEGAN: I'm glad Nate is giving me space and that I was missed. I'll be there tomorrow.

My head hits the pillow and I drift to sleep.

"Do you have experience?" Nate asks.

I fidget in my seat and my dirty mind drifts; I'll be thinking of Nate asking this later but in a very different scenario. I snap myself back to reality.

I clear my throat, "Yes, I served at a diner in my hometown, but I just moved a few blocks away and your reviews are amazing, I want to work for the best place in town."

Nate cracks a smile, oh God he's gorgeous! "We are the best and we intend to keep it that way. How long were you at the diner?"

"I started when I was sixteen. I worked there all through high school, and technically, I'm still working there until I find something else so I'd really appreciate you hiring me so I don't have to drive there," I say sweetly.

Nate smiles again before eying me up and down, "Alright, look…I wish you had more fine dining experience, but I have a good feeling about you and my gut instincts are usually right." He taps his pen on a notebook, "I'm going to give you a chance but I'm warning you, we don't employ anyone who is weak. We expect 100% effort."

"I don't know how to give anything less."

That impresses him. "Everyone's role here is important. That being said, the guys in the kitchen can be intimidating, me included, and my brother and I are Italian so, there's cussing and yelling sometimes."

"My Dad is a cop and a Bears fan. I've heard it all Chef."

That earns me a laugh, "Perfect, you'll fit right in. You start tomorrow." He slides me a handbook and document on the dress code and I glaze over it. "Be here tomorrow at 2. Fill out the tax paperwork and tomorrow, you'll be training with Val." Nate slides me a thick card stock menu, "Memorize this." Another list gets passed to me, "Wine List. Are you old enough to drink?"

"I'm 21, I'll be 22 in December."

Nate holds up a finger and comes back with a small plate of pasta and a glass of red wine. "Tell me what you think. You're already hired so your new job won't depend on if you love or hate this. I want to know what you think."

I look down at the ravioli and can tell they are homemade; a soft orange sauce tops them.

"Take a bite of the food, sip the wine, then take another bite," Nate instructs.

I do as he asks and the flavor explosion is amazing. "The ravioli taste like fall and the wine has a smokiness. It's fresh. It tastes like it's from the garden and the wine makes me want to curl up next to a fireplace."

Nate beams, "Perfect. I knew my instincts about you were right."

NATE

"You invited her?"

Nico looks at me blankly.

"You're a genius!" I add and hug him.

"Hey, hey, get off me!" He playfully shoves me away.

"Thank you."

"She keeps you from going into full Asshole Mode and we need your head on right, the crew will be here any minute."

A few minutes later, Megan comes in looking like a hot librarian. She's wearing a tight pencil skirt, heels, and a white blouse. My cock twitches in my pants. My face splits into a smile and I walk to her and kiss her cheek sweetly. I'm not ready to tell Nico about my feelings towards Megan.

"Nico invited me," she smiles, "Is it okay that I'm here?"

"Yes," I say breathlessly, "You look incredible."

"Thanks. Nico told me to dress professionally but not in uniform, how's this?" Megan spins around and I have to remind myself that I have a job to do.

"It's perfect."

Nico and Raul come around the corner and both greet Megan with a hug. They compliment her outfit and Megan comments on seeing Raul dressed up.

"We asked you two here for an important reason."

They look at us quizzically.

"We're firing you, Megan." Nico blurts out.

"What?! Why?! You guys said you missed me!" Megan panics and Raul, Nico, and I start laughing, "This isn't funny! You made me dress up and come here to get fired?! Nate!" She turns to me, her eyes wide.

"We are firing you from being a server," I say in an even tone.

"But…but…"

"We want to promote you," I say to calm her fears.

Her shoulders slump in relief, "I finally take time off work and you want to…promote me?"

"She's right Nico, maybe we are making a crazy move," I laugh.

"Shut up!" She giggles, "What's the promotion if I choose to accept?"

"We need a maître d' for the front. You'll oversee reservations, seating, the servers, and bussers."

"I know what it is Nate. Are you sure?"

"Yes." My brother, Raul, and I say in unison.

"You'll run the front. I'll stay in the back. The only time I'll come out is when you ask me to for a guest."

Megan straightens her spine like she is considering the idea.

"You'll stay in the back?" She cocks her eyebrow at me.

"Yes. Nico and I wanted more time in the kitchen and you stepped up when we were in Aspen."

"And they missed me," Raul cheeses.

Nico nods his head yes.

"You'll be salary, so you'll have a steady income." From the look on Megan's face, she likes the idea.

"What about the waitstaff?"

"Amira will lead," Nico answers.

"Can I talk to Nate? Alone." Megan asks Nico and Raul and they excuse themselves just as the film crew arrives.

"Nate, I appreciate this but I don't want special treatment because you and I are…dating."

"Technically, I haven't taken you on a real date."

"You know what I mean, can you please not be a smart ass right now?"

"Yes."

"I don't want people to think I got this promotion because of …us."

"Megan, everyone loves you and knows you put in the work, if anyone insinuates something like that, fire them and I'll back you up 100%."

"You will?"

"Yes. Nico and Raul don't know about us yet, we can keep it on the down low if you want or I'll proudly let everyone know. Whatever you want."

Megan closes the distance between us and kisses me.

"Is this your way of saying yes?" I ask breathlessly.

"Yes, Nate."

I kiss her nose, "Tell me what you want."

"Let's keep it to ourselves for now." She kisses me quickly then smooths out her outfit, "Go get 'em." She smiles and shoves me towards the dining room.

Nico and I cook for the film crew so they can get shots of us working our magic. They record us together and separately for when we judge and compete together and against each other. The crew interviews Raul, who we promoted to back-of-house manager, and Megan, we give them her new title to use for the episodes and articles.

We finish with the film crew eating the meals we prepared and they love it, they said it's one of the best they've had. When they leave, Nico, Raul, Megan, and I celebrate with a bottle of champagne.

"You guys did amazing!" Megan beams with pride.

"It's so cool to see behind the scenes," Raul adds.

Nico clamps my shoulder and I can see he is fighting back tears, he is proud of me. Us.

Raul finishes his glass of champagne, "Hate to duck out but it is my day off. I'll see you guys on the 4th."

"Hell yeah! You're manning the grill." Nico claps. He checks his watch, "I'll clean up and then I gotta go."

"Leave it. I'll clean. Go do what you gotta do." I tell Nico, hoping to give Megan and me some privacy.

"I'm not going to say no to that," Nico slides out of the booth and hugs Megan goodbye. Raul does the same and they both leave the dining room. Megan pours herself another glass of champagne and she doesn't speak until we hear the backdoor close behind Raul and hear the rumble of the elevator taking Nico upstairs then back down and the door close behind him.

"I need to get something from the office, I'll be back." I kiss Megan's cheek and clear empty plates from the table.

I return with a leather folder that holds Megan's new employee file. I set it in front of her.

"What's this?"

"Need you to sign, make it official."

Megan smiles.

"Hopefully the salary suffices." I tap the folder and she opens it and her jaw drops.

"Nate, this is too much. No." She slides the folder back and I push it back.

"It's industry-standard plus extra for your time with us."

"I can't, no, it's too much." She shakes her head and drinks the entire glass she just poured.

I place my forefinger under her chin and make her look at me, "Megan, you've been putting up with me for years. You earned it. You're an asset to Due Fratelli."

Megan doesn't question me. She knows her worth. I grab her waist and pull her to the end of the booth. I kiss her passionately and she tastes like champagne. Her lips are glossy and sweet and fuck does she smell good. I want to see more of her. I've thought about what she looks like bare since I saw her sleeping in bed.

"Nate, wait." She whines and I kiss her neck.

"Yes?"

CHAPTER FIFTEEN

Megan

I have a promotion and Nate.

"Today is a great day."

"Want to make it even better?" He moans. I nod.

Nate holds his hand out to take mine. I place my hand in his and he leads me through the kitchen to the elevator. The doors open and when they close, Nate and I make out until we reach the fourth floor. He opens his door and we are all over each other.

I unbutton his chef coat and Nate shrugs it off.

"You look stunning, my God."

I chuckle, "You think this can be my new uniform?"

"Fuck yes," Nate groans and kisses my neck. He grabs my ass and lifts me. I wrap my legs around him and he carries me to his bed. We continue to kiss and Nate slowly unbuttons my blouse and places kisses over my chest. Surprisingly, I'm not overthinking or nervous. This feels right. I've fantasized about this so many times. Nate takes his time exploring my body and I love seeing his facial expression when he sees my tits for the first time. It's like he melted.

I reach for Nate's shirt, pull it over his head, and grip his biceps, "God you're hot." I blurt out and bite my lip.

Nate blushes and stands to takes his pants off. His cock strains against his boxer briefs. Holy fuck. "See something you like?"

I pick up my jaw from the floor and hum, "Mmmhmm,". I wish I had more willpower but this is five years of pent-up feelings and desire.

Nate crawls between my legs and kisses my feet, ankles, calves, and inner thighs. He lifts my skirt to see my panties, "Sweetie, you're soaked," he whispers over my lower stomach then slides my panties off.

Shivers run up my spine, "Nate…"

"Don't be shy. You're perfect," he leans down and kisses me as his fingers trail over my smooth pussy lips, "Mmm so wet and ready."

"Yes but…it's uh, been a long time so…"

"Shh, don't worry. I'll go slow baby."

Baby. He called me baby.

Nate rubs my clit until I orgasm, "Don't hold back, let it out for me, be as loud as you want," his lips meet my neck, and he sucks gently. I let my moan escape me and my legs shake in pleasure, "That's it, that's my girl."

My girl. Is this man trying to kill me?

I ride out my orgasm and Nate slips a finger inside me. Even one finger feels like an invasion. "Ahh, fuck…"

"Fuck Megan, I'm going to have to take my time and open you up ain't I?"

"Yes," I say breathlessly as I look up into his sparkling eyes. Another finger slides in me, "Oh Nate…"

"Are you okay?"

"Mmmhmm."

His fingers move slowly in and out of me and when I look down, his fingers are coated with my arousal. I feel my pussy getting used to him. Just as I feel like I'm able to handle it, Nate positions himself and starts licking my clit while fingering me. Another orgasm rocks through me and quickly another. *Three. I need more.*

"Make love to me Nate, please."

He pops from between my legs and licks his lips. His messy hair falls across his face. "I will. Sit up."

I do as he asks and he slips my blouse off and unhooks my bra. I'm suddenly self-conscious and try to cover myself but he stops me.

"I want to see you, you're so beautiful. Lay down." Nate drinks me in with his eyes, looking over every inch of me before taking my nipple in his mouth and swirling his hot tongue around it.

Another moan escapes me and I writhe on his bed. His fingers return to my pussy and he hits my g-spot while spoiling my tits.

"Nate please, I need you inside me," I beg. *Four.*

Nate takes his fingers out of me and gets off the bed to take his bottoms off and I see it. What a beautiful cock. Nate is trimmed and manly, his cock is long and thick. Goddamn.

Nate catches me staring as he grabs a condom out of his end table. I roll over on the bed and reach for him taking him by surprise. I need my mouth on it. Now. I grip the base and kiss the tip, his precum coats my lips and I lick it off then swirl my tongue around the crown.

"Megan, you don't have to…ahhhhh fuckkkk," he moans as I take him in my wet mouth, "Oh God…what are you…" his knees get weak as I dance my tongue over his shaft and take in more. I look up at him with my hazel blue eyes, mouth full, and he tilts his head back in pleasure. His muscles flex.

I suck him until I can't take him not being inside me anymore. I pop my mouth off and seductively lay back on the bed, grabbing my tits. Nate puts the condom on and climbs on the bed. He pops himself on his knees and gets between my thighs. He rubs over me then slowly presses his thick tip inside.

"Nate…" I sigh as I look up at him.

"You okay?"

"Yes, keep going."

He presses in further and I silently nod, letting my walls adjust to him.

"Relax and take me baby," Nate says as he caresses my thighs and watches himself sink inside me, hitting my cervix. I wince at first then take a deep breath and relax. Nate slowly pumps in and out of me. The way his muscles and stomach flex are so fucking sexy I clench watching Nate please me. It almost doesn't feel real. "How do I feel, is this everything you've ever dreamt about?"

"Yes, oh fuck yes, even better."

"What did you fantasize about when you'd think of me?"

"This, you and me…together." I pant.

Nate presses in deep and I feel so full, "In this position, like this?"

"Mmmhmm, and others…"

"Mmm, we'll have to make your dreams come true," Nate says before he leans down and kisses me softly. I wrap my legs around his waist and hold him as he pumps into me a little faster. "Yeah, wrap those legs around me, hold me close," Nate moans into my neck before kissing it and I orgasm at the sensation. *Five.*

"Don't stop, please…" I beg.

"Oh, I got plenty of stamina for you, I plan to be inside you all day and all night."

Six. "Nate!"

"Yes? Are you coming again?" He smirks and thrusts hard.

"Yes! Yes!" I cry out. The stretch and feeling of being full is overwhelming.

"Your moans and whimpers are music to my ears."

"I need you to come, please!" I pant.

Nate leans back up and pumps into me, my tits bounce and I look up at him, my eyes pleading with him to explode.

"Megan…"

"Do it, do it! Come for me!" I whine.

Nate's eyes widen and he bites his lower lip, "Here it comes, I'm coming for you. Meg…" A primal moan and grunt rips through the air and I come with Nate. *Seven.* Once every drop is drained into his condom, he collapses beside me and pulls me over to lay on his chest.

Our breathing is labored, our skin slick with sweat.

"Are you okay?"

"Yes, Chef."

NATE

"You are unbelievable." I sigh.

"I should have told you how I felt five years ago," Megan laughs and I kiss her head.

"In all seriousness, thank you for being so good to me Meg."

"No, thank you. I can't imagine working for anyone else, even though you're an arrogant prick at times."

"Well yeah, I'm a Chef."

Megan slaps my stomach and knocks a puff of air out of me, she sits up and combs her hair through her fingers, "Is my schedule still going to be the same, is there anything you need from me?"

I pull Megan back down into my arms, "Oooh baby, talking business after sex, are you trying to get me hard again?" I tease.

"Asshole." Megan laughs and twists my nipple.

"Ouch!" I chuckle, "Yes, your schedule is the same and please wear that outfit so I can catch a glimpse of you all night, knowing you're mine."

"Mmm, I like the sound of that." Megan snuggles into me and lazily strokes her hand over my abs as we bask in our orgasm high, "How'd you get started in the kitchen?" Megan asks as she nuzzles into me.

"Nico would pull me on the line when our manager was off, then before I could join, he made me roll 5,000 meatballs."

Megan laughs, "He would."

"It taught me patience and perseverance."

"I'm over being patient," Megan hums before she plants a kiss on me then straddles me. Time for Round Two.

***

"Woman! Are you trying to kill me?" I gasp for air after Round Four with Megan. She's insatiable.

"Food. I need food." She groans.

"You fuck the life outta me and now you want me to cook for you?" I tease.

Her giggles are the fucking cutest.

"Fine fine, I'll raid your fridge," Megan attempts to crawl out of bed and I pull her back into me.

"You're not going anywhere missy, lay down." I kiss her cheek and get out of bed. I toss my condom in the trash and get Meg a bottle of water. She chugs it, then nuzzles my pillow.

"What are you in the mood for?"

"French Toast."

"It's six o'clock at night."

"So…breakfast for dinner is fun."

"I'm running down to get Italian bread from the kitchen. I'll be back."

"Okay," she yawns.

I throw on gym shorts and flip-flops and take the elevator downstairs. I get a loaf of fresh bread and when I return, Megan is passed out asleep. I cook the French Toast and cut up strawberries. I eat first and then wake up Megan. She looks so peaceful when she's sleeping.

"Hey sweetie, wake up." I lightly shake her awake.

"Is it morning?" She grumbles.

"No, you've been asleep for almost an hour. Come on, wake up and eat."

Megan sits up in bed, "Why did you make French Toast?"

"In your post-orgasm stupor, this is what you asked for before you fell asleep."

"Oh my God, how embarrassing!" She laughs at herself and takes a bite, "This is delicious, did you eat?"

"Yeah, I ate and hydrated. I feel like a new man."

"Can you get my phone from my purse? I want to let Hayley know I'm okay."

I walk to her purse and bring the whole thing because I am not reaching into it. I know better. "Do you want to let her know you're spending the night?"

Megan cocks a brow at me, "Oh, am I?"

"You better."

"Yes, Chef."

I don't think I'll ever hear her call me 'Chef' without my balls tightening ever again.

CHAPTER SIXTEEN

Tuesday, July 2nd

Megan

Waking up next to Nate is surreal. I've wanted this for so long and now, I have it. I'm in his bed, he's sleeping beside me, my pussy and bones ache from our sex marathon. Nate is sleeping on his side facing away from me. Even asleep, his back muscles pop and his ass is so cute and bitable. I roll over to kiss his shoulder and trail my fingers down his side.

Nate lets out a sleepy groan, "What time is it?"

"8:23."

"Alarm goes off at 8:30," he grumbles.

I slide my hand over his hip and down to his morning wood, "That gives us seven minutes." I whisper over his bare flesh and start slowly stroking him.

"Mmm, seven minutes in heaven?"

I stroke more.

"You should stop, you're going to get me used to waking up like this," Nate laughs huskily, eyes still closed.

I adjust myself and push him to lie down on his back. I kiss his neck and lips, then over his tattoos and down his stomach. His breathing hitches and I take him in my mouth.

"Megan," he whimpers as he runs his fingers through my hair. I keep sucking and everything about Nate arouses me. His scent, taste, his moans, and whimpers as I take him down my throat, and his touch. I look up at him and he's smiling down at me.

"Best wakeup call ever."

I giggle around his shaft and he hisses in pleasure. I pop my mouth off, "Sorry."

Nate grabs the nape of my neck and pulls me up to kiss him. We make out as I grind my bare wet pussy over his length.

"Fuck that feels amazing, keep doing that," he growls and grips my hips. I glide his cock between my dripping lips and feel his swollen head rub my clit. It is electric. My moans fill the room and, Nate grips my tits and I let out an orgasm.

"Yes, come on this cock Megan, fuck!"

My eyes flutter in pleasure like a butterflies wings. I refocus on Nate and increase the tempo of my grinding.

"Megan, Megan…I'm coming…" Nate groans. I look down and spurts shoot on his stomach, hip, and even as far as his pecs and it's the hottest fucking thing I've ever seen.

"Oh my God, there is so much."

"All for you."

"That's so fucking sexy."

BEEP BEEP BEEP BEEP BEEP!

"It's 8:30, time to get up," Nate smirks.

Nate and I shower together and he makes us coffee and breakfast.

"Want me to take you home so you can change? If you want, I'd like you to stay with me for a few days. I want to take advantage of our time off."

"Take advantage, huh?"

"Not just sex."

"What do you have in mind?" I flirt.

"I want to take you out on an official date. I want to cook for you. I want us to set up for the July 4th party together…"

"I can only stay until Friday evening. My sister and I are going to our parents this weekend."

"That's fine. I'll take any time I can get with you."

Nate drives me home and I invite him up.

"Your sister paints here?" Nate asks as he admires Hayley's work.

"Yeah, she does. Studios are expensive and we don't need a dining room," I joke, "Hayley are you here?" I holler and Hayley emerges from her bedroom in an oversized tee and her hair up in a messy bun. When she notices Nate behind me, she perks up and tugs at the bottom of her shirt.

"Uh, hi," she half waves.

"Hi, Nate Rossi…" Nate reaches his hand out to shake hers.

"I know who you are, we've met remember?"

"Right. Sorry," Nate cringes and takes his hand away.

"I'm here for clothes, I'll be staying with Nate until we leave this weekend," I say as I move past her in the hallway.

Nate tries to follow and Hayley slams her hand on the wall to block him, "Nu-uh. You stay."

"Hayley," I sigh, "Let him pass, we aren't fucking here." Hayley puts her arm down and lets Nate by but she follows him into my bedroom.

"Aww, you really did set up a mini version of the gardens," Nate coos as he studies my bonsai tree and mini fountain.

"I told you I did."

"This is awesome. We need a fountain at my place."

"So, Meg, are you still quitting?" Hayley asks with her arms crossed.

"We fired her," Nate says with a smirk as he turns back to Hayley.

Fire burns in her eyes, "You did what?! Megan, how can you be with this asshole if he fired you?!"

Nate laughs and Hayley pulls her fist back ready to punch him. I stop her. "They fired me from serving, chill. Nate and Nico promoted me. I'll oversee the front of house." I explain. Hayley's expression softens.

"Oh, well. He could have worded it better," Hayley huffs.

"And miss seeing your reaction and the vein pop out of your forehead? Nooo." Nate pokes her forehead and she slaps his hand away.

"I hate you," Hayley grumbles but I can see her trying to fight a smile.

"Show me your paintings while Meg packs?" He offers. That wins brownie points with my sister. They leave the room and I change into a sundress. I put on makeup and fix my hair. Once I'm happy with my appearance, I pack my bag with enough clothes for the next few days.

Nate and Hayley seem to be getting along when I join them. Nate takes my duffle bag from my shoulder.

"Ready to go grocery shopping?" Nate asks.

"Gee, how romantic." Hayley teases.

"I'll make it fun." He sneers, "I want Megan to pick random ingredients and I'll have to come up with an app, entrée, and dessert from what she chooses."

I smiles, "You want to practice for what might get thrown at you during competition."

"Exactly!"

"Oh, this will be fun!" I fold my hands together, "I'm not going easy on you!" I warn him with a devilish smile.

"Good. Let's go." He says as he smacks my ass. "Bye Hayley!" he sings.

NATE

"You really didn't go easy on me, did you?" I ask Megan as I stare at my first basket of four random ingredients.

"I told you I wouldn't," Megan laughs, "I'm setting the timer for 20 minutes. Go!"

My mind races at the speed of light and I can't explain it, but the ingredients come together like a puzzle. Smoked Salmon already cooked. The cucumber needs to be sliced for a base. Crackers, garnish for crunch. watermelon, garnish. I run to the walk-in for cream cheese, herbs, and garlic, and then I'm back at the table mixing cream cheese. I set it aside and the kitchen fills with the sound of me slicing cucumber and dicing watermelon. I glance up at Megan and she is watching my every move in awe like I'm a surgeon performing a procedure.

I run for small plates and assemble my dish. Cucumber slice. Garlic and Herb Cream Cheese spread. Smoked Salmon. Cubed watermelon. Himalayan Salt. Dill for garnish. I smash up a cracker and sprinkle it on top. I throw my hands up before the timer goes off.

"Chef, time's up," Megan mocks in a TV host voice, "And now the judging. Chef Rossi, what have you prepared?" She continues in her man voice.

I play along, "Judge before you is a smoked salmon cream cheese cucumber bite with watermelon."

Megan nods then takes a bite, "Mmm, ohmygod," she says with her mouth full. "Wow, it's so fresh!"

"Perfect! Whew!"

Megan swallows and I try mine. I'm happy with it. "Reset Chef. Next course." She waves her hand like a magician. As I clean up, she preps the next basket for the entrée. I hear her snickering devilishly. Oh shit, this is about to get harder.

Thirty minutes later, Megan's eyes start rolling in the back of her head and it's not from my dick.

"Nate, how did you do this?"

"You watched!" I laugh.

"Who makes liver taste good?"

"Me I guess, you know, you're brave picking ingredients you hate."

"I know, it didn't hit me until I saw you unpacking…liver…" she shudders, "That I realized that I'm the one to taste test it."

God, she's cute. My dish may be perfect to her but when I try it, I notice everything I could have done better.

My dessert round is not a success, to Megan at least.

"Holy crap is that sour!" Her face scrunches and she reaches for her water.

"You picked Warheads, sweet tarts, gummy bears, and lemons. You didn't give me much to work with."

"I should have picked sweet instead of sour."

"You know some foods can be either depending on when they are harvested. Like raspberries."

"Really?"

"Mmmhmm," I grab one from the bowl, "Close your eyes."

Megan glares at me, "Just do it."

"Stick your tongue out."

"Nate," she blushes.

"Do it."

She reluctantly does and I pop the raspberry in her mouth.

"Mmm this one is sweet," she says with her eyes closed.

"Open." I direct and Megan does as I ask. I place a sliver of dark chocolate on her tongue, and she lets it melt in her mouth.

"Mmm."

"Now try both baby," I pop another raspberry in her mouth with dark chocolate and she licks my finger seductively as she takes it.

"Oh wow, this tastes incredible together." Megan's eyes sparkle when she opens them.

"You've had our dark chocolate raspberry cake that Leah makes."

"I serve the food, Nate. I don't eat it."

He argues, "You've had everything on the menu."

"No, I've only really had what you serve for the family meal."

"We need to change that, everyone who serves should know what everything tastes like."

"I agree."

"I'll make a note of it," I say but as I reach for my notebook, Megan grabs me by my chef's coat.

"Nate?"

"Yeah?" I look down and she is licking her lips.

"Taste me."

I lift her onto the cold metal prep table and hike her dress up, "No panties?" She giggles. I growl and bury my face in her pussy. Her fingers trail over my scalp and a sweet moan escapes her.

"Nate, mmm, how's that pussy taste?"

She's bold today, I love it. "Like a world-class dessert baby."

"Mmm, keep going."

My sweet, innocent Megan isn't as pure and shy as I thought she was.

"Potrei restare qui tutta la notte," I whisper over her sensitive flesh, "Paradiso."

"You…speak Italian?" Megan pants.

"Not much, but yes."

"Do it again." She moans as her hips move seeking my mouth.

"La mia Bellissima ragazza."

"Si, sono tuo." She whines. *Does she know Italian?*

"Sono il tuo uomo."

"Nate…I'm…oh yes…" She shakes and I give her one long slow lick, lapping up her arousal. The haze in her eyes is fucking gorgeous.

I reach for a strawberry, take a bite, then feed her the rest. "If I could put you on my dessert menu, we'd earn our Michelin star."

CHAPTER SEVENTEEN

Thursday, July 4th

Megan

After our game, I helped Nate clean up the kitchen then we shared a bottle of wine on the rooftop before turning in for the night.

Yesterday, Nate and I did a little food tour. American for breakfast. Greek for lunch. Indian for dinner. It was like traveling the world but in Chicago. Nate wanted to taste food from around the world to prepare for the competition. He had his notebook and took notes and pictures. Eating with him is an experience. He can pick out ingredients and spices like a pro. He asked to speak to owners and chefs about their flavors and processes. It was incredible I think as I lay in Nate's bed. He left early to pick up last-minute things for the party.

I hear the door open, and Nate comes in holding a beautiful bouquet of red, white, and blue flowers. I sit up and Nate's face is plastered with a smile.

"Good morning," he says as he kisses my forehead and hands me the bouquet. "These are for you."

"Aww, what's the occasion?"

"These are 'thank you for helping me practice and try new foods with me' flowers. I know the past two days were kinda about me, so I wanted to show you my appreciation."

I kiss him softly, "Nate, that's sweet. Thank you."

"You're welcome. I'll put them in a vase for you." Nate takes the bouquet back and walks to the kitchen in search of a vase. "The lady at the flower shop these will last so I'll try to keep them alive this weekend."

"We'll see about that," I tease.

"You have no faith in me?" Nate's jaw drops playfully, and he runs to the bed and tickles me, "I can keep some flowers alive Meg."

"Ok! Ok!" I giggle hysterically.

"Now get up, we gotta get ready." Nate laughs as he pulls the covers off me, lifts me over his shoulder, and carries me into the shower.

NATE

The party is set on the rooftop: Buckets of ice, mixers, beer, and food. The music is bumping, the red, white, and blue decorations are up and the cornhole board is set in place. Raul and Callum are already playing beer pong and Megan, and the girls are dancing. The last thing we need is more liquor and wine and Nico ran out to get more.

I crack a beer and watch Raul and Callum. Megan sits next to me. She looks so fucking good. She's wearing cut-off shorts, a red crop top, and flip-flops. I can't stop staring at her legs. Her hair is French braided, and I want to faint thinking about pulling her hair. Her legs are so smooth, and she smells floral and fruity like the botanical gardens. I've been trying to learn from the mistakes I'd made with Olivia, the last thing I want to do is fuck this up.

I sip my beer and when the music stops. I go to the speaker system and put on another playlist.

"Are you good? Do you need anything?" I ask Megan.

"I could use a kiss."

Her boldness takes me by surprise, "Oh yeah? You want a kiss?"

"Mmmhmm." Her eyes shimmer behind her sunglasses.

I look over her shoulder and everyone is occupied. I take Megan's hand and lead her behind the garden area where it's more private. She leans her back against the brick wall and I kiss her. She tastes like white rum and fruit. My hands are greedy and I grab her ass as we make out.

"Is this okay?"

"Yes, oh yes." She moans into a kiss. Megan twists her fingers in my hair and she starts grinding against my leg. My cock instantly responds. I break our kiss and I'm smiling ear to ear. I caress her braided hair and see the disappointment in her eyes that we stopped. "I really want to keep going but don't want to do it here, okay? I want to take my time with you."

She nods and adjusts herself, "How do I look?"

I kiss her neck, "Fucking sexy, I haven't been able to take my eyes off you."

Megan smiles, "I meant, is my makeup okay?"

"Flawless."

"Let's get back to the party, I need water."

"You go first." I tap her ass and count to ten and then come out from hiding. As I turn the corner, I see Nico coming through the door with liquor and wine in both arms and behind him. Olivia. *Olivia?!*

I hide and rub my eyes, am I really seeing Olivia? *What the fuck is she doing here?* I peek around the corner again and she is unloading bags and Nico is pouring shots. She takes two. I look for Megan and she is distracted dancing until Nico calls out "Who is taking us on? Any takers? Step right up!"

Megan glances up but I don't think she realizes that it's Olivia. Yet. God, I hope she knows I didn't ask Olivia to come. *What the fuck is Anders going to think? He threatened me and told me to stay away from her, but she is here?*

I start walking, not taking my eyes off Olivia. I'm hoping she's a figment of my imagination.

"Raul and I will take you on!" I look at him and he runs to grab another beer.

"You get on Olivia's side, Nate. Raul, you're with me. Let's do this! Get a couple of practice tosses in." Nico directs.

I take my place. I lock eyes with Megan and give her a quick shrug to let her know I have no clue what's happening.

I break the silence between Olivia and I, "It's…um, good to see you. How did you get here? I mean, why are you here?" I try to get clarity.

"Nico and I ran into each other at the store, he invited me for a drink and begged me to be his partner for a game. I hope you don't mind?"

I like my limbs and life. Of course, I fucking mind! I toss a bag and miss the board by a long shot. I look over to Megan again and she is giving Olivia the death glare.

Kill her with kindness Nate, "Uh, yeah, no…I'm glad you came…I just didn't expect it. I'm fine with you being here but what will your *boyfriend* think? He's not going to come for me, is he?"

"I'll tell him I was here." My confidence in her telling him the truth isn't strong.

"Do you two have plans today?"

"We do. I'm not sure what they are, Anders is surprising me. I'm leaving right after this game."

We need to make this the quickest game in history.

"I'm sure he will have something nice planned," I say dryly.

The game begins and it turns out to be the longest fucking game ever. My skin prickles having Olivia within arm's reach.

Megan walks by during Olivia's turn, grabs my forearm, and whispers, "You good?"

I give her a quick nod and say, "Take pictures in case her boyfriend comes for me."

She gives me a quick nod and goes to the table to pour herself a shot. I can't blame her. I can't imagine how she is feeling right now.

"Come on Livy, you got this girl! We need nine to win, sink three bags and we are done!" Nico cheers her on. I'm gonna kill him.

"Three in, pffft." I say under my breath. That's impossible, "She won't get it Raul, we got this! We only need four points!" I smirk over at Olivia and chug the rest of my beer. She hurt me. She deserves some taunting. My taunting only provokes her to turn superhuman and she sinks two bags in. "Fuck!" I grumble. I hate losing.

"Yes! One more!" Nico cheers. I'll never hear the end of him winning.

Olivia misses bag three and I don't know what comes over me, the alcohol or wanting to remind her of fucking her, I lean in close while she's trying to concentrate and say, "I remember getting in a hole pretty easily." Then I step back.

My words sting her, I can see it on her face, and she shoots daggers at me, "Looks like I'm the one on target today." She snarls then launches the bag and wins the game for her and Nico. *Thank God now she can leave!*

Nico runs and lifts Olivia in celebration and everyone claps. She didn't introduce herself to anyone and Nico called her Livy. I don't think anyone besides Megan knows exactly who she is.

"Best teammate ever! Suck it, Nate!" Nico taunts. He is going to pay for this. "Victory shot! Come on!" Nico leads Olivia over to the table and Megan grabs the bottle of Bacardi. She directs Nico to crouch to her level and pours a shot straight into his mouth.

"Your turn Olivia! On your knees!" Megan encourages.

Olivia's eyes are on mine as she gets on her knees and opens her mouth, she tips her head back and closes her eyes and Megan pours a long shot into her mouth. She looks at me when she swallows, and my blood turns to lava. *Why the fuck is she taunting me?* I should bend Megan over and fuck her right in front of Olivia to prove I'm not fucking jealous of Anders.

Megan helps her up and gives her a high five, "That was awesome!"

"Thanks for the shot, I gotta get out of here while I can still walk straight," she laughs.

"Noooo! Please stay!" Megan pleads. *What the hell?*

Nico wraps his arm around Megan and kisses her head.

Megan and Olivia hug goodbye and take a selfie together. Nico hugs her next. "Great game, come back anytime and bring that man of yours with you next time!" *Oh, he is so dead.*

Olivia waves to everyone, "Have a great time! Enjoy!" I watch her leave and as soon as the door closes, I smack Nico upside the head.

"What the fuck? Why did you bring her here?" I raise my voice.

Nico giggles, "I'm sorry, I thought maybe if…"

"I fucking can't with you." I've heard enough. I leave the rooftop and run down three flights of stairs to catch Olivia before she leaves. I run out of the backdoor. She's nowhere to be found. I run to the main street and there she is holding bottles of wine in her arms.

"Tell me he is treating you right and that you are happy," I say as I gasp for air and brush the hair out of my eyes.

Her eyes soften, "He makes me happy. I couldn't be happier."

"Then why did you come with Nico? You knew I would be here, are you trying to rub it in my face that you moved on?"

Olivia's face falls and I see when it hits her, the regret. The admission, "I guess, maybe, a part of me wanted you to see me and make you feel regret."

"I regret it every damn day." *Well, every day until Megan and I kissed.*

"I shouldn't have come, it won't happen again, I told you to leave me alone and you have, I…I'm sorry."

"Are you going to tell him you were here? You know Megan was taking pictures, she posted them already…" Megan did it now so Olivia can't hold this from Anders for too long. He doesn't deserve to have his new girlfriend lying to him.

Olivia looks like she's about to cry, "Yes, of course I am. I don't hide things from him."

Yeah, we'll see.

Olivia's car pulls up, "Go back to your party. I'm sorry I showed up." She gets in the backseat, slams the door and I watch the car drive down the street until it disappears.

Megan

Seeing Nate run after Olivia makes my heart sink.

"He doesn't want her," I say to myself trying to slow my breathing.

"Meg, hey, are you alright?" I hear Julian ask.

"That was Olivia," tears sting my eyes.

"I know but Nate stayed away, he didn't invite her, fucking Nico did the asshole. He's drunk."

"Why's Nate chasing her?" I ask Julian like he has the answer.

"I dunno, maybe he's telling her to stay the fuck away from him. Nate adores you. I can see it in his eyes."

"You can?"

"Yes. Now calm down, okay?"

Instead, I leave the rooftop and try to find Nate. I skip using the elevator, my confusion and anger fly me down the stairs. I run outside and find Nate and Olivia. I hide in the alley where I can hear everything.

Olivia came here to make him regret blowing his chance. That's fucked up. Nate says he regrets messing up with her. I peer around the corner and Olivia looks like she's about to cry. I hide again and Nate says my name but a car goes by and I can't hear what he said. My heart is pounding in my chest. I peek around the corner again and Olivia is getting into the backseat of a car. I hide again as the car drives past.

I come out of hiding and Nate's face falls.

Nate comes to me and kisses me. It's needy and passionate. He picks me up and I wrap my legs around him. "I'm sorry." He whispers against my neck then kisses it. "I just wanted to see why the fuck she came."

"What did she say?"

"She wanted me to regret fucking up and I did until I realized who I always should have been with was here all along."

He's talking about me. "Nate…"

"She won't come around again. It's me and you, okay?" Nate strokes my cheek.

"Yeah," I nod and my mouth is back on his. My hips slowly grind on him and then we hear a horn honking. We turn our attention to it.

Nate hurriedly puts me down and sheepishly waves, "And that's my parents. Wave." He sings between a forced toothy smile.

The car pulls into the alleyway and parks along the building. Nate and I follow and I standby while Nate greets

Giovanni and Maria. Gio pops the trunk and there are two huge food carriers.

"Ma went overboard," Gio says as he pats Nate's back. "Megan! Darlin! How are you?" Gio holds his arms open and I greet him with a hug. He smells like cigar smoke and aftershave.

"I'm great, welcome to the party. Let me help." I grab the first carrier from the trunk. Nate finishes getting both cheeks kissed and pitched by Maria and he grabs the other.

"Megan sweetie! So good to see you. Is my baby boy treating you right?" Maria hugs me.

Oh, he's treating me more than right, I want to say but settle for, "Yes ma'am."

"No ma'am, it's Maria!" She corrects me and I get a cheek pinch too.

Nate leads us to the elevator and when we reach the rooftop, Nate and Gio take the food to the long table we put together and I offer Maria a drink.

Maria leans close to me as she hands me the bottle of wine she wants opened, "I saw that kiss. How long have you and Nate been seeing each other?" She whispers.

I knew they saw us, "It's new." I keep it short and vague.

"It must not seem like it's new though, you've been here awhile, you're practically family dear. I'm happy to see it. Nate needs you. You're loyal, you're in the business, you know how determined and focused on his career he is but…"

"Oh no, there's a but…" My skin tingles and I pour Maria's glass.

She looks at me and grabs my hand, "You can help him see there is more to life than work."

I softly smile, "In all fairness, DF is my life too," I chuckle.

Maria smiles, "Then you need each other. Gio and I work together at his jewelry store, have for almost our entire marriage and I still love him."

Her words fill my heart and she pats my hand and waves down Nico.

The next few hours are filled with food, dancing, and yard games. Amira and Nico lost to Nate and me. I caught us getting looks from our coworkers a few times, like when Nate smacked my ass for a good toss and lifted me after we won but Nico and Amira were even more friendly. He even kissed her a few times.

When the sun sets, we gather around the family table and formally eat together, not just pick and snack.

Before we begin, Nico taps his beer bottle to make an announcement.

"Welcome everyone! Thank you for coming to the best party on the block! Nate and I are so thankful for all of you and this is the perfect time to make some announcements."

Nate stands, "Nico and I will be in the kitchen full time going forward. Raul and Julian will be on the line too. Raul is now our back-of-house manager officially. Callum will back us up on the line."

The dishwashers and bussers boo him but it's out of love and everyone laughs.

Nate continues, "Megan is going to lead the front of house taking care of reservations and guests, making sure the front runs seamlessly. Nico and I are confident she will help DF run even better."

"Oh, that's lovely!" Maria cheers and everyone claps and whistles. That makes me feel good.

"We missed you girl! Never leave us with the Rossi brothers alone again!" Leah adds.

"One more thing," Nate raises his voice to get the attention again, "Julian will be running the line with Raul when Nico and I are gone. I know he's already been in that position, but he did it because he has heart, determination, and initiative."

I look to Julian and he is holding back his emotion. He gives Nate a nod and mouths, "Thank you."

Nate takes his seat and Nico holds out his hand for Amira. She stands and Nico puts his arm around her.

"Last announcement, Amira and I are dating."

Nate almost chokes on his hotdog, "What? How? When?"

Amira smacks him, "You didn't tell Nate?"

"Sorry!" He laughs.

Maria stands and walks to Nico and Amira to kiss their cheeks and hugs them. Maria welcomes her to the family and Gio tells Nico he will help him pick a nice ring for her. Amira has a megawatt smile and she kisses Nico. When the fuck did this happen? How long have they been seeing each other with nobody noticing? Why didn't she tell me? My mind scrambles and I realize, I never told her about my crush on Nate so if we went public now, it would come out of nowhere or everyone but Julian.

I push back from my chair, "Does anyone need anything? Are there any plates I can clear?" I ask the table and everyone laughs at me.

"You're off the clock, we can clean up after ourselves you dork!" Nico teases.

Maria smiles at me, "I'll take a water and another glass of wine, can you get his Dad a beer?"

"Of course," I smile.

The sun sets and Nico has the dance lights he bought off the internet going. He and Amira dance, and Nate's parents dance together. It's the cutest thing ever. I think back to Julian and I dancing at the bar and how much I liked it. I wished it was Nate. Now I have Nate, and it feels almost wrong if I dance with him.

A slow song comes on and everyone pairs up. Maria with Giovanni. Raul and Leah. Amira and Nico. Ava and Hayes. The rest of the staff lounge on the outdoor sofas.

"I'm going to take a piss," Nate kisses my cheek, "You can have the next dance."

"Okay," I smile.

As Nate leaves, Lilah joins the party. She finds Julian and Callum, kisses their cheeks, and sits on Julian's lap. I wonder what the story is there. I wonder if Hayley knows. I type out a text to her.

MEGAN: What's the deal with Lilah? She's here for Julian giving him googly eyes

HAYLEY: They are friends from high school. They have both been through shit. She'll be good to him, I promise

I watch Amira smile up at Nico, it's my first time seeing him with someone. I watch Giovanni twirl Maria.

Leah and Raul act like idiots trying to do 'The Lift' from Dirty Dancing.

Nate comes back and a Dean Martin song comes on and Maria takes Nate's hand.

"We used to dance to this when we were cooking!"

Giovanni takes my hand and teaches me some dance moves. I'm drunk so I think I'm doing wonderful. Giovanni is a great dancer and seeing Nate and Nico dance with Maria is adorable. Damn, Nate can move his hips. *Fuck.*

That's Life comes on next, and Giovanni's voice is incredible. Nate, Nico, Maria, and Giovanni put their arms around each other and sing along. I get my phone to take pictures and videos.

CHAPTER EIGHTEEN

NATE

The joy I feel with my parents, closest friends, and Megan here is overwhelming. What started as an unexpected day seems to be ending perfectly.

We all settle in to watch the fireworks, and Megan, nervous about keeping our secret, hesitates. But I pull her onto my lap, loving the closeness. I've noticed that her love language seems to be physical touch—every chance she gets, she finds a way to touch me.

My parents love Megan and are glad that Nico and I promoted her. My Mom lectured me that it should've been sooner. My Dad's only gripe was that Megan isn't Italian or Catholic, but once she spoke some Italian to him, she won him over.

"Hey, I forgot to ask where you learned Italian," I whisper in Megan's ear.

She turns her focus to me and smirks, "You think I'd work at an Italian restaurant in Chicago and not learn the basics?"

God, I love her.

When the fireworks start, my mind flashes back to the night I met Olivia. She kissed me first that night. Maybe it jinxed us. The colors of the fireworks dance on Megan's face and I see her look over at Julian, whose arm is wrapped around Lilah. I know she's struggling to see him with her. I can't fault her for it. Feelings don't just disappear, and she had to see me play cornhole with Olivia.

"He's fine, don't worry about him," I say as I rub her back. I can feel her heart beating through the back of her ribcage.

"I'm just protective of him."

"I know, me too."

The grand finale starts and Nico cues up a patriotic song. He puts his arm around my Dad who served in the military before opening his jewelry store.

A tear streams down Megan's cheek, and I assume it's because her Dad is a cop or seeing Nico and my Dad makes her emotional. I stand up, wrap my arms around her from behind, and slowly sway her from side to side.

"There's nobody I'd rather be holding in my arms right now, you know that?" I whisper in her ear and Megan nuzzles her head against mine.

When the fireworks are over we all cheer and clap then my parents start to say their goodbyes.

"Party is moving to my house for whoever wants to come!" Raul announces, "Mr. and Mrs. Rossi, I have a spare room if you want to come, no need to drive home this late."

My Mom pats his cheek, "That is so sweet!"

Leah chimes in, "He makes the best pancakes!"

My Dad looks at me for approval and I give him the thumbs up. "Sure, we can probably drink you kids under the table."

I laugh, "Please take care of our parents."

"I'm going so I'll watch them." Nico chuckles.

"I have no faith in you." I tussle his hair. We all say our goodbyes and I see Megan and Julian hugging. Then she hugs Lilah.

"We'll take out the trash and run the dishes through the wash downstairs before we go." Ava and Hayes tell me before they leave. Nico knows I want time with Megan. Everyone else grabs what they can to clear the rooftop. The rest can wait until tomorrow.

"Sunday. Church and Dinner." My Mom points her manicured finger at me before hugging me.

"Sure Ma, I'll be there."

"Have a good night, Son." My Dad hugs me.

"Goodnight Dad, love you."

Megan hugs my parents goodbye. She informs my Mom of her weekend plans but promises to talk to them soon.

When it's just Megan and I again, I take her hands in mine, "Did you have a good time?"

"Yeah, this was great," she smiles softly.

I want to make her forget the blip in our day with Olivia's unexpected appearance, I pull her into me and gaze into her eyes. "You know, I heard once that bad timing doesn't exist. The people your heart chooses at the wrong time are simply the wrong people. The right people fight for you, show up for you, and care in good times or bad. The right people take a chance."

Megan squeezes my biceps tightly and I hear her sniff back a tear, "Thanks Nate, I needed to hear that."

"It's our time now." I kiss her forehead. "Do you want to finish the rest of this bottle of wine with me?"

"Absolutely."

I take Megan's hand and lead her to the outdoor sofa under the twinkling lights and the sound of booms and crackles of fireworks fill the air. I pour us a glass and empty the bottle. I motion for Megan to snuggle with me. We can see fireworks at varying distances.

"It's beautiful up here but do you ever get tired of living in the same building where you work?

"Um, I've never given it much thought honestly."

"Doesn't it feel like you never leave work?"

"Work is my life." I rationalize, "Do you not like staying here?"

Megan sits up, "No! I do! But it kinda feels like I'm at work."

"Because of the location or because of you and I? Do I feel like work?" My anxiety builds.

Megan takes a sip of her wine, "Just being here. Not you." She sips her wine again.

"We can leave and go to your place if you want but I think your sister would strangle me with my shoelaces if she heard us having sex."

Megan snickers, "Oh yeah! You'd be dead for sure."

"What if I just slept there with you? I can behave, I swear."

She raises an eyebrow at me, "You sure about that?"

"I can if you can," I whisper and gulp down my wine.

"Fine. Let's test that theory." Megan stands and finishes her wine, "Nate Rossi, you and I are going to clean up the rest of the party, chug water, then you're walking me home. You will stay the night with me in my bed. Boxers on and we will fall asleep together."

"You're on! But if you can't resist me, you'll never hear the end of it."

"Deal."

It's not easy being in bed next to Megan while I'm drunk and horny, but Megan wants this tonight. She needs to know we are more than just sex. Part of me feels like she wants us to be in a space that hasn't been tainted by Olivia. If this is what Megan needs, I'll give it to her. I'll give her everything.

CHAPTER NINETEEN

Friday, July 5th

Megan

I wake up to the sound of laughter coming from the kitchen. *Nate and Hayley.* I jolt out of bed and tip-toe to my door, cracking it open just enough to eavesdrop.

"She's been obsessed with you for years!" Hayley laughs and I cringe, "I'm as gay as they come but this egg benedict could turn me."

I stifle a laugh. *Nate cooked breakfast and won over my sister.* I must be dreaming.

"You know, I've always liked Megan and held a special place for her, it wasn't romantic, but I've cared about her and looked out for her for nearly six years."

I melt against the doorframe.

"And you never thought to ask my sister out?"

"I don't date my employees."

"When did you start seeing her differently?"

Good question Hayley.

"The night she posted pictures with Julian. You know, I was so jealous that I went over to check on her. God, I'm glad she was in bed alone."

Only because Julian had left already.

"Then you took her to the botanical gardens, which is fucking smooth by the way."

Nate laughs, "I wasn't trying to be. I took her there. I told her about my past and my best friend Trey. It felt good to talk about him. I know it sounds fucking crazy but, Trey's the one who told me Megan is the one for me."

"Your best friend had to convince you?" Hayley scoffs.

"Trey, uh, isn't here anymore."

"Shit. Sorry."

"He talks to me sometimes."

"Hmm."

"You know what, forget I said anything…it's crazy."

"No, no, it's sweet," Hayley coos, "Your dead bestie likes my sister."

Okay, that's enough. I walk out of my bedroom fake yawning and stretching, acting like I just woke up.

"There's the sleepy head!" Hayley announces.

"Good morning," I smile and walk to Nate to kiss him then pour my cup of coffee.

"Breakfast is done," Nate says as he kisses my shoulder.

"His cooking is the best!" Hayley cheers.

"Well, I'd hope so since he's going to be on Food Network soon." I joke.

"I hope you get a breakfast challenge! You'll win for sure!" Hayley compliments as she clears the last bite from her plate.

"Thanks, Hayley," he smiles.

After breakfast, Nate checks his phone. "My parents survived the night at Raul's. The weather looks incredible. Do you want to go for a ride along the lake?"

"Hell yeah!"

"Wear helmets!" Hayley calls.

NATE

I drive Megan and me to a motorcycle shop and let her pick out a helmet. Hayley's right, we both need to be safe. Once we are geared up, I drive along the coast of Lake Michigan. There's nothing like riding on a motorcycle on a beautiful day. I take backroads when possible, driving through small towns brings me joy. You can smell fresh-cut grass, people barbecuing, and the floral scent of a field of wildflowers. It's magical.

Along the lakeshore, I spot a clearing and a small parking lot that looks like it borders a secluded beach. I pull into the parking lot and turn off the engine.

"We're here?" Megan asks.

"I didn't have a destination in mind."

"Oh."

"This looks nice and we can stretch."

We leave our helmets with the bike and I take Megan's hand in mine as we follow a path through a wooded area. The path opens to the wide expanse of the beach.

Megan gasps, "This is beautiful."

"It really is. I love getting on my bike and driving without a plan and seeing where the road takes me. I've found the most beautiful things are unplanned."

"I love that Nate."

I wrap my arms around her waist and kiss her forehead, "I'm going to miss you this weekend."

"Aww, you're not sick of me yet?"

I laugh, "Hell no."

"Do you think work is going to get in the way of us?"

"What do you mean?"

"Well, we have been on this break from work since we started, um…dating. What if work gets in the way?"

A very valid question. Megan knows better than anyone how swept up in work I get.

"Plus, you're traveling to New York soon…" Megan continues.

I cup her face, "Meg, look…yes it will be an adjustment, but we can do this."

"What about dates?"

"We'll go on dates on Mondays and Tuesdays, I can see you before work, and you can stay after your shift. We can go out before or after work. If you need me, we can always sneak away. We will make this work." I ease her worries the best I can.

"What if I need a break from always seeing you?"

"Then go do your thang and it will give you a break and you can tell me all about it when you see me."

Megan laughs, "You did NOT just say *'thang'*."

"I sure did."

Megan rolls her eyes at me and I steal a kiss from her. She deepens it and I can feel her body buzzing against mine.

"Nate...I...I..."

Oh, fuck she is going to say it!

"I *really* want to strip down and run into the lake."

"Wait, what?"

Megan pulls away from me, strips off her shirt, then wiggles out of her boots, socks, and jeans. She runs through the sand and dives into the water as waves crash over her.

I shake my head in disbelief, "She's wild. She's fucking wild."

I remove my clothes with a little more finesse, keeping them out of the sand before running in my boxers to join Megan. The cool fresh water of the lake is invigorating and when I surface, Megan leaps into my arms.

"You didn't have to come in," she giggles. I swear, every time she does an angel gets its wings.

"Where you go. I'll go."

"Nate! Did you just 'If you're a bird, I'm a bird' me?"

"What? What the hell is that?"

"It's from The Notebook."

"Whose notebook?"

Megan slaps my shoulder playfully, "The movie! You never had a girlfriend force you to watch it?"

"I've never really had one, so no."

"Your Mom didn't make you watch it?"

"No."

"Nate Rossi!"

"Are you mad that I spoke from the heart instead of using some line from a movie?" I try to clarify.

Megan ravishes my mouth. All I feel is her mouth and tongue on mine. Her thighs are in my hands and my toes are in the sand beneath me. Waves crash into us, but I stand tall and unmoving like a lighthouse.

"I want you, Nate. Now."

"Ok, I can go get a –"

"No Nate, now, right now," she pants breathlessly and scoots back enough to reach into my boxers for my dick. The memory of the night Olivia wanted nothing but sex when I was trying to be romantic creeps in.

"Meg, hey," I set her down and take her hand out of my boxers.

"Come on Nate nobody is around," she looks to the shore, "It's just the two of us and the lake, it's so romantic."

"You're right. It is. Do you really want to ruin the romance with sex?"

"Sex can be romantic."

"I know, I—"

"Oh shit!" Megan's hands cover her mouth, "I'm being like her!" She shrieks as panic floods her face.

"Hey," I try to reach out to comfort her but she dunks her head under the water and even over the crashing waves I can hear her scream underwater in embarrassment. She pops up rubbing her eyes and flinging the hair out of her face.

"Megan, I'd never compare you to Olivia."

"But…that's why you hesitated!"

"Hey. Stop." I cup her face in my hands and gaze into her eyes, "Yes it crossed my mind for a split second but then I thought, 'The first time I'm bare inside my girlfriend, I want it to be perfect.'"

"Really?"

"Yes."

"And, I'm your girlfriend?"

"If you want to be, yes."

"I do, but what about unplanned things being beautiful? I don't want to put 'first time raw with Nate' on our work calendar."

That gets a chuckle from me, "I promise it won't be planned but a lake full of dead fish, seaweed, and God knows what in here isn't how it will be, okay? You deserve better than that."

Megan sighs, "Alright when you put it that way, I'm glad you're the older rational one here."

I kiss her forehead, "I'll race you to shore. Tag. You're it!" I tap her on the head and run through the water the best I can, but Megan beats me to it. I run to her, pick her up, and twirl her around as the wind whips through our hair.

Late Evening of July 5th

Megan is finishing up in the shower, rinsing the sand from her crevices and long hair. As I wait for her, I check my phone—scrolling through texts, emails, and social media. The usual posts fill my feed, but then one catches my eye, making me stop. Olivia and her boyfriend are kissing and wearing matching hockey jerseys. She tagged a few people. I check their accounts for more pictures. Nothing. Except for the last account Eva Rodriguez. She posted a video of Olivia and Anders kissing and I could see him mouth 'I love you' to her and she said it back. I unfollow her but become keenly aware that I am smiling.

I'm not jealous or bitter or angry. I'm happy for her. The exact opposite of how I thought I'd feel seeing this one day. I'm glad for Olivia. I hear the shower turn off and Megan humming. My heart flutters. Megan walks out of the bathroom towel drying her hair with another towel wrapped around her. Steam billows and she looks like a goddess.

"Nate, what's that smile for?"

I get off the couch and walk to her.

"Nate, say something, babe."

"You are beautiful."

She groans, "I'm all wet, my hair is a mess, I don't have makeup on…"

I cut her off with a tender kiss. "This is when you're the most beautiful. When you're just you." I resume kissing her and creep my finger into the top knot of her towel and tug it free. Now that Megan and I are finally together, I can't shake the feeling that every moment we have is too precious to waste. I want us to make the most of this time, to soak up every second, because I know we won't often get days like this. Most of the time, my mind is consumed with work, and I don't want to let these rare moments slip away. I need this time with her, now, more than ever.

I trail my forefinger between her breast, down her stomach, over her belly button, and down to her smooth pussy. Her breath hitches. Her pussy is hot and slick. I slide my finger inside her.

"Nate, you know I need to be home tonight."

"You don't leave until the morning. I'll get you home." I kiss her neck and shoulder then get on my knees to kiss and suck her perky nipples.

Megan runs her nails over my wet hair, "Nate, I love your mouth and fingers."

"I can tell. You're so wet." I moan over her bare skin and taste her pussy. Her legs wobble and she grips my shoulders to balance herself. I lick her until she orgasms, and her legs give out. I pick her up and carry her to the bed. I kiss every inch of her making sure to please her over and over again.

"Tell me you want me baby."

"No... I *need* you." Megan corrects me, "Please."

I grip the base of my cock and slide it over her wetness. I take a deep breath and then slowly press my bare cock inside Megan. I feel *everything*. Her warmth, wetness, her walls contracting. No barrier between us is fucking heaven.

Megan hisses, "Wow, oh wow. You feel...bigger. Your head feels incredible on my g-spot."

"I feel it all, nothing has ever felt better. Nothing compares to this." I pant before I lean down and kiss her. I take my time pumping in and out in long slow strokes. Looking down and seeing Megan's cream around my cock makes my balls tighten.

Megan's nails rake over my chest and the pain adds more pleasure. I love hearing her moans and panting, hearing her say my name and God's. The only thing I would change is that we should have been doing this years ago.

"Nate, don't stop,"

"I'm not stopping baby," I assure her and seal her lips over mine. I run my hand up her leg and grip it around my arm, getting even deeper. My spine tingles, my balls tighten and I'm getting close. Megan's moans get louder and I feel her walls clenching me tightly. She's so turned on her pussy has a pulse and it's taking everything in me not to explode.

"I'm getting close," I warn her.

Megan's cheeks blush and she bites her lower lip, "Don't pull out, please. Keep going."

Her shyness and sweet voice send me into orbit. Rational Nate from earlier is gone and after a few deep penetrating thrusts, I unload inside of Megan. Her shocked facial expression followed by pure fucking bliss is the best drug I've ever seen. The best high I've ever had.

"I've waited so long for you. I need all of you," she whimpers, and tears of joy spring from her eyes. I empty my cum, fears, anxiety, and pleasure into her.

"You have all of me, forever."

CHAPTER TWENTY

Saturday, July 6th

Megan

Nate makes good on his promise and gets me home with plenty of time for me to pack. Saying goodbye to him was hard. I didn't want to leave our bubble of bliss. After we made love, I cuddled up with Nate and we fell asleep. It was the best sleep I've ever had.

This morning he woke me up with soft kisses, the sun shined through the windows casting his living space in a golden glow and I thought I was dreaming until my alarm started going off.

"Do you need anything before we start our trek?" Hayley asks, breaking up my daydream.

"Do we have time to stop at the pharmacy? I need sunscreen, tampons, nail polish…" I ask Hayley.

"Yeah, we can stop. Need condoms too while we are there?"

I laugh nervously.

At the pharmacy, I get everything I mentioned to Hayley, but I also get Plan B. I hurry up and pop it when she's pumping gas. I'm on birth control but I've been awful about taking it at the same time and I'm not ready to get pregnant. It dawns on me that Nate and I never discussed if I was on birth control, maybe he assumed since I told him not to pull out. I shake the thought from my head, dig out the red nail polish I bought, and begin carefully painting my nails as Hayley drives.

On the way to our parents, Hayley talks about her crush on Kenzie for the 45-minute drive. 'Kenzie's so hot. Kenzie's so talented. Kenzie's mouth needs to devour me.'

"When are you going to see her?"

"I dunno," Hayley groans.

"It's been too long. Why don't you ask her to meet for coffee? Keep it casual, low-key. Talk art and her business."

"I will. I'll do it tomorrow."

"Tomorrow we'll be hung over." I giggle.

"I won't drink… too much," Hayley corrects herself.

When my nails are dry I pull out my phone and scroll through Instagram. "Ohmygod! Holy shit!" I gasp and reach for Hayley.

"What?! What is it?!"

"Olivia launched her relationship with the hot Viking guy last night."

"That was fast."

I scroll more, "Kenzie posted."

"What! When?" My sister grabs my phone and almost runs us off the road. I slap her hand away, "She posted pictures on the 4th, one with... Jake Hudson," she recalls.

"And now she posted a picture with Jake and Trevor Armstrong, the hockey player." Her panicked shrieks fill the car. Kenzie tagged Jake but his social media page looks professional. Trevor, well he plays in the NHL, so his page is mostly hockey stuff like game-day pictures, sponsored posts, and a few pictures of him and his buddies. "The girl likes variety," I snicker, Jake and Trevor are smoking hot. "Guess she's not on your team after all Hay." I joke.

Hayley adjusts in her seat and squares her shoulders, "No! I have to find out for myself. I'm texting her tomorrow. No more waiting."

Ten minutes later, Hayley pulls us into the driveway of our childhood home. It's still early so we have room to park. A few hours from now, our driveway will be packed. We get our weekend bags out of the car and walk through the side door to the kitchen.

"There's my girls!" Our Mom, Lynn, announces and greets us holding a Bloody Mary.

"Hi Mom," Hayley sighs. After seeing Kenzie's Insta, Hayley needs a long Mom Hug.

"Where's Dad? I have some news to share."

"He is out back getting everything set up, cornhole boards, yard games, the tables for all the food and fireworks."

"I'll see if he needs help," I set my bag by the stairs and walk out to the deck and yard where my Dad is cursing at a table that won't cooperate.

"Hey Dad," I greet him with a pat on his back.

"This damn table won't lock!" He grumbles. I gently move him aside and get the table to lock and set it upright. My Dad scoffs.

"Let's get you a beer," I smile.

"I'm on my third, maybe that's the problem," my Dad's laugh bellows. My parents start early on special occasions.

"It's only 11 am." I chide.

"Eh, it's a holiday, fuck it."

This is where I get it from.

"I have some news and I wanted to tell everyone."

"You're pregnant?" he guesses.

"Dad!"

"What?" He laughs, "Everyone I know has grandchildren, I kinda feel left out. Hayley isn't going to give me a grandbaby. It's up to you."

I almost feel bad now for taking the pill earlier, "Dad, Hayley can, there are a lot of options for same-sex couples now, or she can have one on her own if she doesn't meet anyone…"

"I know, I know…but…"

I give him a half hug, "Dad, can we go inside so I can give you my news please?"

My Dad leads the way inside and Hayley and Mom are elbow-deep mixing potato and macaroni salad for the picnic.

My Dad makes our presence known with his bellowing voice, "Megan has news, and no, she isn't pregnant."

"Eww, Dad!" Hayley cringes.

"You hush! Mom and I are the only ones without grandbabies, we can dream."

Hayley chuckles, "Meg, what's the news? And why haven't you told me?"

I ignore her, "I got a promotion. I'll be running the front of house. We *will* earn our Michelin star," I say confidently. "And Nate and Nico got cast to compete and judge on Food Network. The film crew was there Monday filming and they interviewed Raul and me too. Once the episodes air, we are going to take off even more. We are already booked for the rest of the year." I smile from ear to ear. Hearing it come out of my mouth makes it real.

"Honey that's amazing!" My Mom hugs me, trying not to get mayonnaise in my long dark hair.

"Nate better pay you what you deserve," Dad adds.

"He is, I think he's paying me too much, but I'll take it." I smile.

My Dad pats my back and it jolts me forward, "I'm proud of you kiddo. Tell Nate and Nico congratulations for us."

"I will." I smile. "We are going to have a huge party when the episodes premier and I love for you and Mom to be there, not just to show your support for the Rossi's, but for me too."

"Of course, sweetie. How exciting! We know famous people!" Mom's eyes light up, "Hon, we can brag about that instead of little rugrats!"

"Good point. I like it." Dad tips his beer can at her before taking a swig. "Hayley, what's going on with you?"

My parents direct their attention to Hayley and start asking about her paintings and relationship status. No changes in her world. Still single. Still using our dining room as her studio.

I spend the next hour helping with food prep: chopping, stirring, and setting everything in place. Once we're done, I snap a photo of the spread and send it to Nate, along with a selfie of me covered in splatters from the kitchen chaos.

MEGAN: How do you enjoy this?

NATE: LOL You look hot in the kitchen 😊

MEGAN: I'll stick to serving, not cooking, Chef

NATE: Mmm, you make my cock twitch when you call me that

I excuse myself from the kitchen, grab my weekend bag, and carry it upstairs to my old room. I close the door behind me and send Nate a voice memo. "Mmm, you like when I call you Chef? Does hearing it make you hard?" I tease. I walk to the window and see my family in the yard. "I'm still thinking about last night." I purr and hit send. Sex is what I needed to come out of my shell.

My phone lights up: 'Nate'. I answer, still watching my family outside. "Hi Nate."

"Look at your screen," he moans.

I pull the phone from my ear and look at the screen. Nate is stroking himself and my thighs clench. His cock is hard and shiny with lube. His strong, veiny hands stroke his cock and my hand drifts to my left breast. I turn my camera on and lay on my twin bed. I lift my tank top and bare my tits for him and his strokes slow. I hear him moaning. I tease my nipples, trail my hand down my body, and slide my hand into my shorts. "I'm so wet Nate," I whisper and he pumps his hand faster.

"Those red nails will look so good wrapped around me. I can't wait until this is your pussy and not my hand," his voice is shaky and his hand pumps faster.

My fingers are deep inside me, I'm hitting my spot, and my hips ride my fingers. "Nate, come for me," I whine softly. I don't know how much time I have. I finger myself faster and when I see Nate erupt, white ribbons shooting across his tan skin, I orgasm. I try my best to muffle myself.

"Fuck baby," Nate says breathlessly, "I miss you."

I pull my fingers out of me and pull my shirt down, "I miss you too."

His dimples pop with his megawatt smile, "Is it crazy that we miss each other already?"

"If it is, I don't care." I blush.

"Megan! The Jenkin's are here! People are arriving!" My Mom calls up the stairs.

I pout, "I gotta go."

"I'll be thinking of you." Nate squeezes his cock again and more come oozes out. I end the call before I get even more distracted.

NATE

I fucking love her.

I drag myself out of bed and hear muffled moaning coming from downstairs. Amira calls out Nico's name.

"Jesus Christ." I grumble to myself.

I stumble to the shower and blast music while I work out until my muscles are so weak I collapse on the floor. I try to regulate my breathing and my eyes drift closed. I daydream about Megan. My hand drifts to my cock thinking about how tight and wet her pussy is. Feeling her bare was incredible, the best feeling ever, and then it hits me. I came inside her. She wanted it. I delivered. Is she on birth control? She has to be, right? Fuck. I'm ready for a relationship. I'm not ready to be a Dad. Am I?

More moaning echoes through the ventilation system.

"I need to get the fuck out of here." I push myself off the floor, get dressed, run to the garage, and take off on my motorcycle.

Destination: Botanical Gardens for some goddamn peace

Megan

Hayley and I sit in lawn chairs a safe distance from where our Dad and his buddies from the precinct are lighting fireworks. Mom is schmoozing with the neighbors being the perfect host.

Hayley and I watch the neighbor kids and grandkids of my parents' friends play tag around the yard, "Remember when that was us?"

Hayley smiles, "Yeah."

"Do you ever wonder where those kids are now?"

"After Dad's friend and his wife died in that accident, their daughter quit coming."

"Yeah," I frown, "I loved them. I wish Mom and Dad were that in love still." I think back to the couple who were so obnoxiously in love. Maybe our parents but they don't show it. "And the tall skinny boy with the long dark hair, we always teased him about being one of the girls even though he was a grade higher than us," I giggle.

"I think his Mom got a new job or something so that's why he quit coming."

"What about the bitchy blonde girl who always acted like she was too good to be here? Cunt." I mutter and Hayley laughs.

"She's the reason I hate blondes. Remember when you pushed her in the mud puddle and she came out looking like a sasquatch? I could have died." Hayley holds her hand to her stomach laughing, "She cried so much her parents took her home, little shit." Hayley and I laugh and sip our hard seltzers.

"She was picking on that boy! Fuck I wish I remembered their names. I don't like bullies, yeah, we called him a girl, but she was downright nasty to him."

"I really hope her life sucks." Hayley mutters then changes the subject, "What's going on with you and Nate? I thought you were coming home last night."

I think about how to answer this. Hayley is crushing on Kenzie who is best friends with Olivia. Olivia knows me, kinda, but she doesn't know my sister. "It's new." I settle for.

Before Hayley can pry, the sizzle of fireworks fills the air and then whistles, shrieks, and booms follow. Our Mom clumsily joins us and watches our Dad light up the sky, "I'm surprised he still has all ten of his fingers."

When the festivities are over and Hayley and I are ready to call it a night we go to our childhood room. Our parents haven't touched it. Boy Band posters on my side, paintings on Hayley's side.

"Do you have an extra pair of sleep shorts?" Hayley asks then digs through my weekend bag and before I can stop her, she sees it. The empty box.

"What the fuck is this? Did Nate pressure you to get this?"

I snatch the box out of her hand and stuff it back in the empty bag. "God no! He doesn't even know I got it now shut up!" I say between gritted teeth like our parents will ground me if they overhear.

"That's almost worse!" Hayley yelps. "You're keeping things from him already?"

I lower my voice, "Look, I know being a lesbian you don't have to worry about getting pregnant, but I do. Things with Nate are new. I don't need to get pregnant, okay? I'll tell him."

"But you're on the pill…"

"I've sucked at remembering to take it."

"Then you need a new method! Why didn't he wear a condom, please tell me he isn't one of those 'they are too uncomfortable, I'll pull out' types Megan."

"He's not. We wanted to do it without a barrier between us."

"And he…" her fingers do an explosion gesture, "Inside you."

"I asked for it. I wanted all of him. He's the first guy I've ever done it with so chill. I've loved Nate for years, he isn't some stranger from the internet."

"Oh, I know you've loved him. You're just…moving too fast." Hayley whines.

"Too fast? I'm sorry, I'm not waiting another five years to fuck him or tell him I love him."

Her jaw drops, "You told him you love him?" My sister asks slowly.

"Almost."

Hayley scoffs, "Have you learned nothing from me?"

"You've never been in love!" I argue.

She folds her arms over her chest, "I have so!"

"Angelina Jolie, Ruby Rose, and Kristin Stewart don't count! You have no idea about real relationships!"

Hayley steps to me with her chin raised, "Not. True."

I look her right in the eye, "Up until a few weeks ago you were treating Chicago like a fucking pussy buffet. And you want to judge Kenzie for banging two hot guys and shame me for Nate? Fuck off."

"Ughhhh!!" Hayley shrieks and stops out of the room. Are we 16 again?!

CHAPTER TWENTY-ONE

Sunday, July 7th

Megan

I am hung over but Hayley is bright-eyed as she drives us back to Chicago. We still aren't talking after our blowout last night. We arrive home just as the sun burns away the morning fog.

"I am going to the coffee shop by Kenzie's gallery. I'll *casually* ask how her weekend was and see if she wants to join me."

I yawn, "Sounds like a plan."

Hayley fidgets, "How do I look?"

"The same as always."

"I know you're fucking pissed at me. I'm sorry for judging you okay? Talk to me."

Hayley *hates* the silent treatment. "I forgive you. Good luck with Kenzie. Hopefully, she's not getting railed by two dudes when you show up."

"I hate you," Hayley grumbles and leaves.

I stumble to my room, plop on the bed, and text Nate.

MEGAN: Back in town, have a nice day with your parents 😊

NATE: I'll try. Nico and Amira kept me up all night so I'm deadass tired. She is coming with us today. I didn't know you'd be home so early or I would have invited you

MEGAN: I'm sorry they kept you awake. It's okay, next time 😊 Plus, if I walk into a church I may burst into flames. I'm a sinner

NATE: I'm no saint. If you don't hear from me, come collect my ashes at St. Mary's and spread them somewhere nice

MEGAN: The Botanical Gardens?

NATE: Perfect

NATE

Spending an eternity at the Botanical Gardens doesn't sound so bad.

Better than six feet under. I hear Trey. His voice is back. I haven't heard it since the night I flipped out on Megan. It's like he is sitting in the passenger seat next to me. I look over and he's not there.

Of course I'm not you idiot. He laughs. *Tell Nico he's allowed to drive faster than 50, old man*. I chuckle and Nico notices in the rearview mirror.

"What's so funny?"

I snap back to reality, "Just thinking about Trey, you know, he'd say you're driving like an old man, the speed limit is 65 you know?"

Nico looks over at Amira and I see her place her hand on her stomach.

"What the fuck?" I lean forward and slap Nico's shoulder.

"We found out Amira is pregnant. It's early but I'm being cautious."

"Oh fucking her brains out is fine but you can't even drive the speed limit?" Amira laughs at me, "And you! Amira, you were just fucking drinking on the 4th!"

"No, I wasn't. It was just cranberry juice." She corrects me.

My jaw drops, "I am so fucking confused." I try to piece things together. "You've been honest with Amira, right?" I ask Nico.

"Yes." He confirms as he takes her hand.

Amira kisses the back of his hand, "I know about Hannah if that's what you're trying to avoid asking him in front of me."

"You hooked up with Hannah in Aspen and now Amira is pregnant with your child?"

"Nate…" Amira says softly, "Nico and I have been fucking for like, years. We were never exclusive and I guess we weren't very careful." She shrugs, "I missed my period…and…"

I hold up my hand for her to stop talking, "No, nope. I'm not listening to this period talk. La-la-la-la-la." I plug my ears and she reaches back and slaps my arm.

"I did drink at the bar the night we all went to Raul's but I didn't know I was pregnant, once I did, I quit drinking. I told Nico I was late, we got the test together…"

"That's why you announced you are a couple the other night, so in nine months people won't be shocked."

"We are telling Ma and Pops after church. It's early and a lot can go wrong so we aren't making a big announcement yet, but I can't wait to tell them."

I slouch back in my seat. Well fuck.

Congratulations Uncle Nate, Trey laughs. He knew.

Megan

I wake up from my nap and have a text from Amira.

AMIRA: You may want to check on Nate. Nico and I just dropped a bombshell. Congrats on dating him, he told us. Btw, I'm pregnant. Don't tell anyone. Love you byeeee

She's what?!

I don't have time to process it before my sister burst into my room dancing around like Buddy The Elf. I cover myself, "What the hell got into you?"

"Kenzie and I kissed!" She squeals and jumps on my bed making me thrash around practically giving me whiplash before she plops on the bed breathlessly, "It was soooo hot! She plays for both teams!" Hayley says proudly.

"Uh, congratulations?" *Did I wake up in a parallel universe?*

"Is it cool? Since she's Olivia's best friend and you're kinda seeing Nate?" *I'm doing more than seeing him.*

"Yeah, even if I did have a problem with it, you're going to pursue her anyway." I deadpan.

Her jaw drops, "If you *really* had a problem with it, I wouldn't." She crosses her arms over her chest.

"It's fine."

"Kenzie wants me to bring pieces over to the gallery so I'm going to take some to her. God, I'd love to work on a piece with her, both of us creating beautiful artwork together!" Hayley practically floats off my bed and dances out of my room like a damn sugarplum fairy.

"What the hell is going on?" I mutter.

I take Amira's advice and text Nate to make sure he hasn't died of a heart attack or shock.

MEGAN: Are you okay? Amira told me the big news. Congratulations on being an uncle 😊

I don't get a text back.

***

At 11 pm, the buzzer on the intercom goes off. Hayley is closest so she answers.

"Who is it?" She asked annoyed.

"Nate."

She buzzes him in and I run to the bathroom to freshen up. When he knocks on the door, Hayley answers. They exchange hellos and I slip into my bedroom.

"She's in her room. Behave." Hayley warns. I see the shadow of Nate coming down the hallway and I stand. Butterflies flap in my stomach. He enters my room, dressed in his Sunday best, and closes the door behind him. He looks exhausted and like he might have been crying. He holds his arms out for me and I take him in my arms, cradling his head against my chest. I let him melt into me.

"Are you okay?"

He shakes his head against me.

I stand him upright and slide his suit jacket off. I take off his tie and unbutton his dress shirt. I slip it off his shoulders and then remove his white undershirt before working at his belt, shoes, and dress pants. I fold them all and lay them on my dresser. He's only in his boxer briefs and dress socks. I cup his face and kiss him softly before getting in bed and gesturing for him to lie with me. He lays down and buries his face in my neck and shoulder. Nate's hands slip under my tank top as he holds me and he lets out an audible exhale. I rub his muscular back and rake my fingernails over him softly as he moves to nuzzle my chest. I feel his body become less tense.

He finally speaks.

"I'm exhausted. Physically and mentally exhausted." He whispers, "I need you."

"I'm right here." I kiss his head.

We lay in silence holding each other, lost in time, before he speaks again, "Why is everything changing?"

I time my time answering, "Because time never stands still." I say softly, "What changes are scaring you?"

"Nico and Amira are together; he's going to be a Dad. He got a ring from my Pops tonight. He's proposing once they make sure the baby is safe. My parents want me to get married and have babies."

"My parents want that from me too. It's a parent thing." I assure him.

"Ughh. Olivia and Anders are in love, I dated her like, weeks ago…I know we were nothing serious but…it took her no time to fall in love with that guy after me."

I stay quiet and think about how long I've been hung up on Nate and how quickly Olivia moved on from him.

Nate continues to vent, "I need to hire two people to take over for Amira and your serving spot. She's a rockstar behind the bar and you just got promoted. Nico and I are leaving in a few weeks for New York. I need his head to be on right. I need him focused."

"And this baby news will make him unfocused?"

He sits up propping himself over me with one arm, "Well, yeah, I mean…it's life-changing."

I see the pain and worry in his beautiful eyes, I stroke his cheek, "Nate, for some people, having a family is rewarding and life-changing in the best way. We aren't teenagers. Nico is a grown man. Amira is great. Both are stable."

Nate lets out a huff.

"Okay. Nico could use some work, but Amira and the baby are what he needs to grow up. They will have a beautiful little family."

Nate stands, "What about me? What about the restaurant? While they are off playing house, I'll be running everything when we have never been busier!" He stabs my mattress with his finger at each point.

I raise an eyebrow at him but he keeps ranting.

"And they fuck like, all the time! Like knowing that she's knocked up—"

"Pregnant," I correct him and sit up.

"Fine, *pregnant*," he drawls out, "Nico just wants to go at it like rabbits, I mean, is that even healthy?" His voice cracks.

I fight my laughter and kneel on the bed to cup his cheek until he breathes, "First, yes, Amira and Nico can have sex while she is pregnant. From what I hear, the sex drive is crazy when you're pregnant."

"Well... can't they fuck at her place? I need sleep!"

I laugh, "Talk to Nico. Tell him that. Don't you think that maybe they are both excited they don't have to hide anymore?"

Nate softens, "I guess. He said they have been fucking for years. I had no clue! Just like I never picked up on you flirting with me. What else am I blind to? You know, Nico thinks Julian likes you."

I bite my lip and Nate starts pacing with his hands on his head, "Don't tell me you two…"

Time for the truth bomb, "Julian and I kissed. Once. And I fell asleep next to him because he had a nightmare at Raul's but that's it. Oh, and it was his idea for me to post pictures with him to get your attention."

"What the fuck?" He sighs in frustration. "It was a trap."

I get off the bed and hold Nate's waist, he is unraveling, "Nate, baby, can I tell you what I think?" I ask tentatively.

He throws his hands up in the air, "Sure, go for it."

I slink my arms around his neck and gaze into his eyes, I want to show him patience and understanding, "I think you're maybe a teeny bit jealous."

"Jealous?" He scoffs.

"Olivia moved on quickly and fell in love with Anders. Nico, who has looked out for you as your brother and been your business partner, now has two more people to look after. Amira and his baby. Nico has always been your parents' favorite in your eyes, and he's giving them a daughter-in-law and a grandchild. You're wondering where that leaves you in their life and at work."

Nate's eyes fall, "Yes," he whispers, "You say it so much better than me."

"Nate, you're forgetting, you have me. I'll be by your side. I'm not going anywhere." I kiss him softly and continue, "I'll hire two new servers. You focus on the kitchen and practicing for New York. I'll talk to Amira about having Nico stay at her place so you can sleep." I take his hands in mine, "Change is good Nate and when you're ready, I don't want us to hide anymore."

Nate kisses me passionately as if my words opened something in him. "I needed to hear that. God, why are you always right?" He moans and kisses me again. I can't help but smile against his lips.

Nate lays me down on my bed and kisses all over my body, worshiping every peak and curve. He grinds against me and the friction of his boxers against my panties gets me wet, "Wait, Nate…there's one more thing I kept from you."

He looks down at me, his eyes pleading for it not to be bad news.

"I am on birth control, but I've been really bad at taking it when I should. I got the morning-after pill yesterday to be safe. I'm not ready to be a Mom and like you said, things are about to get crazy at work and I didn't want to complicate our lives more. I should have talked to you about it."

It takes Nate a minute to process what I said but then he kisses me, "You did the right thing." Another kiss, "But, start taking your pill because I'm going to want to be inside you any chance I get."

After Nate and I make love, he is back to himself.

"I'll be right back," I kiss his cheek, throw on my silk robe, and scurry to the bathroom. I make a pit stop in the kitchen for bottled water and Hayley has a big smile on her face.

"What?" I groan. I can feel her judgy eyes on me.

She shrugs, "He's kind of adorable when he's spiraling," she chuckles.

I giggle. She's not wrong.

"Are you two okay?"

"Yes, he just needed to talk and bang out his frustration."

"Oh, I heard," she pretends to gag, "I'm happy for you Meg."

"Thanks, I am too."

CHAPTER TWENTY-TWO

Wednesday, July 10th

NATE

Our first service back after the break went perfectly. Megan did incredible running the front of house and it was great being in the kitchen for a full service with Nico, Raul, and Julian. Callum is still learning the ropes.

Before service, we had a family meal like we do every Wednesday, and Megan and I announced that we are dating. I had given Julian the heads up beforehand so he wasn't caught off guard and let him know that I'd take care of Megan. One ass-beating from Nico was enough.

Megan joins me in the office once the last table is gone, "Hayley texted me she's spending the night with Kenzie, do you want to spend the night at my place?"

I stole glances at her all night, she wore a black pencil skirt and blouse and a low heel with her hair in a fancy updo and her makeup was done up, I had to fight my hard on all service. "Yeah, I just have to close up—"

"Nico will do it, I already talked to him."

Fuck I love the way she takes care of business. I don't need any further encouragement. "Get your bag and meet me outback." She skips off and I take off my chef coat, throw it in the laundry, and walk to the garage. I get my bike out and grab our helmets. When Megan comes out she takes my breath away. She traded her heels for combat boots, slipped on a leather jacket, and let her hair loose. *Fuck me.*

"I'm ready." She flirts.

Me too. Jesus, fuck. I hand her helmet over and get on my bike to steady it before I rip a hole in my jeans with my cock. Megan gets on and I can feel the heat of her pussy against me. I speed to her apartment and kiss and feel her until we are inside. After last night, I'm falling head over heels for her but right now, I need to be inside her.

"Bend over," I order as I walk her to the back of the couch. She leans over and I lift her skirt and prop one leg on the back of the sofa. "No panties?"

She shakes her head and I spank her ass. "You worked all day with no panties on?" I crack my hand over her other ass cheek and she whimpers.

"I wanted to be ready in case…" Her voice fades.

"In case what?"

"You wanted to fuck me."

A growl rumbles deep in my throat. I rub her wet pussy until she orgasms and undo my belt. I fish a condom out and tear it open with my teeth then pull my pants low enough to free my cock. I put the condom on and then shove deep into Megan's sweet pussy. She cries out in pleasure, "Is this what you were hoping for all day?"

"Yes, yes Nate."

I pound into her hard. Last night, I was a complete emotional wreck, and the last thing I want is for her to see that as a weakness. I want her to know that, while she can be my strength when I need it, I will always be her man—there to take care of her, protect her, and meet every one of her needs and desires. I need her to feel safe with me, to know that no matter what, I've got her back just like she has mine.

My time with her is never enough. Whether we're out to eat, cooking together, or even enjoying a date night like at the lake yesterday, it never feels like enough. No matter how close we are in those moments, I always crave more of her—more of the way she makes me feel, more of the time we share.

"Fuck you're so hot," I tug her skirt up more then turn her around, "Show me those perfect tits baby," I order.

Megan works her blouse open and tugs her bra cups aside. I lean down and suck her nipples while she pulls my hair and bucks her hips on me. Her perfume mixed with the leather from her new jacket drive me wild. I pull away leaving her aching for my lips.

"Nate," she gasps.

"Yes?"

"I'm going to come...don't stop," Megan pleads.

I grip her hips and pound into her relentlessly until I feel her pussy clench and try to push me out. I pull out and Megan squirts all over my dick and the hardwood floor. It's fucking beautiful. I let her ride her orgasm and then I push back inside. Megan wraps her legs around me and I hold her perfect ass in my hands as I slam my hips into her. I look into her eyes as I fuck her. The past two days I made love to her, I was sweet and romantic but now...I need to show her she's mine.

"Whose pussy is this?"

"Yours Nate, yours. You own this pussy."

"That's right. And my cock belongs to you, baby.'

Megan's nails dig into my shoulders and the pain turns to pleasure, "I'm coming, fuckkkk." I moan and the tingles and heat wash over me. My balls tighten and I empty every drop into the condom. I hold Megan against me, panting. She moans and whimpers and then I hear her sniffle. I pull away and her dark hair covers her face. I pull my pants up then pick her up and carry her to her room and gently lay her down, "Babe, hey, look at me, what's wrong?" I move the hair from her face and wipe her tears. "Megan, talk to me." My heart races.

"That was…it…you…"

"Was it too much?"

"No. It felt…So. Fucking. Incredible." Megan sighs with a smile and my heart fills. I wipe her tears again and kiss her forehead.

"Stay here, don't move." I kiss her cheek. I walk to the kitchen and dispose of my condom then get a glass and look for orange juice in the refrigerator. Luckily, they have some. I pour her a glass and stop in the bathroom to get a hot washcloth for her. I walk back to her room and turn on the bedside lamp and her fountain. I hand her the orange juice and make her drink the whole glass before I undress her piece by piece before I gently clean her up.

I undress and crawl under the covers with her and pull her to me. She lays her head on my chest and lays her hand over my stomach. Her leg loops over mine.

"Thank you."

"Don't thank me, it's my job to take care of you."

She hums in acknowledgment.

"You did amazing today at work. I knew you would."

Silence. I look down and Megan's eyes are closed. I turn off the lamp and lay in the dark with nothing but the sound of the fountain trickling and Megan sleeping peacefully. My paradise.

CHAPTER TWENTY-THREE

Thursday, July 11th

Megan

I haven't seen my sister for days. I decide to stop at Miller Gallery to check in on Hayley. She and Kenzie have been inseparable.

"Hayley?" I call out as I enter the gallery. I notice my sister's paintings hanging on a wall mixed in with ones I don't recognize. Kenzie's. Hayley walks out from the back of the gallery covered in paint and Kenzie slyly peeks from behind her.

"Hey! What's up?" Hayley greets me trying to act casual but her lips are swollen. I hand her coffee and a brown bag containing two muffins from the coffee shop.

"Wanted to pop in and see how it's going and bring you breakfast."

"Thanks," she grins and takes the coffee and bag.

I look from her to Kenzie.

Hayley sips her coffee, "Megan, this is Kenzie, Kenzie, my sister Megan."

Kenzie holds her paint-covered hand out to shake mine, "It's nice to meet you, Hayley has told me so much about you."

I smile kindly, "I would say the same for you but I haven't *seen* Hayley lately," I dart my eyes at her. Hayley's cheeks blush.

"Come, I'll show you what we are working on." Hayley gives Kenzie the paper bag and coffee and leads me to the back of the gallery.

When I turn the corner I see it, "Hayley, this is incredible!" My jaw drops looking at the colorful canvas. I ignore the breast and ass prints on it. Hayley knows I see them and her cheeks get even more red. I lower my voice, "I assume it's going well?"

"Ugh, yes! You will love her!" she whisper yells, "Come out for drinks with us!"

"I work tonight." I remind her.

"After, come out, please! I need my sister's stamp of approval."

That makes me laugh, she has *never* cared what I think of her partners. "Fine, where are we having drinks?"

"Dive bar where Lilah works? It's close to your work."

"I'll text you when I'm done." I smile.

Thursday Night

"Text me if you need me," Nate says as he kisses my cheek before I leave for the night.

"I'll be fine Nate, just drinks with my sister."

"Didn't she practically kill you with shots last time?"

He's not wrong. "I'll be fine. I'll keep you updated."

I change upstairs in Nate's apartment. Jeans. Tank Top. Sneakers. Hair in a ponytail. The night air is warm and I walk to the bar. I meet Hayley and Kenzie inside, and Lilah mixes something strong and fruity for me to drink.

"Your sister is amazing! So talented!" Kenzie compliments her over the music.

"Yeah, she's alright," I tease and Hayley puts me in a headlock until I tap out.

Kenzie and I talk about her artwork, she inquires about my work at Due Fratelli and I let her know about my promotion. She seems genuinely happy for me. I like her. Something about her is...familiar but I can't put my finger on it.

After my third fruity mixed drink, I come up with a grand idea, "I should set up a dinner with Mom and Dad at DF, you can bring Kenzie and Nate will be there," I suggest to my sister and she loves the idea. Kenzie looks scared shitless but agrees. "I'll get ahold of Mom and set it up for next Wednesday," I smile.

"Let's get you another drink!" Hayley offers in hopes I'll get too drunk to remember this idea.

The rest of the night, I'm the third wheel while Kenzie and Hayley dance together. I see Julian come in with the dish crew and Callum. Julian must be the DD. He doesn't spot me and walks to the bar and starts chatting up Lilah. They are flirting and she makes his non-alcoholic drink only…I see her put liquor in it.

I push through the crowd and walk up to the bar, "What the fuck are you doing? You know he can't have that!" I snap at Lilah. I'm protective of Julian.

"Hey, Meg…it's fine…" Julian takes my arm and I rip it away.

"No, it's not!" I scoff. "What the fuck is wrong with you!" I yell again. Lilah focuses on Julian with a look in her eyes that makes my blood boil. Julian wraps his arm around my waist and pulls me away from the bar, but my eyes are locked on Lilah.

Julian backs me against the wall and tips my chin towards him, "Hey, chill. I'm not on probation anymore. I can drink now."

My eyes narrow at him, "So you're drinking as soon as you're clear?" I cross my arms over my chest.

"I told you I wasn't on probation for drinking. I'm not an alcoholic Meg."

"It still feels, wrong," I whisper and lower my arms.

"It's not. I've behaved for five years. I've followed every rule, taken every class, passed every drug test, stayed out of trouble, and now I can finally...*live*." He gives me an attitude and I deserve it. "What are you doing here? I'm surprised you're not with *Nate*." His tone is like poison in my ears.

"I'm here with my sister and her girlfriend." I square my shoulders, "Lilah and my sister are friends."

"You owe her a fucking apology. She would never spike my drink."

"I'm sorry. I'll apologize, okay?" I motion for us to walk back to the bar. I get Lilah's attention, "Hey, I'm sorry, I was just looking out for Julian."

She half smiles, "It's fine, I'm glad you care about him. Want a shot?"

"I'll do one with you, it's my first drink in five years," Julian nudges me. Oddly, I want to share this with him.

Lilah pours three shots so she can join too, and we tip them back together. Julian winces and coughs. Lilah hands him his drink to use as a chaser.

"Cheers," Julian tips his drink to me and walks to the billiards tables.

I go back to dancing with Hayley and Kenzie but an eye lingers on Julian. When I excuse myself to use the bathroom, I text Nate.

MEGAN: Did you know Julian's probation is over? He is here drinking at the dive bar with Callum and the dish crew

NATE: He didn't tell me, but I knew it was coming up, is he drunk?

MEGAN: Not yet

NATE: Keep an eye on him and text me if he gets out of hand

MEGAN: Will do

God, I feel like a snitch, but I care about Julian and so does Nate.

I wash my hands and when I go back to the dancefloor, Hayley and Kenzie are making out. I look at my coworkers and Julian. They are throwing back drinks and playing pool. I decide to go say hi since I don't want any part of the make-out sesh.

A few of the guys see me coming as I'm walking over when a burly man eye fucks me from his barstool and then smacks my ass as I walk by. Callum puts his beer down and stalks my way and before I can even turn around to confront the guy, Callum has him on the floor punching him. A tattooed arm wraps around my waist and carries me away while two more of our crew pull Callum off the man.

"Don't touch women like that you shite!" Callum yells in his Irish accent.

Lilah runs over to see what the ruckus is, and she bans the burly man and his hick-ass friends from the bar. "Callum! No fights!" She warns him.

"He touched Boss Lady, nobody fucks with our family!" He defends himself and I can't help but be filled with pride. The bar erupts and people offer Callum, the guys, and me drinks. I wave them off and become keenly aware that Julian's arm is still wrapped around my waist protectively.

He looks me over and tucks a piece of hair behind my ear, "Are you okay?" he asks and I can smell the vodka on his breath.

"I'm fine, it's not the first time some asshole has done something like that, that's another reason why I rarely ever go out, creeps."

Callum comes over, slinging an arm around my shoulder, drinking his Guinness, and smelling like cigarette smoke, "You good, Boss Lady?"

I laugh, "Don't call me that, but thank you."

He pulls me closer, "You hang with us the rest of the night, we'll protect ya', right Jul?"

From behind me, I hear, "Megan, what the hell?" Callum turns with his arm still around my shoulder and Hayley looks disgusted.

"They work with me. Callum, Julian, this is my sister Hayley and that's Kenzie," I nod.

Callum's arm comes off me so fast as he tries to use his Irish charm on my sister.

That gets Julian to finally smile. He taps Cal's shoulder, "Hey there *mate*, you're barking up the wrong tree."

Kenzie slides her arm around Hayley's waist and kisses her neck.

"'Right, I can handle two of ya'."

"They don't like men," Julian adds.

Callum winks, "Not even an Irishman?"

"Nope," Kenzie laughs, even though she does like men.

"Shite, that always works."

"Sorry pretty boy," Hayley pinches his cheek and I explain what happened to her as the guys start to play pool.

"Shit, I'm sorry I wasn't paying attention, tonight was girls night and I fucked up." My sister apologizes.

"It's okay, my other family stepped in." I nod to the guys. At that moment, I think how much Due Fratelli means to me finally clicks with my sister. It's not just Nate. It's all of them. My family.

NATE

"I haven't heard from Megan in two hours. In the last text, Megan said Julian was drinking with the crew!" I pace Nico's living room area as he rubs Amira's shoulders. Not only am I worried about Julian, but I'm also worried about Megan.

"She's out with her sister, Julian, and the guys are there. I'm sure everything is fine Nate, relax."

"She kissed him, they kissed."

"What? When?" Amira asks, "Tonight?"

"No, at some other point, but…"

Nico sighs, "You have to trust her Nate."

"I do! I just… don't want to lose her to someone like I did with Olivia."

"Stop. Megan would never cheat."

There is a knock at the door. Nico, Amira, and I all look at each other confused.

I run to the door and fling it open. *Megan.*

I pick her up in my arms. Relief washes over me. It clicks in my head that she has keys to the restaurant. I close Nico's door behind me.

I lead Megan upstairs, "What are you doing here? I thought you were out with your sister?"

"I was."

"Is Julian okay?"

"We got him and Callum home."

"Oh, good. Are you okay?"

She doesn't answer until we are in my apartment. I brush a loose strand of hair behind her ear.

"I love you Nate." Megan blurts out and it looks like a weight is lifted off her shoulders, "I love you. I've loved you for so long," her tears swell, "Our crew... Nico, Amira, Raul, Julian, and Callum, everyone, they are our family. We have a beautiful family Nate."

My heart squeezes, I've never thought about it like that but she's right. *We have made a family*. Hearing her say she loves me, I know she will never abandon me for someone else. "I love you too, Megan."

I take her in my arms and hold her tight. I never want to let go. I pull back, look down into her eyes, and kiss her softly. Our bodies talk for us. Megan and I undress each other, and I see a large handprint on her beautiful ass. It's not mine.

"What. Happened?" I ask in a growl.

"Some big burly son of a bitch slapped my ass at the bar and Callum beat the shit out of him."

I fight my smile, "I knew I loved that guy."

"I have a new nickname," Megan smiles up at me as she's naked in front of me.

I slip my shirt over my head and pull my gym shorts down, "Oh yeah? What is it?"

She raises her chin in pride, "They call me Boss Lady."

I laugh, "I'm Boss, so since you're my lady, you're Boss Lady, makes sense."

"They looked after me, Hayley, and Kenzie tonight. Callum was drunk off his ass, but Julian only had a few. I made sure they got home, incident-free."

"That's what family does, they look out for each other," I pull Megan closer and think about our talk. I'm scared to lose Nico to Amira and his baby. I won't be his #1 anymore, but, I have Megan and our crew. Always. I kiss Megan again sweetly then turn her around and get on my knees to kiss her stinging away. When her legs get weak. I take her to the bed and continue spoiling her with my mouth. I kiss and rub her ass, I tease her puckered asshole and she flinches.

"Nate, I've never…"

"One day…" I adjust myself and lick her cute tight hole and she moans in pleasure. I keep going until she orgasms and then I reach for a condom before sliding into her wet pussy.

I make love to Megan, slow and deep. Passionate. Kissing her as I grind my hips into her. "I love you."

"I love you, Nate, so much." She whines as I push further inside.

I keep my pace and momentum until I feel Megan clench and pulsate around me and she cries out my name. I have my powerful release then slump over her. I turn us on our side and hold her through the night.

CHAPTER TWENTY-FOUR

Wednesday, July 17th

"And for dessert, we are having raspberry lemon torte made by Leah," I finish going over the special menu for the King Family tonight with the crew.

"Yes, Chef!" They call out and go to work.

I put the finishing touches on the private room Megan had reserved. I want everything to be perfect for Megan and her family. I'm not sure they know we are dating, but even so, she's my employee and I want them to know I take care of her and value her.

Tonight is also the first time Charlie, our new server, and Jonah the other newbie are on the floor. Megan hired them and so far, I'm impressed. Charlie is a bubbly girl fresh out of college who studied accounting and business management and Jonah oozes charm like me, our customers love him.

"Chef, Kenzie is here." Charlie chimes. I walk to the lobby area and greet Kenzie, she is shaking like a leaf from nerves.

"Hi Kenzie, nice to have you," I reach out to shake her hand, "The rest of the group on their way?"

"Yeah, they should be here any minute." She forces a smile.

"Nervous?" I laugh.

She nods.

"Meg said you're dating Hayley?"

She takes a deep breath, "Yeah, meeting the parents after a week," she laughs nervously, "If you see it start to go badly, can you bail me out like you did for Olivia?" She winces.

That makes me smile, she wants my help, "Of course I can. You'll do fine. Their Mom is super sweet, and her Dad looks intimidating but he's cool. If the conversation becomes awkward, ask him how he thinks the Bears will do this season. He'll ramble about it until the next course comes out."

Kenzie takes a deep breath, "Thanks Nate."

"Anytime. I need to put the finishing touches on a few things, breathe." I pat her shoulder and walk back to the kitchen. I check on the timing of everything, walk to the bar, and open two bottles of wine, with how nervous Kenzie is she is going to need them.

When I return to the lobby, I see everyone greeting each other and I swear Megan is walking in slow motion.

"Wow." Escapes from my lips. Her long dark hair is styled in loose curls, her makeup is done, and her mid-thigh length black dress hugs her in all the right places. I clear my throat and refocus.

"Good evening Mr. and Mrs. King, welcome."

"Good to see you again Nathaniel." Lynn kisses my cheeks warmly as she calls me by my legal name like my Ma does when I'm in trouble.

I shake Mr. King's hand, "Thank you for hosting tonight Son."

"My pleasure." I follow Kenzie and Hayley inside and pull out Lynn and Megan's chairs for them like a gentleman. "Wine and ice waters are here, Charlie will be back with warm bread and salad." I excuse myself.

The kitchen pumps out our courses and I only catch snippets of conversation. It sounds like The Kings are grilling Kenzie and I'm glad I'm not in the room. I join after we drop off the torte Leah made for the night. From the look of it, everything went well. Kenzie looks more relaxed. She and Hayley look like they are in love.

Ruben and Lynn ask me about Food Network, they thank me for believing in Megan and I thank them for raising such an amazing woman.

Megan

Kenzie and Nate survived dinner. Granted Nate wasn't here for all of it, but he passed the test. My parents thank Nate for the meal and I let them know I'm going to hang back to help clean up.

Nate closes the door to the private room and we attack each other with desperate kisses.

"This dress, fuck…you look gorgeous."

I tug on his black tie, "You do."

"Did you wear panties?"

I giggle, "Yes."

"That's a shame, I was hoping you wouldn't"

"It's dinner with my parents Nate."

"So…" He whispers.

I change the subject before I'm on my knees for him, "How did Charlie and Jonah do?"

Nate bites his lip, "If you're trying to change the subject so I won't fuck you, talking about work isn't it baby."

"I'm serious," I laugh.

Nate takes a deep breath and adjusts his hard-on, he lets go of me and runs his hands through his hair, "They did amazing. I knew you'd be good at this hiring thing."

"And the rest of service? Do you need me on?"

"Nico and Amira have it covered. I need you upstairs. It's your uh, annual review."

"I got hired in September," I giggle.

"We are doing them early this year," Nate makes his face serious and adjusts his tie all Boss-like.

"Fine. I'll meet you there in 15." I flirt. I do a quick check-in with Charlie and Jonah then take the elevator to Nate's floor. He's already waiting for me. Naked. I put on a fake pout, "You're naked already."

"I'm efficient with my time."

"I know but I like undressing you myself, especially when you wear a tie."

Nate grabs it off the dresser, "Oh, this tie?"

"Mmmhmm," I purr. "I had an idea of what you could do with it."

"I like it when my employees bring ideas to the table, I'll have to put that in your employee file." Nate keeps up the role-playing, "What did you have in mind?"

I turn around and put my hands behind my back.

Nate walks up behind me and gently wraps the tie around my wrist before giving it a hard pull to make sure it's tight. "I got a complaint that you didn't wear your proper uniform, Miss King."

"I'm sorry, Chef," I say seductively.

Nate leans in and whispers in my ear, "I'm going to have to punish you for that."

"What can I do to make you forgive me? I don't want anything bad in my file."

Nate sits on his leather sofa and motions for me to kneel between his legs. His cock is throbbing and veiny. Precum is already seeping from his tip. "Suck me and look up at me while you do it."

My pussy clenches in excitement. I didn't know Nate had this side to him. I saw glimpses of it but this. Fuck.

"Now." He pushes.

With my hands tied behind my back, I can only use my mouth and it drives Nate wild. He bucks his hips up into my wet mouth in slow thrusts enjoying every second of me submitting to him in this scenario.

"Good girl, you listen so well. Now stand up." Nate demands but he also helps me. He slides the bottom of my dress up and practically salivates when he sees my black lace panties. He buries his face in my pussy and I feel his hot breath over my sensitive skin. Nate's hands feel up my calves, over my thighs, he grabs and spanks my ass then slowly pulls my panties off. I step out of them and Nate pulls my dress down. "That is your proper work uniform."

"Yes, Chef."

"Turn around."

I do and I feel the tie come undone.

"Sit on it."

I hesitate because I know he doesn't have a condom on.

"I said, sit on my cock."

My heart races and I can feel my juices between my thighs. I lower myself on Nate's bare cock and the pressure and stretch of him inside me makes me orgasm before I even start riding him.

"Fuck, you're so tight baby. I had to feel you against me again like this. I'll let you know when I'm about to come, okay?" Nate asks as he grips my hips and starts moving me up and down on him.

"Yes." I whimper.

"This ass is beautiful, all of you is a fucking masterpiece."

I feel my dress lift over my ass, Nate reaches around to play with my clit and I orgasm again. With his slick fingers, he moves to my ass and plays with my tight virgin hole.

"I'm going to try something, breathe and relax okay?"

"Yes."

I feel pressure, then a burning followed by a wave of pleasure of having Nate's big cock in my pussy and his finger in my ass. I cry out his name and move myself faster up and down on him.

"Are you okay?"

"Yes! Fuck yes, it's almost too much but I want more."

His finger pushes deeper and he holds me down on him so I'm taking every inch.

"Nate!" I whine, desperately wanting him to pound me and finger my ass.

"Tell me you love me."

"I love you, I fucking love you!" I orgasm around him, my walls throb and clench and tighten around his shaft. In one motion, Nate has me bent over on the floor, ass up and he pulls out and releases his pleasure all over my ass as he moans and curses.

"I love you, Megan," he says breathlessly then spanks my ass again.

CHAPTER TWENTY-FIVE

Thursday July 18th, 2024

Megan

My phone is ringing but I don't want to move from being wrapped in Nate. This is my happy place. My phone stops and then rings again. Fuck. I lazily reach for my phone.

"Hello?" I ask groggily.

"Megan, where are you?"

"I'm with Nate."

"Can you get home? I..I found something out and I really want to tell you in person."

I sit up in Nate's bed, throw the covers off, and begin gathering my clothes. "I'll be right there." I get dressed and lean across the bed to kiss Nate. He stirs in his sleep but doesn't fully wake up, "Hayley needs me, I'll see you at work later."

"Is everything okay?" He mumbles.

"I hope so."

I run down the stairs, all the way home and the elevator in our apartment building won't move fast enough. I unlock the door and burst in to find Hayley on the couch. It doesn't look like she's been crying but she never cries.

"Is it Mom or Dad? Are they okay?"

"They are fine."

"Are you okay? Did something happen with Kenzie last night?"

"I'm fine. Kenz is…fine."

I plop down next to her, "Please tell me why I left my naked boyfriend in bed…" my patience wears thin.

Hayley blurts out, "Kenzie was the little girl we used to play with at the picnics and parties."

I feel the air get knocked from my lungs, "Excuse me?"

"She was more of a strawberry blonde red then, long hair down to her butt. Now her hair is like the deep red of an autumn leaf and short. She's a woman now. Not a girl. She had parents then, she doesn't now."

I move closer and put a hand on Hayley's knee, "I-I'm sorry. How did you—"

"Dad told her after dinner last night that he knew her parents. He was the one who had to tell her the night of the accident and take her to her Grandma's house."

I hug my sister tightly and try to comfort her. It's crazy that we knew Kenzie years ago and now she and Hayley are brought back together.

"Dad told her he has a lot of stories he can tell her when she's ready to hear them."

"I'm sure she will love that. Dad tells the best stories."

Hayley smiles and then it fades, "Kenzie also remembers the boy."

My eyebrows raise, "She does?"

"Yeah," tears rim her eyes, "His name was Julian."

My chest feels like it's splitting in two. It's like my chest is cracking open to make more room for my heart. "My Julian?" I ask as if it's such a common name. I want to kick myself for calling him mine. He isn't.

"Kenzie remembered hearing her Dad talk about Julian, his Dad abused his Mom so badly, that she moved them away. That's why he stopped coming to parties. Julian's Dad went to jail, some bad people in there killed him for being a narc. His Mom fell into a pattern of dating really bad men."

Tears fall from my eyes and I don't want to believe what my sister is saying, "But, his hair is short and he's not stick thin anymore."

"He cut his hair so his Mom's abusers couldn't grab him as easily. Kenzie tried to stay in touch with him. Her Dad brought him to their house a few times so he could eat and shower…"

I shake my head in disbelief, "No."

"He had it bad. I-I talked to Lilah and she confirmed it all, they met in high school. Lilah had it pretty bad too and they bonded."

"They're wrong." My throat feels like it's closing up, "He would have said something to me." My eyes burn.

"Maybe he didn't want you to. He's a new man."

The tears keep falling and my breath hitches. I don't want to believe it. I run into my room and slam the door. I strip my dress off and change into joggers, a t-shirt, and running shoes. I leave the apartment with nothing but my phone and run.

***

My lungs are on fire and I don't even realize I'm at Julian and Callum's apartment until he answers the door.

"Megan?" Julian looks shocked and confused to see me.

"Are you here alone?" I heave out as I try to catch my breath.

"Callum's in his room what's up? Are you okay? Can I get you a water or something?" Julian moves aside and closes the door behind him then walks to his kitchen. He gets a bottle of water and hands it to me. I chug it and immediately feel like I may spew it back up. "Is it Nate? Are you two okay?"

I haven't thought about Nate since Hayley dropped the bomb on me about Julian. "He's fine." I choke out.

"Sit, calm down." Julian tries to take my hand and lead me to his couch and I pull my hand away.

"Do you know who I am?" I ask with tears in my eyes.

"You're Megan King…Boss Lady…Nate's girl—"

"Me! Do you know me? Have you known who I am since I started?" My voice cracks and I see Julian's throat bob. I walk to him and shove him, "Tell me." I plead up into his azure, blue eyes.

He takes a deep breath, "How'd you find out who I am? Did Lilah tell you?"

I'm almost jealous she knows more about Julian than me. "Kenzie Miller told my sister, my sister told me. Our Dad told Kenzie he knew her parents last night and the puzzle pieces just…fit together like some fucked up mosaic."

Julian can't even look at me, he starts cleaning his apartment of empty beer cans, paper plates, and random dirty shirts lying on the furniture, "You don't owe me anything. I don't want you to feel sorry for me or some shit."

"But…"

"We were kids Meg, what the fuck could you have done?"

"I bullied you, I was mean to you…that's awful."

"You also were the only one who stood up for me."

My tears fall.

"I made it through a lot of shit. I'm a better man for it. The past is the past. I've let it go. So should you."

"You haven't answered my question, did you know who I was when I got hired? Is that why you and the guys picked on me so much? Were you trying to get back at me for when we were kids?"

"Maybe a little," Julian shrugs.

"Why didn't you say anything?"

"I wanted you to know this version of me, not the one you knew then. I didn't want you to see me as the tall lanky poor kid with the long hair covered in scars."

"When you're a kid, you aren't aware of who is rich and who is poor and who is scarred and who isn't."

A puff of air comes from Julian, "Trust me, poor kids know it. We know where we stand in the hierarchy."

Fuck.

"The night I went out and we went to Raul's after…I heard you having a nightmare and I came in to sleep with you. To comfort you."

"That's why you were beside me when I woke up."

"Yes. I care about you. I always have. Why didn't you tell me we had a history?" The tears well in my eyes again.

"You say that like it would have changed anything."

"It may have."

"Which is exactly why I didn't tell you we are long-lost friends. You would have picked me based on history, not what your heart wants. You would have clung to nostalgia."

He's right. I know he's right.

"This is the better outcome. Nate is stable and safe, he will give you the world. I'm broken. Always have been, probably always will be."

I step closer, "Don't say that."

"You still have me. We are family. I love you, you love me, but we won't destroy each other Megan."

I wipe the tears streaming down my cheeks and Julian takes me in his arms and hugs me.

"I'm okay. I promise." Julian rubs my back and I hug him tighter. "So, your sister is dating that crazy redheaded devil?"

I choke out a laugh and look up at him, "Yeah, she is."

He smiles brightly, "At least it's not the fucking blonde."

Thursday Evening

There is a knock on the office door and when I look up, it's Julian.

"Hey man, what's up?"

"Do you have a few minutes? I need to talk."

"Here or the roof?"

"Roof."

I follow Julian to the elevator and we make our way to the rooftop. My heart is pounding. Is he in trouble?

Julian grabs a basket and starts inspecting the garden. He keeps his hands busy when he's nervous or overthinking.

"What's up? Everything okay?"

He shrugs, "I need to tell you something about Megan."

"If it's about the kiss, it's cool. She told me."

Julians' eyes dart to me, "She told you about that?"

"Yeah and she told me about waking up next to you at Rauls, you were gone before I got there."

"Good thing right?" He tries to crack a joke.

"Is there something else besides that?"

"Um, kinda?" His face scrunches.

I walk closer, "What is it?"

"Have you talked to her today?"

"No, her sister called her this morning and needed something and I haven't texted her or anything. I figured it's some sister situation I don't need to be a part of."

Julian scrubs his fingers through his short black hair, he takes a deep breath, "If she doesn't show up for work today, I'm the reason."

I grind my teeth together but try to stay calm, "Why?"

He shuffles his feet, "I knew Megan, Hayley, and Kenzie when we were kids. Before my Dad went to jail and my Mom made us run, I went to every party and picnic their parents had." Julian steps towards me, "She found out this morning and came to my apartment to confront me. I was ten when my Mom moved us. I was tall, skinny as fuck, and had really long hair that's why he didn't recognize me when she started. I knew Kenzie a bit longer. I knew who Megan was when you hired her but I never told her we were friends as kids and I don't think she's handling it well. If she's not herself today, that's why."

Wow. What the fuck and I supposed to say to that?

"I um, thanks for telling me. How was she when she left?"

"We had a laugh about a blonde girl who she pushed in the mud. The girl was nicknamed Sasquatch for a long time after that."

"That's my girl," I laugh.

"Megan wanted to know why I didn't tell her, it's obvious I liked her, you know? But I wanted her to follow her heart, not choose me because of history. Her heart led her to you and I'm so fucking happy it's not me. I would have fucked it up and never forgave myself."

"That's my greatest fear besides failing this place," I admit.

"She loves you, always has. You two are the only people alive who ever looked out for me and I'm grateful for you both."

"You're welcome. Thank you for being a great friend to us."

"We aren't friends. We are family."

I hug Julian. I think we both need it. I pat his back, "I'm proud of you." A creek from the door makes us break apart. We turn to see who it is and it's Megan striding towards us with a smile on her face.

"There are my guys," she jogs over to us, and Julian and I both hug her together. "Are you two done bonding up here? It's almost time for service. You ready?"

Julian and I look at each other and smile.

"We're ready."

CHAPTER TWENTY-SIX

Monday, July 22nd

Megan and I are on our way to Bowl-O-Rama to double date with Hayley and Kenzie. I guess this means I have the 'sister's stamp of approval'. Now I need to win over my ex- fling's BFF. Megan can feel my nervousness. She tightens her arms around me as I drive us through town and it brings me comfort.

Megan and I are working together amazingly. When we're at work, it's all business. Everyone loves and respects Megan in her new position. Megan never missed a beat after the Julian incident. We talked about it that night and she told me stories of Julian as a kid. She's so animated, I felt like I was there.

Megan and I have been spending time at her apartment since Hayley has been with Kenzie. It's nice to get away from Due Fratelli, it feels like I have a work/life balance. I've taken Megan out on rides, we've tried a few new restaurants and we've had lots and lots of sex. Megan makes sex fun and exciting and I'm man enough to admit that I love cuddling with her after. She gives me everything I've always dreamed of having in a relationship.

I find a parking space easily and Hayley and Kenzie are holding hands waiting for us outside. I turn the ignition off and Megan's a pro at getting on and off the bike. She takes her helmet off and shakes her dark hair out. It's so hot seeing her in tight jeans, sneakers, a tank top, and a leather jacket. She slips her jacket off and throws it over her arm, she holds her helmet, and with her free hand, she intertwines my hand in hers.

We greet Hayley and Kenzie and I lead us inside. I pay for the four of us because I'm a gentleman, and we get our bowling shoes. *All these years and they haven't made them look any less dorky?*

While we get ready, I order drinks and appetizers for the four of us. I'm treating Megan and the girls but I get a lecture from Hayley about being able to pay for herself because she's an independent woman.

"You get the next round then, deal?"

She nods in compromise.

Megan and I take the left lane, we are competing against Hayley and Kenzie. In the first game, I purposely suck so that the girls can have some satisfaction for beating a man, but in the second and third game, all bets are off. Megan and I win both which is surprising because I check out her cute ass in her tight jeans the whole time. Every time we switch turns, we find a way to touch each other. I cheer her on and encourage her, and every time one of us gets a strike we kiss. Motivation to win.

"I want Nate on my team!" Kenzie cheers, "Get over here, let's go against the sisters! She sneers at Hayley. Hayley and I switch sides.

It could be because we are a few beers in but Kenzie and I get along. I can't help but ask, "How's Olivia?"

"Great!"

"Have you told her about Megan and me? Does she know you're double-dating with us?"

She pauses, "No."

The expression on her face is telling. She may not have even told Olivia about Hayley. The fact she hasn't told Olivia about this double date makes me think she doesn't want Olivia to know, or maybe Olivia wouldn't care. Olivia is in love. She's moved on and so have I.

Friday, July 26th

Megan

"Hello, Due Fratelli, how may I help you?" I answer the phone as I work on the plan for the night.

A familiar voice comes across the line, "Hello, I'm looking for Megan."

"Speaking."

"They have you serving *and* answering phones?" A man's chuckle fills my ear, "This is Mark."

"Oh, hi Mark! I got a promotion, so I'm no longer serving…"

He cuts me off, "Even better! I know it's a long shot, but can you get me a table for two tonight? I have a date with this woman who is a huge foodie and I want to impress her."

"We are booked solid for the rest of the year, but I'll make it happen."

Mark sighs in relief, "Thank you! What time can you fit us in?"

I check the reservations and notice a regular, one who usually eats and leaves and doesn't loiter, "Make it 7. I'll make sure you two are taken care of."

"Yes! Perfect! You're the best!" He cheers quietly.

"Just one thing," I smile, "Breathe, don't be nervous."

Mark laughs, "This isn't our first date, don't worry. We will see you tonight."

After the call, I let Nate know he's not allowed to come to the dining room tonight as a joke.

"I have you, I'm not stealing the poor bastard's date, okay?" Nate says before kissing my cheek.

Later that evening, Mark comes in with a beautiful older brunette and they are both dressed professionally. Maybe they are co-workers?

"Megan, this is Claudette."

I reach my hand out to greet her, "So nice to meet you, welcome to Due Fratelli. We have your table ready for you." I lead them to the best table in the house. A bottle of wine, ice water, and fresh bread are on the table before they are sat.

Mark pulls her chair out and I place the menu's before them and go over our specials. I open the wine, and pour them a sip, once I get the nod, I fill the rest of their glass. From the look in Mark's eyes, I can tell he is thankful

I gave him credit for choosing it. "Your server Amira will be right with you." I smile politely.

I leave Mark on his date and as I check on guests, I keep an eye on them. His date looks familiar but I'm having a hard time placing her.

This date seems to be going much better than his date with Olivia! Claudette is laughing, they are both drinking, and then it hits me. *She's a Michelin.*

"Chef! Can I steal you for a moment?" I ask Nate as even toned as possible. He finishes what he's doing then joins me at pass.

"Mark's date is an inspector."

"What? How do you know that? They are anonymous."

"I recognize her. She's been here before, Mark said she's a self-proclaimed foodie. We have to get the food perfect," I say softly. I don't want to make anyone nervous. We always strive for perfection no matter who is at the table, but Claudette and Mark's food has to be perfect.

Nate squares his shoulders, "Thank you." He says before he returns to the line and starts directing like he's a conductor and Nico, Raul, and Julian. His instruments.

Mark and Claudette are served their entrees and then order dessert. I have Leah deliver it personally. Claudette's eyes sparkle and she closes them savoring her first bite. This fills me with excitement and pride and I know we pulled it off.

When Mark and Claudette are finished, he waves me down, "Can we get our check, please?"

"It's been taken care of, Mark." I smile, "You're one of our best customers."

"Impressive," Claudette purrs in her French accent, "I love a man with good taste." Her hand laces with Marks, "Should we get going now?"

"Yes." Mark winks at her and stands, I move aside.

"Have a great night, we'll see you soon," I smile and watch them leave hand in hand.

Mark looks back at me and mouths a silent, "Thank you!"

When they are out of sight I practically run to the kitchen, my eyes search for Nate but he's not on the line. I run to the walk-in cooler and find him. "Nate, we did it!" I cheer. He turns around and I leap into his arms and start kissing him. "We did it," I whisper and keep exploring his tongue with my mouth.

"You did amazing Megan, you're so observant…' Nate kisses my neck, "They loved it?"

"Yes," I moan and kiss him one more time. Nate puts me down on my feet and helps me straighten out my dress. "Celebrate after close?" I flirt.

"Oh, absolutely."

CHAPTER TWENTY-SEVEN

Monday, July 29th

NATE

"You're going down!" Nico taunts me as we prepare the kitchen for our test competition.

Amira, Megan, Hayley, and Kenzie are going to blind taste-test our dishes. Next Monday Nico and I leave for New York City and we want to impress the judges and bring out the best in each other.

"Your cockiness is going to be your downfall you know that?" I playfully punch him.

"We got five-star reviews all last week, we are kicking ass, the paper wrote about us, we are on fire!"

I can't fight the smile on my face. He's right. "Are you worried about us leaving for the week when we have all this momentum?"

"Callum is amazing on the line. I have no worries about him filling in with Raul and Julian next week. Charlie and Jonah are kicking ass on the floor with Megan running the front. You and I can focus on the competition and judging next week. Megan and Amira will hold it down."

"Yeah, you're right. How is Amira by the way? Like, with the pregnancy stuff."

"Horny as ever, when she isn't throwing up." He adds.

"Eww."

"Yeah, it's gross but I like taking care of her. I like waking up next to her daily and working with her. Knowing she has my back and cares about me. She doesn't judge me, and Ma and Pops love her. We are having dinner with her parents tonight and giving them the news about the baby."

I shake my head, "It's wild to hear you say that." I laugh as I tie my apron.

"You know I'm still going to look out for you even though I'm with her and becoming a father, right?" Nico asks softly.

"Yeah man, I know. We're family, that's what we do." I pat his back and we share a quiet moment before Amira's sing-song voice fills the kitchen.

"I don't smell any food cookingggg, the girls and I are waitingggg." She chimes. "First course, appetizer. You have twenty minutes," Amira pulls her phone from her back pocket to set the timer. "Ready?" she looks at us both. I give her a nod and Nico ties his apron, "Go!"

Nico and I start appetizers at our stations. This time, Megan wasn't in charge of picking ingredients thank god!

Nico and I can craft our best dishes with any ingredients and any style.

I know that Amira hates tomatoes and Hayley tries to eat as ethically as possible, she's a flexitarian. With that in mind, since they are both judging, I start preparing a vegetarian spring roll with a sweet chili dipping sauce.

I focus on myself and my dish. I get tunnel vision and get in the zone only looking up from my cutting board and sauté pan to check the time.

I get the spring rolls out of the pan and plated before the timer goes off and Nico comes into focus.

"What did you two prepare?" Jonah asks. He is going to serve the dishes but the ladies won't know who made each dish.

Nico starts, "I have prepared a Steak Bruschetta with Goat Cheese and Tomato Jam on toasted bruschetta."

"And you Chef Nate?"

"I prepared a Vegetarian Spring Roll with a Sweet Chili dipping sauce." Nico and I load the tray with our plates and follow Jonah to the dining room. He presents our dishes and I see Hayley flinch at the word 'Steak' and see Amira swallow the lump in her throat when she sees bruschetta. I try my best to keep a straight face.

Megan and Kenzie clean their plates while Hayley and Amira devour mine and only take a sympathy bite of Nicos.

"Judges, please hand me your scores." Jonah prompts. He plays this host role really well.

Nico and I watch as Jonah adds the scores but I know I won this round.

"The winner of this round, it wasn't even close," Jonah mumbles then clears his throat to get back into character, "Winner of this round is…Chef Nate!"

Nico hangs his head.

"You know I hate tomato!" Amira defends her decision.

"And steak and goat cheese, eww!" Hayley adds.

Megan and Kenzie laugh, "We loved them both!"

"I loved the steak and creaminess of the goat cheese mixed with the tart and sweet of jam," Kenzie compliments Nico, "Nate, your spring roll was fresh and unexpected."

"Ready for Round Two boys?" Megan smiles.

Round Two, Nico wins. He took mental notes and adjusted the entree he originally planned. My dish lacked a surprise element. Now we are tied 1-1 and it all comes down to dessert which isn't exactly the Rossi brother's strong suit. With only thirty minutes to prepare, I once again play into what I know the ladies like. Coffee. Amira hates that she switched to decaf so she will love this and Hayley and Kenzie's first date not date was at a coffee shop.

I prepare a no-bake Coffee Cheesecake and the lemon scent coming from Nico's prep station lets me know he is going tart.

When our thirty minutes are up, we follow Jonah to the dining room but this time I can't read Amira or Hayley's reactions.

"For the last course this afternoon we have No Bake Coffee Cheesecake topped with chocolate shavings and coffee beans and a Lemon Lava Cake. Enjoy!"

I can hear my heart beating, and this isn't even the real deal, it's practice! No live audience, no world-class judges, just the woman I love and I guess… my new friends Hayley and Kenzie. And Amira my future sister-in-law.

The four of them moan when they take a bite of my dessert. Women love their coffee, but they all love Nico's dessert too. The scores take longer this time.

"Before Jonah reveals who won, I just want to say, that both of you should be extremely proud of yourselves. You will do amazing next week!" Megan compliments.

"I agree! This is some of the best food I've had, good job guys!" Kenzie smiles.

"Ready to hear who won?" Jonah smirks.

"Hell yeah!" Nico cheers.

"Dessert scores were dead even. Nico you won entrée and Nate, you won dessert so it comes down to who scored the highest overall, and…it was Nate!"

"Yes!" I pump my fist in the air and Megan scoots out of her booth and comes running to hug me.

"That app sent you over the top!" She smiles and kisses my cheek before stepping out of the way for Hayley, Kenzie, and Amira to shake my hand and give me hugs.

"Congrats Nate, but next week, Nico is winning," Amira winks before joining him at his side.

"You killed it, little brother," Nico shakes my hand.

"You did too, fuck this is going to be a battle next week."

"You bet your ass!"

"Can you clean up Nate? We have dinner with my parents to get to." Amira asks.

"Of course, have fun. Good luck telling your parents know you have a bun in the oven."

She sticks her tongue out at me and Nico leads her back through the kitchen to the elevator that leads upstairs.

"Help me with the dishes?" Megan asks her sister before they clear the table and it's just me and Kenzie.

"I told Olivia about you and Megan, she's happy for you," Kenzie blurts out like she's been dying to get the words out all afternoon. "She's happy for you," Kenzie smiles as she squeezes my bicep like I didn't register what she said.

"That's cool, I'm glad she's happy for me. I'm happy for her too," I half smile.

"Anders moved in with her on Saturday. Hayley and I went to the party."

"Wow, that's uh, fast but hey, if it works for them, that's great."

"Are you coming with Megan to the painting reveal party in a few weeks? Olivia won't be there." Kenzie quickly adds.

"I'd be there even if she was," I tell her to let her know that Olivia and her happiness with Anders doesn't scare me. "Megan told me Hayley has something special she's been working on that you helped with?"

Kenzie's eyes sparkle, "Yeah, it's a surprise. You'll love it."

"Looking forward to it."

Kenzie gives me one last smile before joining Megan and Hayley and I take a moment to enjoy my win in the quiet of the dining room. When I turn around, I see Trey. I never see him when I'm awake.

"You kicked Nico's ass! He put up a good fight though," Trey shrugs and walks closer to me, "I'm proud of you bro, you've come a long way, and this place is great." Trey looks around like it's his first time here.

I don't know what to say so I choke out, "Thank you."

"Fuck man, you look like you've seen a ghost, oh wait, I am one, fucking crazy right?" Trey laughs, "Come on! Hit me over the head with a wine glass or stab me with a knife or something. I don't feel a thing!" He smiles bright and his white teeth stand out from his brown skin.

"Trey, why aren't you like…"

"In heaven? Fuck if I know, I saved a girl, I gave up my organs to save lives and I still didn't get to heaven. I guess I have unfinished business here or something." Trey sits down and props his feet on the table.

My stomach is in knots, I want to tell him he can cross over now. I'm okay, but if I do, will I never see or hear him again?

"I hear you talk to me."

"I'm always around, by the way, Megan…fuck…you two are perfect together and she's super hot!"

"You don't watch us, do you?"

"I'll never tell," he sings.

I run my hands through my hair and try to rationalize that I'm not seeing the ghost of Trey and that I'm just fucking crazy when Megan comes back to the dining room.

"Everything's cleaned up! Hayley and Kenz took off…" Megan stops in her tracks, does she see Trey too? "Nate, are you alright? You look pale."

"Pale as a ghost?" Trey jokes and my eyes dart to him.

"Nate…" Megan steps closer and my gaze is back on her, "Are you here with me?"

"We both are hottie," Trey stands up and walks beside me. I see goosebumps form on Megan's arms and see her shiver.

Her eyes widen, "He's here. Trey is here isn't he?"

Trey throws his arm over her shoulder, "Observant. I knew I liked her."

"Yeah," I nod still not able to breathe.

Megan takes a deep breath then licks her lips, "Hi Trey, I'm Megan, Nate's girlfriend. Nate misses you. I wish you were here so we could hang out. I'd love to hear stories about Nate as a teenager. I bet he was wild."

Trey laughs, "You would have hated him then, he's the man you deserve now, back then he was just a troubled little shit like me."

"I want you to know that Nate loves you and I promise I'll be good to him," Megan lifts her hand to my cheek and caresses it with her thumb. "I got him now."

My eyes focus on Megan and she stands on her tiptoes to kiss me. When I open my eyes again, Trey is gone.

"Nate?"

"Yeah?"

"Are you with me?" she asks sweetly.

"I'm here with you," I smile and pull her into me.

"Is Trey still here?" She whispers as I stroke her hair.

"No, I think he's at peace now."

She holds me tighter, "I'm sorry."

"Don't be. He needed closure and I think he got it. He knows I have you, that I'm happy. That I'm not the dumbass kid I was."

"I love you Nate."

"I love you."

CHAPTER TWENTY-EIGHT

Monday, August 5th

NATE

Today is the first day of competition.

Nico and I arrived in New York City before the break of dawn and checked into our hotel located close to the recording studio. We are in a holding room waiting for the director to run down the schedule for the day.

So much goes into production and there is more downtime than people realize. What you see on TV is the magic of the editing team to fit a day's worth of content in a one-hour episode. Nico is pacing and his nervous energy is making me nervous.

The door to the holding room pops open, "Be ready in fifteen!" A man says before shutting the door again. As the door closes my cell phone on the table rings. I reach for it and it's our Ma.

"Hi Ma, we are about to go on." I put the phone on speaker.

"I just wanted to call and say good luck to my boys. No matter what happens today, you both should be so proud. Pop and I love you both."

Nico and I get choked up, "Love you too Ma."

"Go knock it out of the park or break a leg, whatever the kids are saying these days,"

"We will make you proud," Nico smiles.

"Call me as soon as you can and let me know who won, I can't wait until the episode premiere to find out!"

"We will call you when we can, this can take a while."

"I'll be waiting! Love you two!"

"Bye Ma." Nico and I say in unison before I disconnect the call.

My text notifications are out of control, I tap on the icon.

RAUL: Go get 'em Boss!

JULIAN: Remember to keep it simple but unexpected

AMIRA: Don't go easy on Nico, give him hell!

CALLUM: Walk-in is broken

CALLUM: Just kidding

MEGAN: I'm so proud of you. Win and I promise we will have fun celebrating 😊

Mmm. That is just the motivation I need.

***

The lights are bright, so bright I can't see the live studio audience as I'm announced and make my way to the stage after my brother. I am star-struck by the host and special guest judges. I need to defeat my brother before I get to compete against a world-class chef. Today's show we are recording is the one that is the biggest deal.

Being a judge for another competition show tomorrow with Nico is cool but we are just tasting other chefs' food. The second competition show on Wednesday, Nico and I are competing against two other chefs in knock-out rounds, hopefully, Nico and I will be the last two standing.

Today. This. Now. This is life-changing, put your name and restaurant on the map type shit.

I completely black out after Nico and I get the ingredient we have to base our entire dish around. I go into 'Chef Mode' and start gathering the ingredients I need and start firing components. This will be the longest and quickest twenty minutes of my life.

"Chef Nate, how's it feel to be competing against your older brother who got you started in the restaurant industry?" The celebrity chef asks me as I chop cauliflower on the cutting board with precision.

"Today he's just another man in the way of my dreams Chef." I answer coolly and the audience 'oohhs'.

"How do you feel about that statement Chef Nico?"

"I'm about to be the man of his nightmares, Chef." Nico laughs.

"It's getting hot in here people!"

The audience claps and cheers and I keep my head down and do what I do best. Cook.

The bell chimes and Round One is over. I wipe the sweat from my brow. Then Nico and I hug each other.

"We kicked ass, good luck," Nico says in my ear then we face the judges. They taste Nico's first and give him their feedback and critiques and then it's my turn.

Judge One begins, "Chef Nate, this dish transports me to Italy, I love that you took the ingredient given to you and made it into a dish you feel in your bones."

"I agree, I felt like I was at my Grandma's house in Sicily, this was wonderful Chef." The second judge compliments.

"The Chef moving on is…"

My entire career runs through my mind like a montage. Rolling 5,000 meatballs, being a busser and dishwasher, signing the contract with Nico for Due Fratelli, earning our first dollar, and being in Aspen. Everything flashes through my mind in seconds.

"Chef Nate!"

The audience erupts in cheers and Nico comes over and hugs me, "Congratulations, go beat him. Make us proud."

"I will. Love you."

"Love you too." Nico breaks our embrace and exits the stage. I take a deep breath and try to shake out my nerves and emotions.

Round Two: I get to pick the dish we make. I've thought about what I would pick a million times. I've watched this show so many times I feel like I know the chef's strengths, and styles I'd have no chance of winning against him.

"Chef Nate, what dish did you pick?"

"Chicken Cacciatore."

The audience applauds, the bell dings, and the competition is on!

I have 45 minutes to prove myself.

I swear time speeds up and before I know it, my dish is being blind taste-tested by three distinguished judges. I have to keep my poker face on for the praise and critiques we receive. The comments are a mix but they always are.

"And the winner is…"

In slow motion I see the judge point to me and the host is shaking my hand. I won. Nico comes running to the stage and hugs me.

"You did it! I knew you could!"

I hold back the tears stinging my eyes and shake the hands of the judges. I say the show catch phrase then I am led backstage to film the commentary they show during the episode.

"You two did amazing!" The casting director compliments, "We have a surprise for you. Follow me." He jerks his head and Nico and I follow him down a stark white hallway. He stops at an unlabeled door and gestures for us to go inside. Nico opens the door and over his shoulder, I see a cameraman. Nico enters and I see our parents and Megan. Nico hugs our parents and Megan leaps into my arms.

"What the hell are you doing here?" My voice cracks and all of my pent-up emotions come out.

"I brought your parents to see you and Nico compete. We didn't want to tell you because we knew you'd be nervous."

I can't help the tears and I'm glad my head is buried in Megan's neck, her hair swirling around me. I hold her so tight I can feel her heartbeat against my chest.

"Thank you," I whisper.

"You're welcome. I knew you could do it." Megan rubs my back before pulling away. She wipes the tears from my cheeks and then kisses me.

Nico taps my shoulder and I trade places with him, my parents hug me so tightly that I feel like my ribs could break.

"My baby boy won!" My Ma cries into my chest.

"We are proud of you Son," Pops add.

"I'm so glad you two were here to see it." I hold them tighter.

"Megan called us a couple of weeks ago and asked us to come, do you know how hard it is to keep a secret from you?" Ma looks up at me with wet cheeks.

"Meg set everything up, our hotel room is gorgeous, and we got to fly first class. I love that girl!" Pop pats my back.

"How long are you here?"

"Ma and I are here until tomorrow. The shows you're judging don't have an audience and neither do the one you and Nico are competing in on Friday."

"You didn't have to travel…"

"Like we said, Megan took care of it all. We wanted to be here for this."

"Let's all celebrate!" Nico cheers and leads my parents to the exit.

I hang back a moment and catch Megan's hand before she leaves. I pull her into me, "Thank you for making arrangements for my parents and surprising Nico and me. That was thoughtful of you. I love you even more for that."

"I didn't want to miss it and knew they wouldn't want to either."

I brush my thumb over her bottom lip, "Are you leaving tomorrow too?"

Megan cocks her head to the side and looks up at me seductively, "Depends if my boss will let me take off Wednesday to Friday," she flirts.

"Mmm, I think he can be persuaded."

Megan

The Rossi Family and I celebrate Nate's victory at a posh rooftop restaurant in Manhattan. I love seeing the Rossi brothers with their parents. Nico Facetimes with Amira to give her the news but he swears her to secrecy and Maria asks her a million questions about the pregnancy and how she's feeling. Maria is going to be an amazing Nonna.

Over dinner, Nate and Nico start planning a viewing party for when the episode they filmed today premiers. They don't want the staff to know who won so only Amira and I will know. At least I can share my excitement with her.

After dinner, Nico offers to show Maria and Giovanni around the city and take them back to their hotel so Nate and I can have time alone together.

"Are you and Nico sharing a room?" I purr in Nate's ear.

"He's down the hall from me. Do you have a room?"

I sigh, "It's next to your parents' room."

Nate winces, "Oooh, not a good option."

"Your room it is."

Nate and I leave the restaurant and get a cab to his hotel and as soon as we are inside we are all over each other. I want to devour him. I unbutton his dress shirt, slip it off his shoulders, then take off his undershirt. I tug at his belt and get on my knees. I set his cock free and take him in my mouth which makes Nate's knees weak.

"Fuck Meg...my God that feels incredible."

I smirk around his length and smile up at him. I taste his precum and it makes me ravenous. Nate steps out of his pants and pulls me to my feet. He lifts me and I wrap my legs around him. His thickness rubs against my panties and my dress hikes up over my ass. Nate and I moan between kisses and he carries me to the bed. He peels my panties off and buries his head between my thighs, lapping up my wetness.

I twist my fingers in his hair and ride his smooth face.

"Have you been taking your birth control?" He asks before biting my inner thigh.

"Yes," I moan.

"When you're supposed to?"

"Yes."

"Good because I need to feel you." Nate kneels and positions himself between my legs. He rubs my juices over my folds and teases my clit before pushing into me slowly. We both let out a moan of relief. "I'm going to make love to you, I want this to last all fucking night."

Nate grinds into me as we kiss and feel each other. His strokes are slow and deep, he caresses my breasts and gently sucks my nipples. And the eye contact…fuck I love when his eyes are on me.

"I wish we would have started dating five years ago," Nate whispers before kissing me.

"I've been here the whole time, I shouldn't confess this while you're inside me but, I haven't been with anyone since before I started working for you."

"Really? No wonder you're so insatiable." Nate moans and kisses down my neck.

"From the day I interviewed, it's always been you."

"I'm sorry I was so blind."

"We're together now, that's all that matters."

With that, Nate lays on his back and in one swift motion pulls me on top of him. I rock my hips on him, feel my tits and pull on my nipples to give him a show.

"You're so fucking beautiful, I'm so lucky you're mine."

"I'm the lucky one."

I take in the view of Nate under me, every muscle, tattoo, every scar. For five years I pined after him. At one time I thought I lost him to Olivia, and now, I have his love, and he's always had my loyalty.

CHAPTER TWENTY-NINE

Friday, August 9th

NATE

The past four days have been incredible. I beat a world-class celebrity chef on his show. My brother and I got to be judges on two other shows and today we beat out two other chefs to compete head-to-head in the final round of another competition. Nico squeaked out the win this time, but it shows that Due Fratelli has two incredible culinary geniuses in our arsenal.

In addition to our success, I have an amazing woman by my side cheering me on and supporting me through it all.

Nico took the first flight home to home to Amira while Megan and I flew home to Chicago together. It's near the end of dinner service when we arrive and the staff is excited to see me back. They want all the details but Nico and I want to see their reactions when we win.

While Megan checks in with the front-of-house staff, I check on Raul, Julian, and Callum even though I know Nico did before retreating upstairs with Amira.

"How'd service go all week?" I ask Raul.

"Perfect as always. Callum did good, I'm impressed. How was the competition? Did you win?"

I chuckle, "Nice try. Julian, how's it going?"

"It's going Chef. Another hour of service and then time to clean and welcome you back. Rooftop celebration?"

"I'd be down with that."

An hour and a half later I'm taking shots of Jameson with Callum, Nico, Julian, and Raul. Callum that fucking Irishman insisted. Megan pops a bottle of champagne and everyone but Amira toasts Nico and me.

"Thank you all for holding it down when Nate and I were in New York, as soon as the network gives us our premiere date, we are planning a party for all of you to see the results."

"We are all taking bets!" Raul laughs and Megan and Amira roll their eyes.

"Eh, well just get ya' drunk enough to tell us all your secrets!" Callum offers.

Nico shakes his head and tips back his glass of champagne before putting music on and dancing with Amira.

It feels good to let loose and relax. I've been so stressed out about competing lately that I can finally soak it all in.

Megan shimmies over to me and puts her arms around my neck. "Dance with me?"

I oblige. Having her close and grinding against me makes me rock hard and the liquor kicks in sending any inhibitions I do have out the window.

Wednesday, August 14th

Megan

"I have to go, Hayley needs me," I groan as I lay naked in Nate's bed. We have been splitting time between here and my apartment. When Hayley is spending the night with Kenzie, which is almost every day, Nate and I stay at my place. When Hayley is home or has Kenzie over, Nate and I stay here. "I'll see you at work later," I lean across the bed, kiss his cheek, and get dressed before heading home.

When I arrive, Hayley is pacing the apartment.

"Oh God, you're pacing…what's wrong?"

"I need to talk to you about something and I don't know how you're going to react."

I slump on the couch, "Just tell me…" I sigh.

Hayley inhales sharply through her nose, "You know Kenzie and I have been spending a lot of time together."

"Yes, I've noticed. You're working on that painting and dating each other, kinda like Nate and I."

"Exactly, but you and Nate have *years* of history, and Kenzie and I have like, a month. I'm not counting our childhood."

"What's your point?"

Hayley fidgets with her hands, "Kenzie asked me to move in with her and offered me part ownership of the gallery. I told her I needed to think about it."

I sit up on the couch, "Damn, I knew lesbians moved fast but, holy shit. How do you feel about it? What do you want?"

"I want to do it, but should I? What about you and the bills here?"

"Hay, I make enough to cover everything and have plenty saved too," I reassure her, "If you move in with her and it doesn't work out you can always come back or get an apartment."

"There has to be a reason we were brought together again and Kenzie is…everything."

"You two are having fun working together and spending all this time together? You're not getting sick of each other?"

"No," Hayley smiles. "Meeting Mom and Dad didn't scare her away and she told Olivia about us. She gets along with you and Nate. It all feels…right."

"Follow your heart and move in with her. It would be nice not to inhale paint fumes and turpentine at home and have a dining room again." I tease.

Hayley hits me with a throw pillow, "I'll miss you. We have lived together since coming to Chicago."

"I know, but for the first time, we are both in love, in relationships, and growing up. Finally." I giggle, "Don't be like me and waste years, if you feel it, take the risk."

Hayley hugs me tightly then pulls away, "I'll start purging things, and Saturday at the party, I'll tell Kenzie."

"I'm happy for you."

"Thanks. I'm happy too."

CHAPTER THIRTY

Saturday, August 17ᵗʰ

NATE

I am thrilled to be the one escorting Megan to her sister's event tonight. She looks nothing short of breathtaking in her knee-length summer dress, effortlessly elegant. Her makeup is flawless, and her hair tumbles in soft, romantic curls. As she walks into the living room, every step seems to linger in time, and I can't help but feel my heart skip a beat. It's as if she's walking toward me in slow motion, and at that moment, my mind flashes to a future where she's in a wedding dress, walking toward me to say her vows and be my wife.

I shake the thought from my mind, "Wow."

"You like it?"

"You're taking my breath away." The dress has spaghetti straps and is a mix of deep violet and orange hues. Like a summer sunset. My go-to navy button-down compliments it perfectly.

"You look handsome as always."

"I'm honored to be your arm candy tonight," I say kissing her sweetly.

"You're going to be on your best behavior, right?" She arches her eyebrow in suspicion.

My cheeks blush, "I'll behave tonight until we get home, but I'm telling you, this dress won't make it easy. I kiss her shoulder, collarbone, and neck, taking in the intoxicating scent of her Valentino perfume.

"Nate…" she whines.

"Yes?"

She kisses me but not hard enough to mess up her lipstick, "Quit distracting me, we need to go."

When we arrive, we are greeted by servers handing out glasses of champagne, just like the Open House I came to. Megan and I take a glass and she searches the gallery for Lynn and Ruben. Ruben is at least 6'3" and stands out in the crowd and I point him out and let Megan lead the way. They hug her and Lynn hugs me and Ruben shakes my hand.

"Nice to see you again, son."

"Nice to see you, Sir, are you ready for the first Bears first game of the season? Preseason is looking good; they got the wins!" Again. I know nothing about football but it's a topic I know will keep him talking while we wait for Hayley and Kenzie. I looked up the stats while Megan was getting ready earlier.

When her Mom is done chatting with her, I see her trying to hold back a laugh as I pretend to know what Ruben is talking about.

"Dad, may I steal my date away?" She interrupts before he can catch on. Megan drags me away, "Football, really? How did you know all that?"

"A simple internet search," I smirk.

"You're an ass."

The bubbly blonde who convinced me to buy a $900 painting—now hanging proudly in the restaurant lobby—takes the makeshift stage and grabs the crowd's attention. She introduces Kenzie, who steps up to the stage holding hands with Hayley. Megan slips her arm through mine and gives it an excited squeeze. From the look of it, Kenzie is nervous. Hayley gives her a look and I see her gently stroking her thumb over the back of Kenzie's hand.

Kenzie takes a deep breath and the confidence I know she has shines. "Thank you all so much for your love and support tonight." Clapping fills the gallery, "Tonight's reveal wouldn't be happening if it weren't for one special person, Hayley." More cheers and whistles. "I've never collaborated on a project with anyone before. For the past six years, I've been a solo artist. I've taught classes here, but that is the most I've ever shared my space. Hayley changed that."

Hayley looks like she is holding back tears and I hear Megan sniffle.

Kenzie continues, "I had rules that I imposed on myself. Don't let anyone get close. Don't depend on anyone. Make your dreams come true alone. I told myself that I could be happy flying solo."

I look down at Megan. I can relate to what Kenzie is saying. It's easy to get wrapped up in the rules of life and your dreams.

"I broke all my rules and didn't get punished for it, I got rewarded." Hayley wipes tears from her eyes. Lynn is sniffing back tears and Megan's grip on me gets even tighter. "Sometimes in life, we need to throw out the rule book and do what feels right. The painting we made together shows that." I applaud with everyone. "We took Hayley's strength with oils and watercolors and my strength in acrylics and blended mediums. We put our hearts, souls, and quite literally, pieces of ourselves into this. We hope you enjoy." Kenzie offers the microphone to Hayley but she is too choked up to speak. It's nice to see Hayley be vulnerable for once.

The light in the back of the gallery comes on and so many people shuffle past us I can't quite see the painting, but Megan gasps and takes my hand. "I have a surprise for you, but you need to close your eyes."

"For me?"

"Yes!" She beams, "Eyes closed. Take my hand and I'll guide you."

I do as she asks, saying sorry to people I bump into along the way and I feel Megan position me. She intertwines my hand with hers and leans her head on my shoulder, "Okay, open!"

I open my eyes and it's a blank wall but then my eyes scan upward and my heart jumps into my throat. There are two paintings beside each other, one of the butterfly on Megan's shoulder and one of the butterfly on my chest.

"How did you—"

"I showed Hayley the pictures we took and asked if she could turn them into paintings for me. Now that we are a couple, they are for us."

I have no words. I take Megan in my arms and hug her tightly. Gently swaying us. "You're amazing. I love you so much." I hold back tears. When I got home that day after dropping Megan off, I looked up the meaning of butterflies and there were articles online stating that butterflies are signs from loved ones trying to send you a message. Other sites said a transformation was in your future. Was the butterfly my Nonni or Trey? Maybe. But I can say for certain, I have been transformed since that day.

"How'd Kenzie and I do? I suck at painting butterflies," Hayley interrupts our tender moment, and Megan and I both hug her.

"It's better than I could have ever imagined." Megan hugs her, "I'm going to miss you."

"Miss her?" Myself, Lynn and Ruben ask in unison.

Hayley smiles, "Kenzie asked me to move in with her and asked me to be her business partner and I said yes."

"Awesome!" I exclaim.

Lynn starts crying, again and hugs Megan and Hayley, "I'm so proud of you girls."

Ruben rolls his eyes at me, "Alright dear, turn off the waterworks and let our girls get back to their dates," Ruben gently pulls her away.

"I'll drop the paintings off tomorrow," Hayley gives us a little wave and she skips off to rejoin Kenzie.

"So, sister is moving huh?"

"You didn't notice her things slowly leaving the apartment?"

"Her bedroom door was always closed and I guess I didn't notice her easels were gone."

"I'll be able to have a dining table again," Megan jokes.

"Does this mean we don't have to try to be quiet when I'm there anymore?"

"Mmmhmm."

"Fuckkkk yesssss," I practically moan and get hard just knowing Megan and I will have the place to ourselves now.

"There's one thing you need to do for me though."

"Anything. You name it."

"We need to change the fucking locks."

Megan

Nate agrees to change the locks and also offers to help move Hayley out. He is eager for us to have a place that is ours.

"We can stay at my place, no more hearing Nico and Amira. You won't have to hear a baby crying in 7 or 8 months."

"Hayley can't be mean to me," he adds teasingly, "If I'm changing the locks, does this mean I get a key?"

"Hmm, I don't know…you may be moving a little fast for me Chef."

Nates' knees buckle and he holds back a moan before gaining his composure and leaning close to my ear, "You know what it does to me when you call me that."

Out of the corner of my eye I see Hayley and Kenzie sneaking upstairs and I could use a kiss from Nate right now. I take his hand and lead him to the door to the upstairs and its locked. Shit. I punch in 1,2,3,4 on the keypad. No luck. 4,3,2,1. Nope. 3, 2, 1, 0. Green. The door unlocks and I go up a few stairs then turn to kiss Nate passionately.

"Say your goodbyes, I'm taking you home," Nate moans into my mouth. I hear cheering and squealing coming from upstairs and I take Nate's hand and finish our accent.

"Hayley! You up here?" I call out stupidly. Of course she is.

Hayley runs to me as soon as Nate and I make it to the top. "We got offered six figures for our painting!"

"Oh my God!" I hug my sister and I haven't seen her this excited since my Dad bought her the Bob Ross DVD collection. I look past her at Kenzie and she's in shock.

Hayley walks to her and frames Kenzie's face in her hands, "Baby, look at me, this is life-changing for us, we have to sell it."

"But we created it together, don't you want to keep it, for us?"

My sister tears up and caresses Kenzie's cheek, "Kenzie, we are going to make masterpieces together, we can let this one go."

Kenzie looks around the room. I didn't even notice Jake and Trevor in the room with us. Kenzie gives me a smile then turns her attention back to my sister, "You're right, this is just the start of something beautiful."

They kiss tenderly and my heart swells with happiness for them. Trevor breaks up the love fest and grabs the card from Kenzie, "Before you sell it, are we sure they are legit?"

Jake grabs the card from him and punches his arm, "Don't rain on their parade." Jake turns the card over and freezes. His face goes pale. "No fucking way."

"The offer is insane right?" My sister laughs.

"It's Alyssa," Jake says in almost a whisper.

Kenzie snatches the card back from him and looks at it closer, "That's Alyssa?! THE Alyssa?"

My sister grabs the card next, and her jaw drops, and she looks like she's going to be sick, "That's not just Alyssa. That's Sasquatch."

Nate chuckles, "What?"

I drop his hand and step between Hayley and Kenzie. "It can't be."

Hayley gets her phone out to look up the website printed under the picture of Jean Luc and Alyssa Laurant.

"Who is Sasquatch?" Nate asks.

"This horrible wretched bitch we grew up with, she was awful to Hayley and I and Julian. But how do *you* know her, Jake?" I ask.

"She's my ex," he says plainly, "She's fucking married!?" Jake yells.

Kenzie shakes her head, "She has to be fucking with us."

"You think her husband who put up six figures of his money is in on it?" Hayley asks.

I step in, "You two didn't recognize her. She probably doesn't remember us."

"It's me," Jake says, "She had to have seen your Instagram pictures with me and Trevor. She's a nosey cunt."

"If she came to see you, why wouldn't she have flaunted her new husband to you, you didn't see her down there?" Trevor asks.

"No!" Jake snaps at him, "She had to have known I'd find out she's the one who bought their painting so I'd contact her and, thank her? I don't fucking know!"

Trevor tries to rub his back to calm him down and Jake shoves him away.

"Do we still want to sell it?" Hayley asks Kenzie.

Kenzie sighs and looks at Jake, "Jake, what do you think?"

"Tell them you got a higher bid," Trevor growls. "That bitch is not worthy of owning your work. I'll match or beat their offer."

Jake shakes his head, marches through the kitchen, and runs down the stairs. Trevor chases after him.

"Hay, Kenz…you need to get back downstairs. Everyone is here for you. Remember that. Forget Alyssa."

They nod, give each other a quick kiss and go back downstairs.

"Do you want to join them?" Nate asks sincerely.

"Right after I see what Alyssa is up to."

I pick up the card and dial the number on the back and I hear, "Bonjour, c'est Jean-Luc qui parle."

"Hello, I am calling on behalf of my clients, Kenzie Miller and Hayley King."

"Oui! Their painting is magnifique! Are you calling about the offer?" He asks in a heavy French accent.

"Before they're willing to accept your offer, they want to know how you intend to use the painting."

"I own a private gallery in Paris. I want to show it. I want to own l'original."

"How did you hear about the painting?"

"Ma femme, she is from Chicago and a fan of mademoiselle Kenzie and Hayley."

"I'd like to you ask your wife how she knows them and their close friend Jake."

"Jacques?"

"Jake Hudson is a close personal friend of the artists."

"No." He sounds stunned. He knows who Jake is.

"Oui! Your dear wife terrorized the artist and others when they were children. People I care about and she left Jake."

"No, she said he broke up with her!"

"She's lying. She's always been a liar."

"Mon Alyssa?"

"Oui."

There is a long pause.

"Miss King and Miss Miller do not want their work in the wrong hands, you understand?"

"Oui. My apologies. I was not aware." Jean-Luc admits. I feel a little bad for exposing Alyssa but when it comes to people I care about I am fiercely loyal and protective. "My offer still stands. Their work deserves to be in Paris. If not with moi, I know someone else. S'il te plait?" Jean-Luc pleads, "It could change their life."

"Send me the information."

I hang up and Nate's jaw is on the ground, "That was the sexiest fucking thing I've ever seen."

"Nobody fucks with my family."

Moments later I get a lengthy apology text and the contact information of a prestigious art curator in Paris. I jot the number down and leave it on the table.

CHAPTER THIRTY-ONE

Monday, September 23rd

Megan

Tonight is the night Nate and Nico's competition episodes premiere on Food Network. The episode where Nico wins is first followed by the episode where Nate wins big. I'm at Kenzie and Hayley's getting ready. Their painting arrived in Paris and found its home at one of Paris' hidden gem galleries. The money they earned was split and Hayley paid my rent for a year. She felt bad moving out and even though I told her I'd be able to afford to live on my own, she insisted.

Hayley and Kenzie's lives blended so well that it's impossible to tell where one's belongings end and the other's begin. The gallery is so popular that Hayley and Kenzie can't keep up. The walls are empty so the gallery is only open when Kenzie teaches painting classes on Wednesdays, which is now offered for free for the community. She also rents out the studio which Nate and I took advantage of. A painting we made together now hangs in the bedroom.

"Megan! Hello!" My sister snaps her fingers in front of my face.

"Sorry, I was daydreaming."

"Are you ready?"

"How do I look?" I ask as I spin around. My long sleeve burgundy dress twirls and my hair flows around me.

"Beautiful. Don't be nervous. You know the outcome!" She smiles.

"I know, but tonight is a big night for Nate and Nico and the restaurant. Their parents will be there."

"They love you. Stop worrying and relax."

She's right. Nate and I have been dating for almost four months and Nate and I have taken off a few Sundays to go to church and dinner. I'm still standing so we didn't burst into flames. I love spending time with the Rossi's.

"Move your ass!" Hayley pushes me to the door and the three of us Uber to Due Fratelli.

When we arrive, the dining room is full of employees, friends, and family of our staff. My parents are here to celebrate and my Dad and Kenzie are super close.

"Oh, Megan you look gorgeous!" My Mom says as she hugs me.

"Beautiful honey," Dad adds as he hugs me.

"Thank you for coming. It means a lot. I'll be right back I need to find Nate."

I make my way to Nate, and his face instantly lights up. "There's my girl," he says, lifting me into a hug and spinning me around. He acts like he hasn't seen me in days, though, in reality, I woke up next to him this morning. Ever since Hayley moved out, Nate's been staying with me almost every night. He's even brought his touch to the place—buying pots and pans for the kitchen, upgrading my coffee pot to an espresso machine, and helping me choose a fresh paint color for the dining and living area

We're slowly turning the apartment into *ours*. It's been a beautiful process. We turned Hayley's old room into a walk-in closet, and now, every time I walk in, it feels like a little more of our life together is taking shape. I finally have my dining table back, and it feels like a small victory. Nate brought his Bonsai tree into the bedroom, and now it's become our little slice of paradise. At first, he wasn't keeping up with it, but now we tend to our trees together, nurturing something that's truly ours. We haven't officially called it "living together," but I can feel it coming. Every moment, every decision we make, is pulling us closer to that reality.

"Ma. Pops. Megan's here." He says as he taps their shoulders and I'm immediately kissed on the cheeks and asked a million questions about Nate. Is he eating? Is he eating enough? How's he treating you? How are you doing? How's business? Typical Italian Mom questions.

The sound of a fork clinking against glass fills the dining room, which Raul, Julian, and Callum have transformed into a viewing party. A large flat screen is set up, and the dining chairs are arranged in rows. The front row is reserved for Nate, Nico, Maria, Giovanni, Amira, and me. Everyone turns their attention to Nico.

"Welcome everyone! Nate and I want to thank you all for being here this evening. Our success is only possible because of you. You're our family and we love you all!"

Clapping and whistles fill the air, "Place your final bets with Raul!" He laughs before taking his seat between Amira and Maria.

The tension in the room is thick as everyone leans forward, on edge, during the final round between Nate and Nico. The silence is so intense, you could hear a pin drop. My heart races as the host pauses, stretching the moment. Finally, the verdict comes—Nico is the winner. A burst of applause erupts, cheers filling the air, and Nico stands tall, taking a dramatic bow. Behind us, a few groans break through the celebration, the disappointed murmurs of those who had bet on Nate.

"Before the next episode, there's some business I need to take care of." Nico walks to Nate and he hands him a small velvet light blue box. "Amira, will you join me up here?"

Amira just had her four-month checkup and their baby is healthy and strong. She's concealing her bump well but in moments, everyone is going to know she's expecting.

Nico helps Amira up and he leads her front and center. He gets down on one knee and her jaw drops. He opens the box he holds her shaking hand. "Amira, I know I'm not perfect and I'm probably far from the man you dreamed of marrying and starting a family with…" Gasps fill the air. Maria sniffles trying to hold back tears and I hear Amira's Mom behind me quietly laugh. "I can't promise I won't let you down, but I do promise to love you and I'll try to make you happy every damn day. I'll be the best husband and father because I had the best one raise me." I look over and Gio wipes his tears, "Amira Jones, will you marry me?"

"Yes! Yes! I'll marry you!" She cries as Nico places the diamond ring on her finger then kisses her softly and envelops her in a hug. He kisses her little bump and it's so damn sweet to see him turn to mush.

Maria, Gio, and Amira's parents join them and I hurry to take pictures of everyone before the next episode begins.

NATE

Seeing my older brother propose is surreal. I'm happy for him and Amira and hearing him mention our Dad in his proposal got me choked up, I could barely hold it together. Megan didn't cry, which got me thinking—how would she want to be proposed to one day? Knowing her, I imagine she'd want something private, no crowd, no spectacle, just a quiet, intimate moment between the two of us.

"Alright everyone settle down. There will be plenty of time for pictures and celebrating soon!" I try to settle everyone before the opening credits. I take my seat next to my Dad and Megan and intertwine my hand with hers.

"I love you," she whispers in my ear.

Competing and then seeing how TV editing magic unfolds feels like a dream. The suspense is unbearable, with no hints as to who will win. I know I do but it's surreal. When I beat Nico, our staff goes wild—everyone, even those who didn't bet on me, can't contain their excitement.

During the commercial break, Nico pulls me into a hug, his pride in me palpable. "Trey would have loved to be here," he says softly, his voice thick with emotion. "He's proud of you." His words hit me like a wave, and for a moment, it feels like Trey's spirit is right here with us.

"I know he would be."

When the show resumes, everyone in the room is rooting for me.

"Let's go Nate!"

"You got this Boss!"

My hands sweat watching myself on TV. My heart pounds against my ribcage and I feel myself beginning to sweat. Seeing the judges critique me and eat my food makes it real. I wasn't dreaming. I'm declared the winner and I get hugged and patted on the back from all angles but I hug Megan. She's my rock. She hugs me so tight it's like she is seeing it for the first time too.

"This makes it real, doesn't it?" She asks.

"Yes, baby," I say and kiss her. When I do it's like everyone disappears and it's just the two of us. "I couldn't have done it without you."

After Megan kisses me, my parents hug me, and Nico and I take a picture with them and then a picture with our entire staff. The phone ringing from the lobby area catches my attention and I excuse myself. Who could be calling? We are always closed on Mondays.

"Due Fratelli, Nate speaking. How may I help you?"

"Nate. Perfect. Just the man I needed to talk to. I can't say who I am, but I wanted to call and tell you personally, Due Fratelli has earned one Michelin star."

"What?" *Did I hear him correctly?*

A chuckle comes over the line, "We get that a lot. We have received numerous reviews, all of which have been exceptional. Your commitment to using fresh ingredients, the quality of your menu and specials, the inviting atmosphere, and the overall dining experience are consistently outstanding and truly deserving of recognition."

Tears sting my eyes, "Thank you so much."

"A formal announcement will go soon. But on a personal note, I want to express that I am a great admirer of both you and your girlfriend. Tell her that, while she may not yet fully recognize her passion, it is clear that her true passion lies in connecting with people."

"I'll tell her," I choke out.

"Extend my congratulations to your brother and staff."

"I will. It's an honor to have your recognition."

The line disconnects and I feel hot tears running down my cheeks. Every obstacle and sacrifice has led to this and I'm so damn thankful.

"Nate? What are you doing? Come back to the party." I hear Megan say behind me. When I turn around she freezes.

"Nate, what's wrong?"

"The phone was ringing."

"Really? We're closed."

"I answered and…we earned a star," I say in shock.

"What?! Really?" Megan squeals in excitement.

"The man said you are exceptional."

Her face scrunches in confusion, "Wait, he mentioned me?"

"Our food, atmosphere, and menu too but yeah, he said your passion is connecting with people."

Megan's hands shoot to her mouth in surprise.

"Do you know who it is?"

"Mark." She whispers.

"Mark? Like Olivia's date Mark?"

"That night he asked me what my passion was and I told him I didn't know. I thought his date was a Michelin. I didn't expect him!" Megan squeaks.

"Maybe they both are. He said a formal announcement will go out, but he wanted to call."

Tears rim Megan's eyes, "You did it," she smiles.

"We did it."

EPILOGUE

One Year Later

It's a crisp fall day here at the botanical gardens, and I find myself reflecting on how much my life has changed in the past year. I've developed a new passion for cooking, a renewed love for life, and I've found the perfect partner in Megan. We officially started living together in October of last year.

When the weather is nice, I ride my motorcycle to work, and during the winter, I walk. Each evening, Megan and I either ride home together or stroll hand in hand. It's a simple routine, but it's our special time to talk, plan, and enjoy the beauty of the city together.

I conspired with Hayley and Kenzie to bring Megan here today. Hayley and Kenzie got married during Pride Month in June, and it was the most fun wedding I've ever attended. Nico and Amira also tied the knot. Amira wanted to ensure that she, the baby, and Nico all shared the same last name, so this past spring they had an extravagant, over-the-top wedding on the rooftop of Due Fratelli. I didn't expect anything less from him.

Attending two weddings and becoming the best uncle ever to Amelia gave me the motivation I needed to commit to something forever, aside from my career, which has always been my top priority. I've achieved more than I ever dreamed, but there has always been a missing ingredient: Love.

Megan has supported me and my dreams since day one. Her loyalty has always been to Due Fratelli and me. Now it's time I commit to her.

I reach into my pocket and for the millionth time, convince myself Megan won't be able to see the ring box in my coat pocket. My Dad helped me customize a gorgeous emerald-cut diamond ring. It's one of a kind, just like Megan.

As I approach the fountains where Megan is waiting for me, I see Hayley and Kenzie hiding to take pictures and record my proposal. My heart is racing but I'm filled with the best adrenaline rush of my life. Leaves crunch beneath my boots and Megan turns around. When she sees me, her eyes sparkle.

"Hey Nate, I thought you'd never get here," she smiles.

I swallow the lump in my throat, "Neither did I."

Want to know Olivia's side of the story?

Read *Stars In Her Eyes*, Book One in the Lakeshore Love Series. See things through Olivia's eyes with Nate and discover how his shortcomings lead to Olivia meeting Anders.

Want more Kenzie and Hayley?

Book Two in the Lakeshore Love Series *Breaking All The Rules* follows Kenzie, Jake, and Trevor on their journey of love and self-discovery.

Need more Jake and Trevor?

Their story from *Breaking All The Rules* will continue in Book Four of the Lakeshore Love Series coming in June 2025

To stay up to date on all things Lakeshore Love and Events scan the QR code below

ACKNOWLEDGEMENTS

Thank you for reading *Nate's Redemption*! I never planned on writing Nate's story but fans of *Stars In Her Eyes* demanded Nate get his happily ever after. I cried more writing this book than any other thus far. I wanted everyone to get their happy ending and as always, characters you've read about and grown attached to may show up again (Ahem, Julian, Lilah, and Callum when I start the Lakeshore Lunatics Series)

I want to thank my husband Stephen for listening to me read chapters and brainstorm nonsense for hours. Regardless, he is glad to finally be home from deployment and is excited to attend book signings with me.

Thank you to my in-laws Ron and Linda who always cheer me on and support me (Who also hear me ramble on about my characters like they are real people.) If I could bring them all to life, I would.

Thank you to my ARC readers who are eager to sign up and read my books. I love your reactions and hearing your thoughts on my wild stories.

Thank you to everyone who has come to a book signing, bought a book, downloaded the e-book, or read on Kindle Unlimited. Your time is important and I always have you in mind while I write. As an avid reader myself, I always strive to make you laugh, blush, kick your feet, cry, and reach for that secret drawer you have *wink wink*

ABOUT THE AUTHOR

Ashley Snyder is a self-published author from Erie, Pennsylvania with roots originally in the Pittsburgh area. She is married to her husband Stephen and is a proud Army Wife and Army Mom.

In her free time, she loves to read and go wine tasting in Ohio and Upstate New York. She loves sports and her favorites are hockey and motocross. Ashley is also a self-proclaimed Swiftie and a hardcore fan of Sleep Token.

You can follow her socials on Instagram and TikTok @authorashleysnyder

Did you love *Nate's Redemption*?

Please share it with a friend, post on social media, and leave a review on your favorite sites!

Made in the USA
Middletown, DE
22 January 2025